BLACKFUNK II

WHATEVER IT TAKES

BY

MICHAEL PRESLEY

This is a work of fiction. The author has invented the characters. Any resemblance to actual persons, living or dead, is purely coincidental.

Interior Design by Nancey Flowers
Edited by Chandra Sparks Taylor
First Blackfunk Publishing trade paperback printing July 2004

For more information, or to contact the contributors, address correspondence to:

Blackfunk Publishing, Inc.
P.O. Box 23782
Brooklyn, New York 11202

Or visit: www.Blackfunk-book.com

Library of Congress Cataloging-in-Publication Data
ISBN: 0-9705903-3-4

10 9 8 7 6 5 4 3 2 1

First Paperback Edition

Printed in the United States

Dedication

To my Mom and my first born who has changed the way I look at life.

Acknowledgements

I thank God for my talent as a writer. Without Him none of this would be possible.

I would like to thank the legion of fans who pushed me to finish Blackfunk III. You have been patient and extremely understanding throughout this process. Now you can enjoy the end of the Blackfunk trilogy.

It is with the utmost respect and honor that I give thanks to the book distributors, booksellers and street vendors.

I would like to thank my family for their constant show of love and support. You all are the best, especially David and Patricia.

Zane, thanks for your continued support. To my proofreader, Sheila, thank you. A special thanks to: Minerva, Jason, Wynston, Crystal Lacey Winslow author of Life, Love & Loneliness and Nancey Flowers my publicist (Flowers & Hawyard Publicity and Entertainment), and best friend in the world (author of Shattered Vessels)!

Acknowledgments

Prologue

"Penguin, we don't have all night here," Dwayne Phillips said, flipping the keys he held. Dwayne was a short, paunchy black man with an oversize gut that stretched the buttons of his blue New York City corrections uniform. His face was round and his eyes, nose and mouth seemed to have been dropped in without any kind of uniformity. Gary Coleman was the only entertainer with similar attributes.

It was 1:00 A.M., and the only cell door that was opened belonged to Penguin whose real name was Edwin Thomas. 'In the pit', which was what most people call Rikers Island, any cell opened that time of night would be a hurtful privilege. It would mean that either someone was getting rape, battered or killed with the help of a New York City corrections officer. In Penguin's case, the status quo stood. Dwayne was the supervisor on duty for that particular cell block, therefore, it was on his authority that the cell door was unlocked. Dwayne hated the night shift, but tonight was different. He had an important job to do. A loud rumbling came from four cells to Penguin's left. It sounded like plane wheels coming down. Penguin was informed earlier that it was coming from Tennis Balls' cell. Tennis Balls, he was told had pig nostrils that explained the way he snored. The noise had kept Penguin up but tonight it was particularly irritating, yet Penguin could do nothing about it. He was in protective custody, and protective custody in the pit meant isolation although not totally. Penguin looked down at his tubby hands, which were becoming red from the constant ripping. The small black-and-white sheets that lay in a small pile next to him were made with a thick cloth as a precaution to someone ripping them apart and committing suicide.

"Can you stop making that noise with the keys?" Penguin asked, pulling apart another large part of the sheet. Penguin looked over at Dwayne who was swinging a bunch of keys on his right pinky. Penguin didn't like Dwayne who reminded him of a large Italian sausage you only get in Little Italy next to big China Town just before you hit the Village. The Village itself had its own history, for which Penguin did not particularly care.

"If that will make you hurry up, it's done. Please, Penguin, hurry up." Dwayne got up off the lone hard iron chair in the cell. He stood underneath the door and reached up in an attempt to touch the top of the gate frame. He failed, the same way he had when he tried to touch it upon his entrance. "Richard, keep an eye on Penguin. I have to go outside and take a smoke and get some food."

"You should give that up, Dwayne. They say that stuff will kill you." Richard Lawson leaned against the washbasin with the New York *Daily News* in his hand. He hated the tabloid because of its racist headlines but that's the paper Dwayne had brought in today. Dwayne had no particular convictions—money and food was his driving force in life. Richard was much taller than Dwayne with a straight Jewish nose that hooked at the end. Unlike Dwayne, his uniform was form fitting with no unnecessary bulges.

"When AIDS surfaced they said the same thing about pussy. Have you given it up?" Dwayne started down the hall without waiting for a response. He lifted his knees high because his cousin, Cornel, had said walking like that would make him lose his gut. Cornel told him to eat anything he wanted but just make sure he walked with his knees high.

"To each his own. Bring me back a Diet Pepsi," Richard said, not sure if Dwayne had heard him. Richard sighed and went back to reading the paper.

"You guys will be sitting well after this, won't you?" Penguin asked, continuing to rip into the sheet.

"Well fifteen grand goes a long way on a down payment for an Escalade. And the good thing is there won't be any tax involved. That's the thing about dirty money; the government doesn't get paid. You feel me, Penguin. I know you do. When was the last time you paid taxes?" Richard asked.

Penguin shook his head.

"I thought so. Do you know how much tax I've paid in my lifetime? Let's say it would make you piss in your pants. Yeah, all I do is give money to the government. That's what taxes are, it's fucking giving money to the government to pay for wars. Check this out, if every American stop paying taxes to protest the war in Iraq, the troops would be home tomorrow. Penguin, you can listen and work at the same time. Continue what you're doing," Richard said, looking over at Penguin who had stopped for a minute. "Pull on the knot to make sure it won't come loose."

Penguin did as Richard advised. The knot that held the two pieces of sheet together got smaller but didn't come apart.

"The government is the biggest crook in the country. If a man killed a hundred innocent people, I bet you the government killed a million. The thing about this country is that most people know that, too, yet they go around acting like the government has their best interest at heart. The government doesn't have a heart. Have you ever seen a politician with a heart? Would you sit down and have dinner with an old woman at her house, then when you finish rape and kill her? A politician would do that without blinking. And what makes up the government? Politicians. Exactly. And to be honest, it doesn't matter if they are white or black, they are all fucked up. Look at this!" Richard slapped the middle of the newspaper with the back of his right hand. "Another one got arrested for taking a bribe. I'm not hating though because given the opportunity I would do the same thing."

This time Penguin nodded in agreement to get Richard to shut the fuck up.

It didn't work.

"Well, that's what the government will do. Penguin, I don't think Dwayne will be happy to come back and see you haven't finished your task. Now me, I'll give a guy a break but Dwayne, he will put you in the cell with Tennis Balls and his big pig nose. I'm a good man; I don't believe a man should be unnecessarily hurt. By the way, did you get that phone call?"

"No. What phone call?" Penguin's eyes lit up. A dying man had received news and with most dying men, news was always important, whether it was good or bad.

"Hold on, Dwayne is coming back. He might know what's going on."

Dwayne walked into the cell and immediately sat down on the bed, pushing aside the pile of shredded sheets to make room for his expanding rear. He seemed relieved to be making this scheduled rest stop—lifting his knees were starting to bother him.

Richard and Penguin stared at him.

"What?" he exclaimed, staring back at them. "This is my turkey wrap. This is not your last meal, motherfucker." He pointed at the plastic bag in his hand.

Richard shook his head. "Where's the Diet Pepsi?"

"Man, you didn't tell me about no Diet Pepsi. Penguin, you ain't finished yet?" Dwayne looked at the torn sheet in Penguin's hands. "I told you there are two ways we can do this—the easy way or the painful way. I don't care; I get paid either way. And to be honest, I kinda like the painful way but it involves too much paperwork. This way it's clean, and everyone leaves feeling happy. Even you, Penguin. You leave feeling happy too. I like that we are one big happy family." Dwayne smiled as he took out the sandwich. He picked up the strips of lettuce that fell on the bed, tilted his head and dropped them in his grinder. He slapped Penguin on his back, his fingers leaving an imprint that quickly disappeared.

Penguin flinched.

Dwayne laughed. He took out a blue Nokia cell phone and laid it on the bed next to Penguin.

"Richard told you about Tennis Balls, didn't he? Well let me tell you why they call this big black motherfucker Tennis Balls. Those extra-large condoms made by Trojan won't do a damn thing for him. You heard of Blackfunk, ah? Anyone who agrees to have sex with Tennis Balls is signing an agreement to be blackfunked because their insides will be shredded. The last guy who happened to wander into Tennis Balls' cell, we found him knocked out on the floor, blood oozing from his head and ass. Tennis Balls stood over him grinning as if he had won the Lotto. We rushed the guy to the hospital before the motherfucker could bleed to death because it takes forever to get blood out of the creases on the floor. The guy spent six months in intensive care. They tried to sew him up so that he didn't have to wear diapers for the rest of his life." Dwayne took out a piece of tomato from his sandwich and dropped it on the floor. "Like that, shit would just fall from the guy's ass. Did you know that a tennis ball could have slipped in and out of this guy's asshole with no resistance at all? We are not talking about a golf or ping-pong ball. A motherfucking tennis ball."

Dwayne put his hands together, making a circle with his fingers to show the size of a tennis ball, exaggerating it by about an inch.

Penguin shuddered.

Dwayne used his teeth as a saw to rip apart the bread from the sandwich. He took out a twenty-ounce bottle of regular Pepsi and twisted off the cap.

Richard looked at him.

Dwayne put the bottle to his mouth and made a guzzling sound. When he rested the bottle on the floor between his legs, it was half empty or half full, depending on what part of the world you are or your way of thinking.

"No man should have to suffer that much," Richard said, shaking his head. "That's not right. Tennis Balls is cursed. He is a black man with an abnormal-sized dick. This is why he is in prison. Women would consent to having sex with him, then once he starts, they want to stop. A man can't always stop on the dime. You feel me. "

"Alright, Richard, let me continue. So we put the inmate on suicide watch for a year after the incident and he received every kind of counseling in the world. And do you know what he did?" Dwayne asked Penguin.

Penguin shook his head.

"He killed himself the day after he was taken off suicide watch."

"I would have done the same thing. A man can only live with so much pain. Penguin, you're a good man. You're also a smart man. There is a better life away from here for you. Go into it with a clean body." Richard played with the buttons on his uniform.

"And you guys get to live well off my dead body," Penguin said solemnly.

"Twenty thousand dollars is not bad. Can you believe that, Penguin? I'm getting paid twenty thousand dollars to watch. Do you know how many times I have paid those strippers five and ten dollars to watch?" A far-away look came into Dwayne's eyes as he started to salivate. "My wife doesn't understand it, paying all that money to see a woman dance for a group of men. She doesn't know, for that minute when they look you in your eyes, there are no other men in the room. They're just dancing for you. This beautiful, gorgeous, vivacious woman is putting on a show for your eyes only. Well sometimes I pay the extra twenty for a lap dance but I always walk with an extra boxer so whatever happens in the boxer stays in the boxer."

"The flesh is the best way to get to a politician," Richard said.

"Rich, you still on that shit about politicians?" Dwayne looked at him, raising his eyebrows in a look of-I can't believe we are here. "Brother, you should be thankful for the politicians. They're the ones who keep us in business."

"No, stupid brothers keep us in business. Look at those rappers, they make a ton of money, and they can't wait to go to jail. They are all jumping around 'me, next please pick me.' Stupid brothers pay us to hold them down."

The phone chimed 50 Cent's song "In da Club."

"I guess it's your birthday, Penguin."

Dwayne picked up the phone and listened before saying, "Yeah, he's here. Unless you heard about a jail break on the island."

The men looked at him.

Penguin stopped ripping the sheet.

Richard looked contented; an I-told-you-so expression came over him. He liked people who were true to their word. People who said they were going to do something and did it. Not like the politicians. No, the politicians would tell you they were going to clean up the shit then they'd come and bring more shit.

"Here." Dwayne handed the phone to Penguin and wiped his hand on the sandwich wrapper before he dug into the bread. "Roundtree doesn't have a sense of humor."

Penguin took the phone, his hand shaking. "I'm so sorry, Mr. Roundtree. I don't know what got into me but I won't say a word. I promise. They could send me away for five lifetimes, and I won't say a word. Give me one more chance." Tears flowed down Penguin's face as he held on tightly to the phone. He pushed the sheets aside as he concentrated on the voice on the other end.

Dwayne looked away.

"Maybe Mr. Roundtree might change his mind," Richard said, looking at Dwayne for confirmation.

"I don't think so, Rich. Guys like Roundtree never change their mind." Dwayne said.

"Here's the phone, thank you," Penguin said, returning the phone to Dwayne.

"That was short. What did he say?" Richard asked.

"He said he wouldn't kill the rest of my family." Penguin resumed ripping the sheet.

"I told you he was a good man. Like I said, Penguin, you are a good man too. I won't ever forget you," Richard said, looking at the clock.

"I hear you, my brother. I'm thankful that you were able to save your family. Now, let's get this thing over with. We wish we could help you but we aren't even in this room with you. The shift will be changing in a few hours. Let's get it over with now," Dwayne said, looking up at the iron bars and wondering how long it would take for a man to hang himself. He looked at Penguin's neck. It was extra thick. He hoped that thickness had nothing to do with the time it took a man to die from hanging.

"Damn." Richard hit the side of his head with his palm. "After this we'll have to do overtime."

"Yeah fool, we gonna be making more money," Dwayne said, picking the last bit of turkey from his teeth.

"Penguin is a good man. I don't want to make more money off him," Richard said.

"Richard, just shut the fuck up. Penguin, hurry up!"

Penguin continued to methodically pull the sheet apart, taking time to test each ripped strip for durability. He didn't want the sheet to break because he knew he would have to do it again. No, he wanted to go out like a man.

"You're a good man, Penguin, and you're doing the right thing. I wish more politicians would visit prisons. They too can learn to be good men." Richard stood to stretch his long legs.

"Penguin, you got a half hour left." Dwayne shoved the white greasy wrap from the sandwich into his pocket. He inspected the bed and the floor for any trace of his meal.

Penguin stood and finished laying out the ripped sheets across the bed. He looked at the men in the room and quickly picked up the strip closest to him. He bent once more to retrieve another strip off the bed. He knotted them together, then pulled to make sure they were strong enough. Tears started to roll from his eyes.

"Here." Dwayne handed him a photograph.

Penguin looked at it, and the tears flowed heavily. He kissed the picture and laid it down in the middle of the bed.

The picture was of two young boys, neither one older than

twelve. Looking at Penguin and looking at the boys one could understand the arguments against cloning. He had made a replica of himself just by fucking.

Richard wiped his eyes. "Penguin, you are a good man," he said.

"Sir." Penguin had stopped tying the sheets.

Dwayne looked at Penguin who was pointing at the cell phone.

"Yes?" Dwayne asked.

"The cell phone is off. He might change his mind and call back," Penguin said as he reached out to the iron rod outside the cell.

"I doubt it but I'll keep it on if it will make you happy," Dwayne said.

"Please keep it on, Dwayne. Let's make him happy." Richard said, his voice devoid of irony.

"Thank you," Penguin said as he continued to slip the sheet over the outside steel bar. As Penguin made his preparations, he kept his eyes on the blinking green light on the small Nokia phone in Dwayne's shirt pocket. If the light changed signaling a call, maybe he would see some more pictures of his children getting older. It was all he could hope for.

Chapter 1

"Rashaun, wake up." Andria Jackson nudged Rashaun Jones in the shoulder.

"What? What?" Rashaun sat up on the bed, looking all around as if under attack. He was wearing a gold-and-black striped pajama top and black silk boxers. Andria had told him they were the ugliest pair of pajamas she had ever seen. Rashaun had told her to say it loud enough for his mother to hear. She bought the pajamas.

Andria clicked on the bedside light.

"My water broke," she said, trying to ease herself off the bed.

"Your water broke. What does that mean?" Rashaun started pressing the bed looking for the wet spot.

"Feel your ugly boxers," Andria said, looking at Rashaun.

Rashaun felt his boxer shorts. There was no way in hell he had sweat that much.

"Shouldn't we call the doctor?" Rashaun asked, pulling off his boxers and dropping them on top of the gray hamper next to the bed.

"I'm calling her now. My water broke, which means that the baby will be coming soon. Uh-uh."

"What's that now?" Rashaun asked, looking at Andria bending over.

"Contractions. I'm having contractions," Andria said, finally easing herself off the bed.

"Baby, where are you going? You can't go anywhere while you're having contractions." Rashaun held on to Andria's arm. "You have to wait for the doctor."

"Rashaun, go get your mother. I'm going to call mine."

Rashaun gave Andria the phone and started up the stairs.

"Rashaun, please don't wake up the whole house," Andria called out as he left.

"What do you mean don't wake me up? My grandchild is about to be born and you don't want me up." Rashaun's mother, Albertina Jones, came down the stairs with Rashaun in tow. "Where's your overnight bag?"

"It's over in the corner of the living room." Andria stood and tried to stretch but she held onto her stomach midway through the process. "It hurts like hell."

"How many minutes apart are you?" Albertina asked, putting the overnight bag down next to the bed.

"I think about five minutes," Andria said, getting a dress from the closet.

"Girl, sorry to say it has just begun. You will feel pain you've never felt before. And that fool of a man you got, I don't know what he'll do."

As if on cue, Rashaun walked back into the room, a foolish grin on his face. "You ready, Andria?" Rashaun asked. He was dressed in a blue shirt and blue slacks.

"Look at him. He's dressed like Rupert the mechanic," Albertina said

Andria looked at Rashaun and started to laugh.

Rashaun looked at himself over and over.

Albertina pulled the wet sheets off the bed and bundled them under her arm.

"Let me go and take a shower," Andria said, taking her dress and moving toward Rashaun.

"Andria, are you sure you can take a shower now? Won't that hurt the baby or something?" Rashaun asked, looking at both Andria and his mother.

"Boy, move out of the woman's way. Do you want her to go and stink up the hospital?" Albertina asked.

"Baby, do you want me to make your breakfast or something? It's five-thirty in the morning," Rashaun said.

"Rashaun, Andria can't eat any breakfast now. She's going to the hospital. I think you should get something to eat though because I'm not picking you up when you pass out."

"Mom, I won't pass out. I've seen a lot of things in life that haven't made me sick. Why do you think my child being born will make me faint?" Rashaun lifted the red bag that Albertina had put on the side of the bed. Andria had packed it about a month ago. He didn't know what was in it, and he didn't ask. Over the months he had learned that a woman knew a lot more about having babies than a man. It wasn't because he didn't care, it was just that women seemed born with that extra info.

Andria came out of the shower holding her stomach. Rashaun ran to her before she fell.

"Are you okay?" he asked, trying to put all her weight on him.

"The contractions are very painful."

"Can you take anything for them?" Rashaun asked.

"No," Andria replied, sounding irritated.

"I'm just trying to help, honey," Rashaun said, looking away from Andria.

"I know, honey. I didn't mean to snap at you."

"What are you apologizing for?" Rashaun lifted the bag again. "If my mom hears you apologizing, she will curse me."

"You're right, she surely will," Andria said, smiling. "I think she wants this child more than us."

"Well, let's head out before you have the child in the basement," Rashaun said as he held onto Andria's hand and they started up the stairs.

"Rashaun, you got the car keys?" Andria asked.

Rashaun stopped and extricated his hand from Andria's. He riffled through his pockets.

Andria smiled.

At the same time the door up top opened and Albertina looked down on them.

"I heard. He forgot the keys. I think he was planning to push the car all the way to the hospital," Albertina said. "Andria, come up, girl. Let me give you something for this boy to eat at the hospital. He will act worse on an empty stomach."

"I love you, too, Mom," Rashaun said as he headed back down the steps.

"Rashaun, they're in the dresser drawer by the bed," Andria shouted.

"Baby, don't talk so loud. You might hurt yourself," Rashaun shouted back.

"He will be a good father," Albertina said as she handed Andria a cup of tea. "You just have to ignore the bumbling."

"I know he will. You have raised a beautiful son."

"I wish all my children were like Rashaun. Henry will be coming from Florida with his wife and kids to spend a week. I know you've never met him but he's not a bad boy; he just isn't Rashaun. Henry had so much potential as a young boy. I think he's even smarter than Rashaun but lazy. This boy just always likes things the easy way." Albertina sat down and sipped her tea. She gave Andria a travel cup to give to Rashaun. "Getting him to drink this will give you a head start on taking care of the baby."

"You guys talking about me?" Rashaun asked, dangling the keys, his prize for everyone to see. "Baby, why don't we get married in the hospital after we have the baby?"

Andria grimaced in pain as she had another contraction.

"That's why, because hospitals are for sick people and the pain doesn't end when the baby is born," Albertina said. " And it doesn't end right after birth. And knowing you, you will be so goo-goo eyed over the baby you won't pay any attention to Andria, much less get married."

"Rashaun, I only plan on getting married once, and believe me it's not going to happen in a hospital." Andria got up off the chair. "And I told you, I want all that legal stuff going on with you to be over with before I get married."

"I agree," Albertina said.

Rashaun looked at Andria then at his mother.

"I love you," he said to his mother and reached over and kissed her on the cheek.

"Let's go bring little Rashaun into this world," he said as he took Andria by the hand.

"And don't you dare leave that room. I heard a lot about switching babies and all that stuff. Call me if you need me. It would only take me a minute to head down to the hospital," Albertina said.

"That's okay, Mom." Andria said. "My mom is already on her way to the hospital."

Albertina walked them to the door, stood and watched as they headed down the stairs. Rashaun's car was parked in front of the house. She shook her head and smiled as she watched how gingerly Rashaun walked down the stairs with Andria. It was 5:50 A.M. and fall in New York was announcing its presence. One of the noisiest cities in the United States was quiet as a sleeping baby.

"Rashaun, I'm not an egg," Andria said, tugging at his hand but not letting go of it.

Rashaun held her hand tighter as he reached out to open the car door.

"Rashaun, look out," his mother screamed as she pushed the door open and jumped out on the top of the steps.

Rashaun looked up and saw a red-and-white star-spangled baseball bat heading toward Andria. His hands couldn't go out fast enough to prevent the impending blow.

Andria screamed at the top of her lungs.

Two uniformed officers fast asleep under a big maple tree a few car lengths down jumped up and immediately drew their weapons as they pushed the car doors open.

The baseball bat came down in a murderous rage.

Albertina grabbed onto the railing on the steps to stop herself from falling.

Rashaun pulled Andria down as he extended his body. The red-and-white star- spangled bat swung, and the world as Rashaun knew it existed no more.

He sucked on her breast as the experience of his young life had taught him. Gobble, gobble, bite and pull.

"Stop," Kim said as she pushed the shiny black bald head away from her.

"There is no breast milk coming from these breasts."

"What am I doing wrong now?" he asked, his anger contained in the tremor of his voice.

"There are sensitive parts to a woman's body that when aroused correctly can give great pleasure," she said, "but what you are?"

"I have never had any complaints before. The girls, love me. They call me Dark Chocolate," he said.

"How old are you, Roger? If all you had were girls maybe we shouldn't be talking."

"You know I'm twenty-seven. You did a complete investigation on me before you hired me." Roger Nelson sounded perturbed.

"Then you should know never to refer to women as girls. This is not kindergarten, and you are not playing poke the hole nor are you a lion tearing out a piece of flesh from the hunt. Now I want you to listen to me and do exactly what I say and as the book I loaned you illustrated," she said sternly. "I have had many men in my life, and those who remained were the memorable ones. There is more to being a man than a big dick. Do you want to remain?"

"I have adored you from the time we met. I would do anything to please you," he answered, a dreamy look coming into his eyes.

"Now let's start over."

"Tell me where."

"First, I'll tell you how. When you kiss my body, make sure your lips barely touch my skin. Let your tongue reach out to caress me. Brush me with your lips. Do not suck on any part of my body. Sometimes less is more. Whenever your mouth is on me, your hands should also be on me, caressing the opposite side of where your mouth is. This provides an unbelievable sensation. Now start." Kim laid back on the bed as an offering to the Creator. Her legs were shoulder-width apart and her breasts, which no child had sucked, waited for him.

Roger took her left hand and gently started to kiss it as Kim had advised. As he did so, his other hand reached over to Kim's right elbow, touching it as the book Kim had lent him illustrated. He started with the tip of her elbow and moved his hand back and forth.

Kim closed her eyes as he moved beyond her fingers. She was back in college again, and Rashaun had come to her dorm after studying at the library. He was wearing a long white sweatshirt that he had folded at the elbows. What brand name, he never could tell. He told her so many times that he didn't care about brand names. The faded Guess jeans that covered the white-and-gray Adidas sneakers were in stark contrast to his glistening blackness. She watched him take off his clothes.

Rashaun came to the foot of the bed, blacker than midnight. He reached down and grabbed her toes, kissing them gently as his right hand ran up her side, creating a current so strong that her body trembled. His tongue moved beyond her toes and up to the back of her heel. No one else had found that sensitive spot and as his soft lips reached down to kiss her while his tongue applied pressure to the muscle that ran from there straight to her womanhood, she could hardly keep her body still. Rashaun worked his tongue on the inside of her thighs while his fingers reached up and started to play with her belly button. He created circles around it, which intensified with his touch. His tongue ran up her legs, taking up all the juices her body had secreted. As he did so, he reached up to her breasts and started to make circles around her hard nipples.

She reached out to grab his neck, her head thrown back as she opened her legs. His tongue darted outside the lips of her vagina as her head started to spin. She didn't know if she could last that long. The intensity was building up in her body so fast. She wanted his tongue inside of her. She wanted him to release her demons. She couldn't wait any longer. She grabbed his head and pushed her womanhood onto his tongue.

"Stop!" she shouted.

"What's wrong?" Roger asked, a look of total shock on his face.

"What are you, a Chihuahua? You don't give oral sex like you're chewing on nuts." Kim got up off the bed.

Roger sat up, his head hanging. "What do you want from me, Kim? I'm trying my best." The hurt was evident in his voice.

"I need a drink," Kim said and walked out of the room.

"Can I¯," Roger started to say something but Kim interrupted him…

"No, because when I come back I want you to have your clothes on and for you to be walking out the door."

"What? You can't treat me like this."

"I can't?" Kim looked at him as if he was the killer of her unborn child. "Watch me."

There was complete silence as Kim walked out the room.

When Kim walked back in she had a glass of wine in one hand and a bottle in the other.

Roger was dressed. In his hands he held a picture frame. "He looks just like me," he said.

"How did you get this picture?" Kim asked.

"I kicked it as I was getting my underwear from the side of your bed."

Kim quickly went to Roger and snatched the picture frame

out of his hands.

"Don't fuck with my things," she said. "Turn the bottom lock on your way out."

"Can I call you?" he asked.

"Go home, Roger." She sat down on the bed with the wine glass and bottle in one hand and the picture frame in the other.

"Give me another chance. I know I can make you happy," he said as he opened the bedroom door.

"Not in this lifetime, Roger. You are not the man I want in this lifetime. I'll see you at work tomorrow," she said as she took the remote and turned on the TV. She took the picture of Rashaun and stared at it as if to make it materialize into a real person. She poured herself another glass of wine and drank it quickly, then poured herself another.

When she awoke, the TV was on, and the empty bottle lay right next to the picture of Rashaun. She squinted to check the time on the cable box on top of the TV. She didn't normally look at Channel Nine, the "ghetto channel" but the TV was on that station. When she saw Rashaun's mother screaming for her son, a jolt of sobriety hit her as she turned up the volume using the remote.

"No, it wasn't meant to happen like that. No, he can't be hurt," she said. With shaky hands and tears running down her cheeks, she reached for the phone. She looked at the wall and found the number for Black and Pink cab service. "How long?" she asked as she went over to her closet and pulled out a pair of black stretch jeans and a multicolored blouse.

"I'm going to Brookdale Hospital to set things right," she said.

"Alright, ma'am," the man on the other end said, totally ignoring Kim's last statement.

"How soon can he get here?" Kim asked.

"Twenty to thirty minutes," the cab dispatcher said.

"I'll be waiting downstairs," Kim said and hung up the phone

Kim climbed into the black Chevy Caprice with the tinted windows and a sign that told her she was being photographed.

"Brookdale. How much?" she asked as the car weaved into traffic on Clinton Street.

"Nice weather we're having today," the cab driver said, adjusting his mirrors so he could get a better look at Kim. "You are a very beautiful woman."

"Do I have to repeat myself, Ahmed?" Kim asked.

"No, ma'am. I heard you when you said you were going to Brookdale. The look on your face and the fact that you are going to the hospital can't be a good thing. I'm just trying to make conversation," he said, turning on Atlantic Avenue and heading northbound.

Kim's look didn't change; neither did her mouth open again.

"Forty dollars, and I'm sorry about whatever is ailing you."

Kim opened her purse and slipped her district attorney's's ID into the small opening of the glass partition that separated her from the driver.

The cab driver took the ID and looked it over as he moved around a gray PT Cruiser that was double-parked on Vanderbilt Avenue. "Brookdale, the hospital on Rockaway Avenue?" he said, pretending he had misunderstood her earlier request.

Kim was silent. She looked out at the trees that lined Eastern Parkway. She wasn't in the mood to be fucked with. Even though

Rashaun had completely humiliated her by making her strip then walking away in her office after Tyrone's trial she still loved that man. She honestly believed that Tyrone should be doing prison time right now. Tyrone had killed Judy Francis, a wife and mother. It didn't matter if he did it with his dick or a gun. The result was the same, death. But Tyrone was Rashaun's friend and the jury believed that accident bullshit and now Tyrone was free to walk the earth. Kim thought she would never see Rashaun in court again but when Rashaun got home and found his pregnant girlfriend¯ Kim couldn't remember the bitch's name at the moment—at home with her ex, he shot the ex to death. Now as a twist of fate or pulling strings would have it, she was prosecuting Rashaun for murder—. An attorney's past relationship with a defendant becomes a problem if the attorney understand it to be a problem therefore the law is a subjective one. Kim didn't see any conflict of interest in prosecuting Rashaun therefore she did not turn the case down. Kim knew the only way to get Rashaun was to give him one choice. She intended to do just that. Rashaun didn't know it but she was the best thing for him. He had loved her unconditionally before, and Kim was going to make certain he did it again. Whatever stood in her way she would just have to push it aside, including the bitch with his child. Rashaun would always be her man.

"It's twenty dollars for the ride to Brookdale." He pushed the ID back through the glass. The driver made the left from Linden Boulevard and pulled up behind an ambulance that was parked in front of the hospital.

Kim slid the multicolored twenty-dollar bill through the glass and exited the cab.

"Flowers for the sick." A tall hawkish built black man thrust a bouquet at Kim.

She did not break stride as the automatic doors opened as she stepped into the hospital. She walked over to the information desk where two ladies were conversing. A big heavyset woman about the age of fifty and a young woman half her age with gold bangles in her ears and a piercing in her nose were discussing relationships.

"My man is studying to be a rapper. Every evening when I come home he kicks those lyrics to me. I can't wait. One day he's going to be bigger than 50 Cent," the young woman said, "then I'm going to be riding down Flatbush in a green Hummer with my name on the Sprewell rims."

"I told my husband if he don't find a job, I'm kicking him out of the house. I can't support two kids and a grown-ass man on my meager salary. People come to America, and they think everything is easy. If I knew what I know now, I would have left him in Trinidad." She stretched out her index finger to Kim as Kim came up to the desk. "Girl, America ain't easy. People at home think it's a bed of roses and they're the ones going to the beach on the weekends. Hold on, let me see what this woman wants."

Kim had chosen to ignore the disrespect. "Good morning. Can you tell me what room Rashaun Jones is in?"

"Rashaun Jones?" she asked, looking at the younger woman who shook her head.

"He was brought in very early this morning."

"Mr. Jones. Is he young or old?" the woman asked, looking at Kim as if she didn't want to be bothered.

"Maybe you can check the book," Kim said, looking down at the patient book in front of her.

"Excuse me. Are you telling me how to do my job?" the woman asked Kim.

Kim stared at the woman, her face expressionless. She wasn't in the mood for this shit.

The woman flipped through the book.

"Here he is," she said, pointing at a name. "He's in Room 912."

"Thank you," Kim said and turned around.

"You can't see him. Access is restricted. The cops are up there," the woman said, a big smile coming over her face.

Kim showed the woman her D.A. ID and started to walk toward the elevator on the right.

"So big deal she's a lawyer. These people get a degree and they want you to bow to them," the woman said as she saw Kim heading to the elevator.

"My man listens to me sometimes," the young woman said as Kim became a distant memory for the women.

Kim rode on the elevator with a nurse who wore a tight shirt. She looked at him and wondered exactly what he was working on.

"Visiting?" he asked.

"Yes," Kim replied.

"I hope he doesn't stay in the hospital too long because a beautiful woman like yourself should not be left alone. My name is William," he said, taking off his white glove to shake Kim's hand.

"Nice to meet you, William," Kim said, looking him up and down.

"I'm a nurse but I ain't no fag," he said. "Everyone thinks because you're a male nurse you are gay. But I could give you references."

"I never said you were," Kim said, smiling for the first time this morning..

"You are beautiful, and I can tell that you're educated, two of the main qualities I'm looking for in a woman. Let me get your number. We can have dinner at the Crab House in Manhattan."

"I would love to take you up on the offer but I only eat fish, if you know what I mean," Kim said, emitting a wicked smile.

"I could take you both out. I don't mind watching, and I'll only join if you ask me to because I'm sure you all are tired of the electronics," William said.

"This is my floor. Nice meeting you, William," Kim said.

"I'm on the eleventh floor if you're in the mood for some vegetable besides squash," William said as Kim stepped out of the elevator.

Kim walked over to the nurses' station.

An Indian nurse with a dot on her forehead was jotting something down in a book.

"Can I help you, miss? This is a no visitors wing," she said to Kim.

"I'm here to see Rashaun Jones," Kim said.

"Rashaun Jones is in a coma, and he is under twenty-four-hour NYPD protection due to the nature of his assault. I'm sorry, he's only allowed family visits," she said and looked at her watch. "Where is William?" she mumbled.

Kim took her ID and placed it in front the woman. "I'm with the Brooklyn district attorney's office. I have to see the victim."

"I'm sorry, ma'am. He is down the hall, the second door on the right. There's an officer at the door. Just show him your ID."

There was no officer at the door to Andria's hospital room, which was located on the opposite side of the building.

"How is Rashaun doing?" Andria asked as she lay on the

bed, her legs spread apart and wires hooked up to her stomach to monitor the baby's heartbeat. She had her finger in a tester that monitored her blood pressure, which had started to rise. She had been confined to that particular position on the bed for about five hours.

Her mother, Joyce Jackson, had removed Andria's bedpan.

"Andria, don't worry about Rashaun," Albertina said. "I know my son. He has a hard head. He'll be okay. I want you to concentrate on delivering that baby."

"Yes, Andria. Albertina is right. You can't worry about Rashaun. That will put too much stress on the baby. Remember, whatever you are feeling the baby is feeling too," Joyce said. "Rashaun is in God's hands and nothing that wasn't meant to happen to him will happen."

"I say an Amen to that." Albertina sat back on the white-and-brown flowered couch. "This place is very nice. The hospital today gives you your own private room with a bathroom and TV. It is very spacious with a window so you can see outside. Women today are so lucky. When I had Rashaun, there was a roomful of pregnant women—some screaming in pain, others cursing out their husbands."

"Like that," Andria said as loud crying from a patient down the hall filled the room.

"That woman needs to take something. She'll drive everyone on the floor crazy," Joyce said as she adjusted the pillow under Andria's head.

"Oh, oh," Andria said as she squeezed her mother's hand.

"Try to breathe, Andria. It helps," Joyce said as Andria relaxed the grip on her hand. "Your contractions are coming faster. When is your doctor getting here?"

"She should be here any minute now," Andria said.

"I hope she comes soon because someone has to deliver my grandchild," Albertina said, getting up. "I'm going to call and find out how Rashaun is doing. I think he'll come out of the coma soon."

Andria's eyes lit up. "How do you know? Did you talk to a doctor?"

"A mother knows these things, Andria. Soon you'll understand what I'm talking about," Albertina said. "Rashaun will not leave his child."

Rashaun did not see Kim enter the room, neither was he aware what was going on with him. He just lay there staring out into space. The coma had left him totally incapacitated. There were a number of tubes hooked up to him, and he was currently wearing an adult diaper, which the nurse checked every three hours.

Kim walked into the room after explaining to the officer in front of the door that she was there on official business.

"Rashaun, what have they done to you?" she asked as she walked alongside the bed. "I'm here now," she said, caressing the only part of his face that didn't have a tube sticking out.

Rashaun's eyes remained blank, staring into space.

"I came here to tell you that my love for you will never die. I'm really sorry for hurting you. If I knew then what I know now, you would never be lying here hooked up to these machines. They say every good man needs a good woman beside him, and I'm the woman for you. We could conquer the world together. I've dated men from all walks of life— lawyers, doctors, professional athletes and politicians, and no one can hold a candle to you. You're special. I didn't know that when we were together but I know it now. It drains me whenever I have to go up against you in court but I will stay in your life any way I can. I knew that we were soul mates from the first time we laid eyes on each other. You with your weak lines," Kim smiled. "I saw that beauty in you that I don't think anyone saw before and no one ever will. Your heart is pure and full of love. I know sometimes I don't say or do the right thing, but my whole life I have had to protect myself, and sometimes protecting is attacking. Even though you lie here barely alive I can see the promises of a great future ahead for us." Kim lifted up the hospital gown from Rashaun's right side. "I'm always amazed at your skin, so smooth yet firm and tender."

There was a knock on the door.

"Who is it?" Kim asked.

"I'm just checking to see if everything is alright," the officer replied.

"Everything is fine," Kim said. "I'll be out shortly."

She slipped her hand under the gown, tracing the outline of Rashaun's chest.

"Many nights I stay awake playing with myself as I imagine tracing my hands all over your body. You remember the times when you would sit on a chair and watch me play with myself? You used to get so turned on. You couldn't even wait until I came before you would jump on me and we would make love for hours."

As Kim ran her right hand over Rashaun's chest, she took her left hand and started to caress her breast.

"I'm getting so turned on just by touching you and imagining what it would be like to make love to you again." Kim eased down the diaper that held Rashaun's manhood. "They say there are a few things that work on a man regardless of his state of being."

Everything that people say to do to relieve the pain in labor wasn't working at the moment. Albertina was on one side of the bed and Joyce was on the other as Andria squeezed both their hands in an attempt to fight the pain that seemed to want to render her unconscious.

"Breathe, Andria. Take deep breaths and relax," Joyce said as Andria maximized the pressure on her hand.

And as quickly as the pain came, it left, and Andria released the ladies' hands.

"I don't know if I could do this without the epidural," Andria said, trying to make herself comfortable.

"If you want the epidural, we can call the anesthesiologist to give you the shot," said the nurse, a middle-age woman who had earlier given them some info on her short stay in the Pink Houses on Linden Boulevard. Presently she owned a duplex on Staten Island. "You don't have to go through the pain. I took the epidural for my delivery, and I didn't have any side effects as everyone told me I would."

"Andria, it's up to you. When I was having you, there was nothing you could take for the pain, but I also understand times are different now, and if you don't have to put up with the pain then don't do it," Joyce said.

"Mom, are you okay? I can't believe you said that." Andria looked at her mother in disbelief. "Thanks, but I think I will try it without the epidural."

"Suit yourself," said the nurse and continued to jot down information on Andria and the baby's vital signs. "I think the next time the doctor comes in you'll be having the baby."

"Here it comes again," Andria said, tightening her grip on

her mother's hand as she was hit with the contractions.

"Rashaun will be very proud of you," Albertina said.

"He betta, otherwise he'll have the next one. Did I tell—" Andria gritted her teeth as the pain came on much stronger than before.

All of a sudden a loud ping came from one of the monitors. All three ladies looked at the nurse who had gotten up from her chair. She checked all the sensors going to Andria as Albertina and Joyce backed away. When she lifted Andria's hand she saw the fallen plug that was hooked up to Andria's right thumb.

"Here it is," she said and slipped the sensor back onto Andria's thumb and the pinging stopped.

The door opened and Andria's doctor, Dr. Rice, came in. She was a short black woman with freckles.

"How you doing, Andria?" she asked.

"In pain," Andria replied.

"Well let's see your dilation," she said and lifted up Andria's gown.

Kim adjusted herself on the edge of Rashaun's bed as she slipped her hand over Rashaun's penis. He was semi-erect.

"I guess the saying is true. Your penis still works even when your mind is gone," she said as she started to slowly rub his penis.

"I wish you were conscious for this, Rashaun. Look at me. I'm trembling in anticipation of having you. You hurt me so much when you walked out on me at the office. I hated you so much then but I understood what you were going through. I knew you wanted me. And God knows I wanted you desperately. I was so hurt when I lost you in law school. " She continued to rub him as her eyes swept the room. They settled on a small plastic cup next to his food tray. "I hope God will forgive me."

She went over to the tray and scooped up the cup. Next to the cup were two test tubes with Rashaun's name written on them. She took one that had a red label and walked back to where she was sitting. She looked deeply into Rashaun's eyes and kissed him on the cheek then quickly nudged the lipstick from his face. She went back over to the tray and took the napkin that was sealed in plastic wrap with a white plastic knife and fork. She wondered why they left food for a person in a coma who was hooked up to feeding tubes but this was New York City.

"Damn," she said as she almost tripped over the tubes going to Rashaun's mouth and hand. "Kim, calm down. You are too nervous." She took a quick look at the door. She walked back to the other side of the bed, wiping the lipstick off her lips. This time when she got back to the bed she did not sit down. Instead she leaned over as she pushed up Rashaun's gown and took his penis with both her hands.

As her head started to descend down onto him, she heard another knock.

"Andria, it's time for us to deliver that beautiful baby of yours. You're ten centimeters and fully dilated," Dr. Rice said as she pulled over a tray containing an assortment of tools. "I want you to relax and do exactly as I say. When I say push, you have to push. It will be painful but you can do it."

Andria looked up at Albertina and Joyce who stood on each side of the bed. She brought her hands to hold on to them.

"Now, Andria push," Dr. Rice said.

Andria inhaled deeply and exhaled, pushing down.

"That's good, Andria. I could feel the head. He is coming. Now let's go again."

"It hurts," Andria said, rolling her eyes in pain as she moved her head back and forth.

"Andria, I know you can do it. Inhale deeply and push out as you exhale," Dr. Rice said as she maneuvered the baby's head.

Andria inhaled as deeply as she could and exhaled again, pushing.

"That's it, Andria. You're doing great. Now let's go again. He's coming."

Andria had never felt pain like that before in her life. It felt like as if her vagina was being split open. Her anus felt like it was about to deliver its own baby. She kept turning her head from side to side as the pain increased. Andria did not know why she was still conscious because she didn't want to be. Her friend, Hilma, had told her she had never experienced pain like this before. She had to give Hilma credit for doing it three times. If Rashaun wanted another child, he would have to deliver it himself or have someone else do it for him. She pushed again as Dr. Rice instructed, and with each movement she felt like she was losing the lower part of her body.

"You're doing great, Andria. He's coming. Give me another big one."

Andria didn't know where she was getting the energy from, but she was finding it. Each time she inhaled deeper and deeper, hoping it would be the last. She had pain in places she didn't know could hurt. *What have women done to have to endure such pain?* she asked herself. Sweat was running down her face. She looked at the ceiling then down to the doctor who was hidden by her legs.

"You're doing good, Andria. Don't give up," Joyce said, taking a handkerchief from her bag and wiping Andria's forehead.

Chapter 2

Rashaun opened his eyes slowly. The constant drumming in his head made him want to close them quickly. He didn't. Fragments of what happened to him came back as his blurry vision cleared. He remembered walking with Andria down the steps of his mother's house then going to open the door of his car. He saw the bat lifted in the air. He had bowed down to open the door of the car for Andria. The bat was headed for her stomach, for his child. He knew he couldn't lift his hands in time to stop the blow so he had to do whatever it took to save his own. The only part of his body that could stop the blow was his head. He didn't question whether the blow was going to kill him or damage his brain for the rest of his life. He wasn't going to let anything hurt two of the most important people in his life.

Rashaun couldn't make out the figure sitting in the chair on the left side of the bed. He knew she had a dress on but that was it. She was sitting too far away from him. As if hearing his mental appeal, she got up and moved forward. That fresh, sexy perfume was very familiar. A physically forced smile came to his lips. It was Andria. There was a God, and again he was blessed. She adjusted his hand with the IV in it alongside his body so that she could sit next to him.

"I thought we had lost you," she said, cradling him ever so gently.

Rashaun wanted to speak but the tubes in his mouth only allowed him to repeat the previous gesture.

"Don't try to speak. You have a feeding tube in your mouth."

Rashaun looked up at her, his eyes opening wide.

"Rashaun, you've been in a coma for more than eight days. You have a gash in the middle of your head that took numerous stitches to close. You have a beautiful son that looks just like you," Andria said, smiling.

This time Rashaun blinked twice, and he looked up at the ceiling.

He looked at Andria again with a big smile. He looked around the room.

"Do you think your mother would let me keep Wisdom in the hospital?" Andria asked, looking at her cell phone. "I called her a few minutes ago, so I'm sure she's on her way here. You gave us quite a scare, baby. It happened so fast. I heard your mother scream and I turned around to look at her. At the same time, the man swung the bat and it hit you squarely on the head. The force brought us both down to the ground. You were completely out. I put up my hands to fend off the blow but it never came. Gunshots rang out loud, and I covered my head. When I opened my eyes the man with the bat was lying down next to us with a few holes in his chest. There were two cops talking on their radios, summoning the ambulance, and your mother was with us putting a towel on your head to stop the blood." Andria adjusted the pillow underneath Rashaun's head.

The door opened.

Rashaun grimaced as he turned to the door.

"How you feeling?" A black doctor with a heavy southern

accent asked as he went around to the right side of the bed.

Rashaun nodded.

The doctor shone a light in Rashaun's eyes then listened to his breathing.

"You took quite a hit there, young man. I've seen lesser hits kill men twice your size. You're a lucky man, but then again I could understand why you didn't want to die. You have a lovely wife, and I heard she just gave you a beautiful son. You're recovering pretty well but you have to rest," he said, looking at Andria.

"I know, doctor, but his son is on his way, and I don't think Rashaun will rest until he sees him," Andria said.

"I understand, but let him get some rest as soon as he sees his son. I'll be back tomorrow to check up on you."

The doctor held the door open for Rashaun's mother to come in with the baby.

"Rashaun, you're going to give your mother a heart attack," Albertina said as she took Wisdom from his infant carrier.

Rashaun tried to sit up but the tremendous pain in his head wouldn't let him.

"Don't try to sit up, Rashaun. You can see him from here." Andria pressed the button on the bed that she had seen the nurse use to raise the bed up earlier. Albertina gave Andria the baby, and Andria immediately kissed Wisdom on the cheek.

Andria took Wisdom and held him right in front of Rashaun.

For the first time, Rashaun did not feel the pain in his head. He looked at the tiny little being in Andria's arms, and tears started to flow. He didn't know why Andria said the baby looked like him but he believed he was the most beautiful baby in the world. Rashaun tried to lift his hand to touch the baby but the pain came back with a vengeance.

"Rashaun, don't try to move. You'll have the rest of your life to touch him. He's not going anywhere," his mother said, looking at the bandage on top of Rashaun's head. "I think this bandage needs to be changed."

Wisdom started to cry, and Andria put him in her lap and took out one of her breasts.

"This child is as greedy as you were," Albertina said as she rang the nurse's bell.

The knock on the door jolted the occupants in the room.

Rashaun turned his head slightly to look at the door.

Andria's breast slipped out of Wisdom's mouth.

Albertina's face held a scroll. "Who is it?" Her voice betrayed her feelings as she moved to the door.

"I'm with the district attorney's office. Can I come in?" The masculine voice filtered through the door.

Albertina opened the door slightly.

"I cannot believe you people. The man has been in a coma for over a week and the minute he opens his eyes you all are here already. This is my son. He isn't running away from the law. Why don't you all just leave him alone?" Albertina closed the door, without waiting for a response.

Andria brought Wisdom to Rashaun and once more everyone concentrated on the new entry into the world.

"I don't understand what the DA's office wants with you. They can't even keep their prisoners alive. A week ago one of their prisoners who was supposed to testify against a Brooklyn drug dealer named Roundtree hung himself."

Rashaun kept blinking as his mother spoke. Neither Andria nor his mother knew his connection with the dead prisoner. Penguin was the only man besides Mr. Roundtree that could connect Rashaun with Paul, the man he had killed in his apartment.

"Mom, come hold Wisdom for me. I have to go to the bathroom," Andria said. When she left, Albertina continued holding Wisdom in Rashaun's lap.

"Rashaun, Andria was willing to die for you," Albertina said.

Rashaun's eyes grew large.

"After the man hit you and you were down, the gunshots started, and I thought for sure you and Andria were going to be killed. Andria covered you with her body and she didn't move until I pulled her away. She didn't care about her safety. All she wanted was to protect you. I want you to always remember that because there will be times when you want to walk away from Andria because the relationship might not be working."

Rashaun shook his head.

"Listen to me, Rashaun. You and Andria are both crazy in love with each other now. This kind of love doesn't last forever. There will come a point when the glow fades and reality begins. There will be more attractive women competing for your attention, and the strain of fatherhood will make you look at the front door. I want you to remember the woman who was willing to die for you. When I'm gone and you're all alone, I guarantee you she will stand by you."

Again Rashaun shook his head.

"Yes, Rashaun, Andria has cut the strings between me and you. I thought I would be bitter when that time came but I'm not. My love for you is everlasting."

Rashaun nodded.

"Yes, I know you feel the same way," Albertina said, smiling, "but the torch has been passed, and many mothers have spent their life with sorrow because their son's choices would only bring pain, but not me. I believe in Andria and you. When you were born, the doctor said you were the blackest baby he had ever seen. When he put you in my arms I saw the most beautiful baby in the world. God had blessed me, and over all these years you've never disappointed me. You've done some dumb things and I've beaten your butt because of them."

Once again Rashaun shook his head.

"But you've made me proud and happy. Sometimes a mother says she wishes all her children could be like this one, not meaning lack of love for one child but an exemplary standard. I feel that way about you. You've become a father now. I never thought this day would come. I'm not even worried about the court case because I know you'll be exonerated. The expression in your eyes when you look at this child tells me one thing: you will be a great father. In this day and age, I know sometimes women make it difficult for men to be fathers but I don't believe that will be the case here. I believe Andria will let you be a great father. I'll do one last thing for you. You've given me thousands of dollars over the years. I know you thought I had spent it but I didn't. As you fight your battle so you can be a father and a husband, I'll plan your wedding with your woman."

Rashaun shook his head.

"No is not an answer to this question. I know you have money, but you have a family now, and that should go toward making a life for them."

Rashaun smiled as his mother slipped her hand in his.

"Why are you guys looking at me?" Andria asked as she walked back into the room.

"I don't know what's wrong with this boy. All he does is do head movements and squeeze. He needs to get out of that bed and come home and change diapers." Albertina started to put baby clothes in the diaper bag.

There was a knock on the door followed by the entrance of a nurse.

"People, we have to break up the party. I have to change the patient, and he has to get some rest," she said as she went over to Rashaun. "Now that Mr. Jones has regained consciousness, I'm sure you'll have him home soon."

"Praise the Lord for that," Albertina said as she picked up the infant carrier.

Kim watched the man Captain Bennet introduced as Officer Phillips, the supervisor on duty the night of the suicide. He was about six feet tall and when he shook her hand she immediately took out a tissue and wiped it. She needed more than one tissue to get the clammy sweat off her hands. She shivered as he devoured her body with his eyes. The other one called Lawson was a lot more respectful. He said good morning then went and took his seat without drooling.

Kim immediately knew that Officer Phillips was somehow responsible for the death of Penguin, a key witness in Rashaun's prosecution for murder. Penguin had told Kim that he and a drug dealer called Mr. Roundtree had gone to Paul's apartment and roughed him up as a warning from Rashaun Jones. His testimony would have dug a deep hole in which it would have been impossible for Rashaun to come out of without a key from her. Now, this fool Phillips, she was sure had ruined her plans.

"We're very sorry about what happened to your witness, Ms. Rivers. An internal investigation has concluded that it was a suicide," the captain said.

"The problem I have with this suicide is that the prisoner was supposed to be in protective custody. Tell me if I'm wrong but doesn't that mean that he was being watched twenty-four hours a day," Kim said, staring at Dwayne Phillips.

"Ms. Rivers, protective custody and suicide watch are two different things. Protective custody is when we keep the prisoner from being hurt by other prisoners whereas suicide watch is when the prisoner has shown he is a danger to himself. This particular prisoner never showed that he posed a danger to himself," the captain responded.

"Captain, I do agree with you, but I believe that the prisoner was assisted in carrying out his suicide."

"What the fuck are you saying?" Dwayne asked as he got up from the chair. "I was on duty that night."

"Sit down, officer!" Captain Bennet said, raising his voice for the first time. "Ms. Rivers, we do not live in a perfect world. Due to the nature of the prisoner's death, we did an investigation. We didn't find any inconsistencies with the suicide ruling. The results were forwarded to the DA's office and I'm sure you received a copy. We're here to grant your request to speak to the guards who were closest to the prisoner, so if you don't mind, Ms. Rivers, I will give you the opportunity to speak to the guards at this point. Please bear in mind that this is not a courthouse and my officers have a right to refuse to answer any of your questions."

"Okay, Captain, we'll play it your way. I would like to question the officers individually. I'll start with Officer Lawson."

The captain motioned for Dwayne to leave.

"I don't know why you're giving this bitch all these privileges Captain, but I'm going to contact my union. I didn't take this job working with the scum of the earth to go through this." He grunted some obscenities under his breath then stepped out of the room.

Kim looked at the captain who sat at the head of the table. Richard Lawson sat directly across from Kim.

"I'm not leaving." The captain's tone left no room for discussion.

"Mr. Lawson, you were on duty the night of Mr. Thomas suicide."

"Yes, ma'am. Mr. Thomas was a good man. I don't know why he would have done that to himself." Richard tapped his knuckles lightly on the table.

Kim kept her eyes on him, trying to establish eye contact, but Richard wouldn't let her. "Did you talk to Mr. Thomas anytime on your watch?"

"I spoke to him briefly around 1:00 A.M."

"Did he seem nervous, anxious or relaxed?"

"I can't recall his composure at that time, but I would guess he didn't show any emotion that was out of the ordinary. Prisoners go through a variety of emotions when they're on lockdown. I personally did not know anything about Mr. Lawson's case, and he didn't volunteer any information to me." Richard stopped tapping on the table. He slipped his fingers in and out of each other as if he was getting ready to put on a pair of boxing gloves.

"So you had no idea why Mr. Thomas was in protective custody?"

"No, ma'am."

"When was the next time you saw Mr. Thomas?"

"I saw Mr. Thomas around 3:00 A.M. when I was making my rounds. I assume he was sleeping then."

"What time did you discover the body?" Kim asked, looking a bit puzzled.

"At 5:30 A.M."

"Were there any other patrols after you and before your discovery of Mr. Thomas' body?" Kim asked. She concentrated on Richard's interlocking fingers. There was a small puddle of water forming under his hands.

Richard looked over at the captain.

The guards were supposed to patrol the floors at least once every hour in the protective cells. It was a rule instituted after there was a series of mishaps resulting in some high-profile acquittal.

"My supervisor wanted to stretch his legs so he took a walk around for me."

"Did he find anything out of place or abnormal?"

"I don't know. He didn't discuss anything with me."

"So what you are saying is that when both you and your supervisor saw Mr. Lawson, everything was okay."

"I guess you can say that."

Kim moved her elbows from on top of the table and looked over at the captain. "This really puzzles me. I'm not a psychiatrist but a suicidal person usually shows some signs of positive or negative emotions. The time of the patrols and the time of the suicide don't add up. Thank you, Mr. Lawson. Please send Mr. Phillips in," Kim said as she made a note on a yellow pad she had taken out of her bag at the beginning of the meeting.

Richard remained seated.

"You are excused, Lawson," the captain said. "Send Phillips in."

Richard got up from the chair and quickly wiped up the puddle of water with a napkin with a Subway sandwich logo on it.

The captain averted his eyes so that they wouldn't meet Kim's who was waiting for a reaction from him.

Dwayne walked in and took a seat next to Kim.

Kim pinched the top of her nose.

"I'm sorry. My wife has me on this garlic diet. She says it reduces high blood pressure." Dwayne slipped a peppermint candy in his mouth.

Kim got up and walked around the Captain and sat opposite Dwayne.

"Patience, Ms. Rivers. The scent goes away very fast." Dwayne sniffed into the air.

"Mr. Phillips, did you see Mr. Thomas between the hours of 3:00 and 5:30 A.M."

Dwayne shuffled his feet, rolled his eyes and leaned back on the chair. "I think I did patrol the cells during that time."

"Can you be specific on the time?"

"Not really."

"Is there a specific time in which Richard was supposed to patrol the hall?"

"Between the hours of three and six," Dwayne said, smiling.

"Do you think this is a joke, Mr. Phillips?" Kim asked as she slipped her legal pad into her bag.

"No, Ms. Rivers. I think the correction department is one of the most overlooked parts of the justice system. When you guys put people who would rather kill you than look at you behind bars, do you think these people welcome us with open arms? One of the guys chooses to help taxpayers by killing himself, and there is this big investigation. I think you people are a joke. If we try to protect every prisoner in the system from himself, everyone would be screaming invasion of privacy and the cost would be prohibitive. That would mean that we would have to put enough video and audio equipment and manpower the equivalent of an MTV *Real World* show in every cell. I don't think you or America is ready for that."

Kim started to clap, the sound echoing the room. "Great speech, Mr. Phillips. Was this rehearsed or did a prisoner hanging from a bed sheet under your command inspire you? What you fail to realize or maybe you do is corruption of officials are what's killing the justice system. Sloppy, hungry men who would sell their mother, much less a prisoner for his or her own gain are what's bringing this system down. There is nothing more that I can do here, and you and Richard have been cleared of any wrongdoing. I don't believe you are innocent. I smell a rat and it stinks. My office will launch an ongoing investigation that will look at every penny you and Mr. Lawson have received."

Dwayne adjusted his collar.

"The only thing that either one of you will be able to do with any monetary gains from this incident is buy Twinkies from the grocery store. And it is obvious that you have already had your fill of those."

Kim turned to the captain. "I don't know what kind of investigation the corrections department did but I don't see how a man who didn't demonstrate any suicidal tendencies killed himself. The time frame of the patrols and the suicide leaves a lot of unanswered questions." Kim stood.

The captain stood also.

Dwayne remained seated, staring at Kim's empty chair.

"I'm very sorry about the incident. I hope this doesn't destroy your case, Ms. Rivers. I'm sure you'll be able to work around this unfortunate incident," the captain said, reaching to shake Kim's hand.

Kim picked up her jacket and ignored the captain's outstretched hand.

"Captain Bennet, some things just make things difficult but never impossible. A man was killed, and I will make sure someone pays for that." She turned to Dwayne. "Our office will be watching you."

Dwayne remained seated. His eyes did not leave Kim's chair.

"How did it go?" Roger, Kim's boyfriend, asked as Kim closed the door of the meeting room.

"Just as I expected, a lot of bullshit. This meeting did confirm my suspicion that there was foul play in Penguin's death," Kim said as they walk through the prison.

"Roundtree walks, doesn't he?" Roger asked.

"Roundtree isn't my case, but I'll assume he does. Without Penguin, everything becomes hearsay. Thanks for coming and picking me up," Kim said as they walked to the parking lot. She adjusted her skirt as she slid into the black 350 Z, pulling out a silver Nokia phone, she punched the keys as she adjusted the seat.

Roger pulled the car out of the parking lot, showing the guard his assistant district attorney's.

"Yeah meet me at 40/40 around 7:30." Kim put the phone back into her purse.

"You don't seem upset about losing a key witness," Roger said.

"Roger, let me give you a little bit of advice: You can never depend on one witness to make your case. There's always the what-if scenario. Penguin would have helped solidify my case against Rashaun¯ I mean Mr. Jones¯ but he was only one small part. Mr. Jones killed a man, and I think he did it because of jealousy. I'm sure he had exerted this behavior before."

"Kim, I read the court case, Mr. Jones was defending his pregnant girlfriend. I don't know if I wouldn't have done the same thing if I were in his position. Why do you want to get him so bad? Roundtree, now that's one bad motherfucker. Have you read the file on that guy? He must have killed at least twenty people, and that's a conservative estimate. Now that guy, I think you should go after one hundred percent." Roger came off the Brooklyn Bridge and made a U-turn that took him into the Edison parking lot next to the Brooklyn Marriott.

"I don't care about Roundtree and people like him. For every one that you take down, twenty spurt up. People like Rashaun¯ I mean Mr. Jones¯ believe they're above all the rules. Mr. Jones sets a bad precedent, if every man goes around and kill his lover's ex, can you imagine? Do you know how many men would love to get rid of their spouse's ex? Men don't want to know that there was someone there before them. They want to fuck everybody else then go and find a virgin from Idaho and marry her. They want the innocent, the untouched, and the thought that someone else had their woman climbing the walls in most cases is enough to warrant murder. And that's what I think happened. Mr. Jones killed Paul because of jealousy. He came home and found his girlfriend in a compromising position with her ex, and he went ballistic. I'm sure somewhere in his past he had demonstrated this kind of violent behavior, and it's our job to bring witnesses to testify about that. Now go to Wendy's and get me a grilled chicken salad," Kim said as Roger pulled between a white Camry and a blue Volkswagen Jetta.

"I'm not like those men," Roger said as he got out of the car.

"I know you're not, Roger. That's why I'm still talking to you. Make sure they give you the right salad and pick me up a carrot juice at the natural health store on the corner of Jay and

Willoughby," Kim said, walking away from the car, each step more pronounced than the other.

Roger stood shaking his head as Kim walked away.

Chapter 3

Utica Avenue was crowded as usual at two o'clock in the afternoon and Rashaun scolded himself for even trying to make it down the street. He brought his mother's green Mercedes Benz ML 320 to a stop in front of the West Indian vegetable and fruit store located between Church and Lenox Avenues in the heart of the bumper-to-bumper traffic. He remained in the car for a few seconds, looking up and down the street for a policeman or ticket agents. He knew that the likelihood of getting a park at one of the meters was the equivalent of a young black man hitting the New York Lottery. He waited a few more seconds while the line in front of the Chinese cashier dwindled to one person. Rashaun hit the big red hazard button located on the steering column and jumped out of the SUV. He ran inside the store and quickly went past the aisle that had all the green leafy vegetables: he found the green thyme leaves next to the hot red peppers. He scooped up two packs of the thyme and shot a glance outside before hurrying up to the cashier. He tapped his foot as an old lady in a purple coat inquired about the freshness of the pigtails. Rashaun put the thyme down and went out to look for cops or traffic agents. In the age of the $110 ticket, double parking had become a serious offense. He went back and paid for the thyme thanked the cashier. As he stepped into the Benz, he saw a cop make a U-turn to his side of the street. Rashaun quickly put the car in gear and headed to downtown Brooklyn.

It took him twenty minutes to get there. Rashaun again hesitated inside the car. He scanned the streets, looking for anything out of the ordinary. The police had told him that an eyewitness had seen the man who attacked him and Andria get out of a black Lincoln Town Car that sped away after the incident. He was told he should be careful and always look around whenever he was in public because the police didn't think it was an isolated attack. It seemed to be well planned, and the person who was killed didn't have the capability of planning a simple grab-and-run robbery. The man who attacked them, Robert Lee, was a thirty-five-year-old crack head with a long record of violent robberies. The talk on the street was that he would whack his mama and leave a note if someone gave him twenty dollars. The fact that he died at the scene left the case wide open. No one saw the driver of the Town Car who sped away after the incident. Lee's death wasn't a tragedy but an end to an existence without much substance.

Rashaun was told to be extra careful when he visited familiar places because most planned attacks happened in places like homes, jobs or areas frequented by the victims. He was also told to try to protect Andria and their son because the cops did not know at whom the attack was aimed. Rashaun hated leaving Andria and Wisdom home alone but Bob Yelram, Rashaun's lawyer and mentor, had told him to come into the office to discuss the death of one of the prosecution witnesses. Rashaun had contacted his ex-cop friend Lethal to drive Andria and the baby wherever they wanted to go. Lethal was always a phone call away.

Rashaun took his key out and opened the door, again looking up and down the street. He hadn't been to his office since the assault. Yelram had taken over his office to prepare his defense.

The prosecutor, his ex-girlfriend Kim Rivers had offered him eight to fifteen years instead of twenty-five to life if he was convicted. Rashaun had turned it down when Yelram presented it to him.

"Good morning, Mrs. Louis," Rashaun said, trying to sound as upbeat as possible. Karen Louis was about sixty-eight years old. She had been recommended by Andria's mother and of course approved by Andria. Mrs. Louis had retired from twenty-eight years of employment as a schoolteacher in Brooklyn. She started working in Rashaun's office as a secretary one month after he opened the office.

"Rashaun, it's so nice to see you. How are the baby and Andria?" Mrs. Louis asked. Rashaun told Mrs. Louis to call him by his first name but he called her by her last name to show his respect.

"They're both doing fine," Rashaun said as he took off his cap which hid the bandaged on the side of his head. He couldn't keep it on for too long because his head would begin to sweat, and only God knew what that would do to his wound.

Mrs. Louis looked carefully at Rashaun's head. "And how are you doing?" she asked.

"I'm doing good, just a little pain here and there," he said, eager to move onto his office. "Is Yelram in?"

"He's there. I don't know what he's doing but he's there," she said, rolling her eyes. "When are you coming back, Rashaun?"

"I don't know yet. I have to see how this case goes first. My life is in Yelram's hands."

"Rashaun, are you sure you want him to defend you? My sister has a good lawyer. He got her son off attempted murder last month. I could get his number now for you if you want," she said, picking up the receiver.

"No. I have full confidence in Mr. Yelram," Rashaun said

and made his way to his office. He knocked on the door.

"Did Andria get my reply for the christening?" Mrs. Louis Asked.

"I'm not sure. Give her a call at home. She's there now," Rashaun answered.

"Come in." Yelram's muffled voice came through the closed door.

Rashaun stepped into his office, feeling like a stranger. Yelram was sitting in his chair with a Dunkin Donut coffee cup in his hand.

"Rashaun," he said, standing and coming around the table, "you look worst than you sound."

"It was the best of times and the worst of times," Rashaun said, taking Yelram's hand for a brief handshake followed by a hug.

"Fatherhood has changed the color of your eyes, Rashaun," Yelram said as he went back to Rashaun's pricey office chair as Rashaun pulled up his client chair. If Yelram only knew what he and Andria did in the chair he was sitting in.

"Fatherhood alone would be enjoyable, but all the other things that are going on in my life make it very trying time," Rashaun said, getting comfortable in the chair.

"You were telling me that the cops think the attack on you was a deliberate hit against you or Andria or both," Yelram said, picking up the Dunkin Donut cup.

"Yeah. I think we have enemies out there. I don't think the person was going after Andria though, even though social workers have received threats before. Taking a child from a parent whether it is for the good of the child or not could create some enemies," Rashaun said, looking around the office. "The cops went through Andria's client portfolio, and none of them seemed to be threatening."

"And you?" Yelram asked.

"I can't think of anyone who would want to come after me with a baseball bat—maybe shoot me, but not attack me with a baseball bat," Rashaun said.

"Maybe they're trying to get to you through Andria. If that bat had connected with Andria's stomach, you would not be a father today," Yelram said, taking a legal pad from the right side of the table.

"I try not to think of someone wanting to kill a child to get to me because that gets me angry and afraid for my family. The most difficult thing with this is not knowing where the next blow is coming from. It's even worse than this case. This case I know who's out to get me, but with this assault, I'm flying blind. The next attack can come from anywhere at anytime, and that's scary."

"What are you doing to protect those at home?" Yelram asked.

"I have this ex-cop who takes Andria around for me, and my friends are there if he isn't available. I don't like living that way but sometimes choices are made for you that you have no control over."

"I know what you mean. In the end, it all works out, whether it's for better or worse."

"That's what they say. I'm just hoping that the big man up there is smiling on us. A lot of things have happened since Andria and I got together. It's almost as if someone is trying to keep us apart."

"It's more than you and Andria now. You have Wisdom to think about."

"Yeah, I know. I never knew that I could love someone the way I love Wisdom. I get absolutely no sleep, at night because every time he sniffles I wake up. Andria tells me to go back to sleep but I can't help myself. I just want to be there for him. He's part of me. I want to protect him and give him nothing but the best," Rashaun said, looking at the phone on the desk.

"I see you won't be at peace until you call them. Go ahead. Call home. Let me get this stuff together," Yelram said and pushed the phone toward Rashaun.

Rashaun spoke to Andria for a few seconds then pulled the chair up next to Yelram.

"One of the key prosecution witnesses who was able to link you to Paul committed suicide in Rikers. His name was Edwin Thomas. Now, as you might know, this doesn't mean that the case will be dismissed," Yelram said. "I think Mr. Thomas was connected to a recent client of yours by the name of Roundtree. The police said his death was a suicide, but there is talk that it might have been fixed. There is no proof of that."

Rashaun didn't want to tell Yelram that he knew that Edwin Thomas, or Penguin as Roundtree called him, was a dead man when he opened his mouth to Kim. Money and the willingness to use it to reach an end usually equated removal of obstacles. Rashaun knew that Roundtree, a drug dealer he had defended, would not let Penguin send him to jail for life. Kim underestimated Roundtree's power. The only way Penguin would have survived to take the stand was if he was put in federal prison.

"What does that mean for us?" Rashaun asked.

"In the absence of a motive, I think it will come down to how believable you are on the stand."

"Is there any way I can avoid taking the stand?" Rashaun asked.

"Rashaun, you already know the answer to that. Only you can describe how you felt as you watched a man threaten to hurt your woman and kill your child. I think what we have in our favor here is that when Paul raised his fist to Andria's stomach it's like he had a gun pointed to a child's head. Your proximity from Andria and Paul will be very important. That would determine your course of action. If the jury thinks there was some other way you could have protected your woman and child then that could create a problem for us. We'll go over the specifics of your distance another time. Whenever people hear anything about threats on children, automatically they have empathy. We have to put the jury in your position so they understand your reaction. This is where you and Andria come in. Your testimonies will be the key to an acquittal or guilty verdict. There is no other evidence that could convict you. The police report is very good because it showed that you were distraught over the whole situation. Andria also gave an account that backs up your action. There are no other witnesses to the incident. The gun charges will be dealt with after the murder trial. I don't think Kim has much of a case—unless there is something you're not telling me." Yelram waited for a response.

"I don't have anything else of relevance to the case, but knowing the way Kim works, there's got to be something I'm overlooking." Rashaun tapped his hand on his knee.

"Kim is very intelligent. Not only is she willing to use her brain but unlike the modern businesswoman who shuns her sexuality, Kim knows how to make it work for her. In Tyrone's trial, I saw the way she played the males in the jury. You weren't a slouch with the women either, Rashaun, but I'm too old for that, so we have to counteract Kim's persona with you looking the part of a sophisticated, intelligent, hardworking member of our society willing to do whatever it takes to protect your family. There are eight African Americans, one Hispanic, one Asian and two Caucasians on the jury. The alternates are African Americans. The ages and sexes are almost identical with the exception of the two male alternates. We definitely don't want them in the trial. I basically like our chances providing there are no surprises. The trial starts in two weeks. In the meantime, go home and relax the best way you can, and we'll see what happens." Yelram stood and waited for Rashaun to do the same. "I know you don't like spending time away from your family so go home and I'll take care of the rest."

Rashaun stood. "Thanks for everything. I don't think I could have defended myself on this one. Things get very muddled and emotional when your life is hanging in the balance. I hated to take you out of retirement but you've always been there with the answers."

"Well, let's hope I can spin my magic one more time. My hair is graying but I think the faculties are still there."

"Metaphorically, you're like a rare wine that gets better with age." Rashaun jumped as his cell phone rang. He quickly dislodged it from his hip and flipped the cover up. "Hold on a minute," he said and turned to face Yelram.

"I'll call you if anything else develops. Give my love to Andria and Wisdom," Yelram said.

"Thanks, I will," Rashaun, said. He opened the office door and quickly said good-bye to Mrs. Louis. He stepped outside onto the sidewalk, quickly bringing the phone to his ear.

"Freedom is always good," Roundtree said on the other end of the phone.

"For you, that might be the case, but I still have a murder trial pending," Rashaun said, walking around his mother's SUV before he stepped up into it.

"Let's meet," Roundtree said.

“I don’t think that’s a good idea,” Rashaun said as he started the truck, looking in the rearview mirror and the two side windows. He put his left blinker on.

“I’m not a fool, Rashaun. Being seen in public will only create questions. My friend owns a sixty-foot yacht. Meet me there at 10 o’clock tonight. Unless the cops can see in the darkness, we’ll be okay. I will see you then.” Roundtree hung up the phone without waiting for a response from Rashaun.

“But I don’t know the—” Rashaun hadn’t finish talking in the car when his phone flashed that a text message had been received. Roundtree had sent the address of the meeting and the name of the boat. Rashaun pressed two buttons on the phone and was connected to Andria.

“He’s sleeping,” Andria said.

“You think you know me, don’t you,” he said, smiling.

“I want some escoveitch fish from Apache. And don’t come in through the front with it. Your mother thinks I shouldn’t eat anything that has any taste to it while I’m breastfeeding,” Andria said.

“Maybe she’s right. After all, look at the excellent job she did bringing me up,” he said, turning the car onto Flatbush Extension in the direction of Apache.

“And maybe I won’t be home when you get here,” she said.

“Escoveitch fish coming up,” Rashaun said.

“But seriously, Rashaun, I’m going over to Paula’s in a few minutes but I’m not taking Wisdom. I’ll see you when I get back.”

“Did you call Lethal?”

“Yeah. He is on his way to pick me up,” Andria replied.

“Be careful.”

"Paula, Tonia is so adorable," Andria said, picking up the baby who had walked over to her.

"Thanks, but why did she have to come out so dark?" Paula picked up the bottle with about an ounce of milk left in it.

"Paula, don't even start that up again. The child looks exactly like her father. She even has blue eyes. She is absolutely gorgeous."

"Could you imagine if she was light skin with blue eyes? Then I would say she was pretty. I don't know what happened. I'm not dark, and neither is her father. Where in the hell did she get this blackness? Is God trying to punish me," Paula asked, returning to the couch.

"I don't think he has to do that. I think you're accomplishing that all by yourself," Andria said, kissing Tonia on the cheek. "I could kiss you all day. You are so beautiful."

"Nothing has gone right for me my whole life. Everything I ask for I get the opposite. I purposely chose a light skin man to have my child with, and look what happened." Paula took a white onesies undershirt from a pile of baby clothes she had in a hamper next to the couch and folded it.

"Paula, don't do that to Tonia. Do you know that Rashaun hardly ever talks to his father because of the way he treated him? Rashaun said his father refused to take him to his job. His father hated taking him out on family outings. He felt ostracized. Now his father is all over Wisdom, and Rashaun hates it. I don't think you want your child growing up hating you for not loving her because she's too dark. You know how this society is. She'll be battling enough of that. Right now I'm trying to get Rashaun to say more than two words to his father. He doesn't even want him to stand next to him in the wedding," Andria said, playing with Tonia's hands.

"It's not as easy as you think."

"Most good things are never easy. Tonia, why are you beating your godmother in her face?" Andria kissed Tonia again. she giggled as she continued to slap Andria in her face. "She is growing so fast."

"I know. Her father came by a few times to see her," Paula said.

Andria looked at her.

Paula looked away.

"You did it, didn't you? After all he put you through," Andria said, putting Tonia down on the hardwood floor.

Tonia immediately headed for her mother.

"What difference does it make? It's not like he can't get it anywhere he wants. This stuff between our legs is not gold. If you have a halfway decent looking man he's inundated with offers," Paula said, moving the clothes away from Tonia. "Besides, he's working now."

"Yeah, but just because gold is cheap on the market doesn't mean you have to give yours away. Did he give you anything for Tonia?"

"He brought her some onesies and some winter clothes. Anyway, enough about me. How are you holding up?" Paula asked. "You are becoming the queen of drama."

"I guess I'm okay. I'm on edge all the time, but that's how it is when the next person you meet might be your killer. I'm always worried when Rashaun leaves the house. I stay home most of the time with Wisdom."

"Do the cops know anything else about the man who got away?" Paula asked.

"They say he might have been light skin or Hispanic. An eye-witness said he had a hood on his head."

"That doesn't help in a city that has millions of people. You said that the cops think the one who died was paid to attack you." Paula watched as Tonia tried to climb onto the couch.

"Yeah. They said he's a street hustler. I really don't know what to do. Rashaun is about to go to trial, even though he suffers from terrible migraines. There is no mistrial for sickness in a murder trial. Rashaun doesn't want to wait any longer to get married because he's afraid that something will break us up. I want to get married too, but I don't want a cloud hanging over my head when I do." Andria put her face in her hands. "I'm tired, Paula. I'm tired of fighting."

Paula scooped up Tonia who had climbed up on the couch and was headed to the lamp next to it. "Andria, you're the one who always told me that I have to be thankful for what I've got. I think this time you must do the same because as you well know, things could be much different today. You have a man who adores you, and you've been blessed with a child who has a nice caramel complexion." Paula extricated Tonia's hand from her hair. "I think that you, Rashaun and Wisdom will be just fine."

"I hope so," Andria said, getting up off the couch. "Come here, Tonia. Give your godmother a good-bye kiss."

Tonia did not budge from her mother's arms. Instead she started playing with Paula's face.

Andria reached out and took Tonia from Paula.

"Now give your godmother a kiss," Andria said, pulling Tonia closer to her.

Tonia kept looking at her mom.

"I don't think you're getting any good-bye kiss today," Paula said.

"I'm going to take one," Andria said bringing her lips toward Tonia's cheek. "Love you, beautiful girl."

Tonia smiled, showing her three teeth—two at the bottom and one up top.

"It's time to be heading back. I have to go and feed Wisdom."

"Breastfeeding. I don't know how you do it—I lasted two months with that stuff. The pump was the worst. Not only did it feel like I was about to lose my breasts but that pumping was killing my hands." Paula took Tonia from Andria. "How are you getting home?"

"Rashaun's friend Lethal is downstairs waiting for me," Andria said, putting on her coat.

"Hold on a second. Let me show you the dress I brought for Tonia for Wisdom's christening." Paula took Tonia and headed to the bedroom.

Andria put on her shoes and stood on the mat in front of the door.

Paula came back with a red-and-white dress.

"Paula, it's absolutely beautiful. Turn it around. Let me see the back."

Paula held the dress at arm's length to prevent Tonia from having her way with it. "I love this butterfly cut in the back. I picked it up on the clearance rack at Gymboree. I love that store. It's expensive, but if you get the right sale, their clothes can be washed over and over."

"Rashaun doesn't like me taking the train because he thinks it's too easy to get away with an attack. He promised to take me there on Saturday but that was two Saturdays ago," Andria said, putting her hand on the doorknob.

"I guess you can always go on-line and shop." Paula walked toward the door.

"I don't like buying kids' clothes on-line. I like to see and feel what I'm getting. Paula, got to go. Bye, Tonia," Andria said, waving to the baby.

"Wave good-bye to Auntie Andria," Paula said, lifting Tonia's hand.

"I guess I can't get no love today," Andria said as she stepped through the door. "I'll call you later."

"I'll give you a call tonight after I come back from my mom's house," Paula said as she watched Andria get on the elevator.

Finding love or anything of that sort was not what was on Kim's mind when she stepped into the new hot spot, Jay-Z's 40/40 bar and entertainment center. The two big black bouncers at the door did not look at her driver's license as they did the two young girls before her. All they did was smile and say, "enjoy the night." She stepped through the huge double doors, not knowing what to expect. Maybe Jay-Z or whatever he called himself, depending on the product he was pushing, would be performing to anyone who came out on this cold winter evening. She could tell that Jay-Z was not there by the sprinkling of chicken heads and 'gimme-the-light girls', but the R&B music blaring loudly paid homage to the club's owner. The theater-size screen above the bar highlighted the Knicks' losing ways. Behind the bar were a few booths, which were tightly occupied by various sexes. Kim held her coat in the crook of her arm as she looked around for a coat check and her friend Tracee Waters. To Kim's immediate right were some suspended swing seats, perhaps reminiscent of Jay-Z's hustling days in the parks in Bed-Stuy. The major difference was the subtle leather as opposed to the hard cold plastic of the city parks. Behind the seats was a small space that someone had mistaken for a dance floor and was now filled with the few who felt the music in their bones. Kim looked at the steep stairs that her friend told her would lead up to the special rooms on the top floor. She wondered how long it would take for an intoxicated person to reach the bottom of the stairs headfirst—or in the land of suing for the almighty dollar a wish list that equated broken bones with a new Lexus 430. Kim caught the eye of a black woman with a pen and writing pad.

"Are you for the special party?" she asked as she came over, ready to riffle through the names on her pad.

"No. I'm here to meet a girlfriend. Can you tell me where the coat check is?" Kim asked, bringing her coat between her and the hostess.

"It's all the way upstairs. You'll see the sign," she replied.

"I was hoping I didn't have to train for the NBA season today but I'm sure I'll be okay," Kim said, smiling.

"I have to do it about four times a night. The waiters and waitresses do it about a hundred times, but they're young, and I'm sure they don't even feel it. Have a good night," she said and turned to an older couple who seemed to have lost their way.

Kim walked up the stairs wondering why her girlfriend always insisted on meeting at whatever new spot seemed to be jumping for the moment. At the top of the stairs were a bar to the right and the restroom to the left. In the middle were a few couches for those people who were totally exhausted from the long climb up the stairs. Kim made a mental note of the position of the bathroom; she would definitely be coming back to it.

"Kim, what a surprise seeing you here." The voice came from a tall gentleman making his way toward her. He had on an NFL throwback jersey and some Prada jeans with black sneakers, which were a significant reflection of his status because everyone else in the place was semi-formally dressed.

"Reyser, I didn't expect to see you here. Are the Pacers in town this weekend?" Kim asked, receiving a kiss on the cheek from the basketball player.

"Yeah. We're playing the Knicks tomorrow night. How have you been?" he asked.

"I've been very good, and you?"

"I got injured the beginning of the season, so right now I'm just traveling with the team. I should be back starting in about a month. How come you haven't called me? I keep calling your cell phone number but I guess you've changed it."

"Yeah. Someone slipped my cell phone out of my handbag. I lost all my numbers," she said, looking around to see if she saw Tracee.

"Well it's easy to get in touch with me. All you had to do was call the organization and they would have left a message for me," he said, flipping out a cell phone.

"Uh-huh." Kim continued scanning the hallway, trying to find Tracee.

"Are you looking for someone?" he asked, slipping his phone back into his pocket.

"I'm sorry, Reyser. I'm here to meet my friend Tracee. I'll be very upset if I got here before her."

"Well, in the meantime, let me buy you a drink," he said.

"Are you Reyser, with the Indiana Pacers?" One of two young women who had presented their ID to the bouncers ahead of Kim had found their star. Their smiles were cartoon-like and their tight black pants and low cut blouses were an open invitation.

"Yes, I am." Reyser said. "Give me a minute. Kim, do you

want that drink?"

"Maybe later, Reyser. I have to find Tracee first," Kim said and headed down the hallway.

"I'll be looking for you," Reyser said before turning back to his fans who had not lost any of their teeth.

Kim was walking down the hallway when she felt a tap on her shoulder. "Hi, sexy. What you doing in a place like this?"

Kim turned around. "Tracee, you just got here, didn't you?" Kim said, turning around to face her friend.

"I was waiting to use the bathroom. You know they only have three or four stalls, and they're unisex so the wait is long and the seats are wet. I'm sure Beyonce doesn't have to use those bathrooms."

"I don't think Jay-Z would have the baddest woman in show business soil her precious ass," Kim said.

" Let's get a drink and go into one of the rooms. It's the only place you can hear yourself talk without shouting like we're doing now. I saw one of your basketball flings. The one you called the freak," Tracee said. "The first drink is on me."

"Yeah, I saw Reyser. The first time we got together, the brother brought out a whole lot of S&M shit. He wanted me to spank him on the ass, then he wanted me to strap on a dildo and have him suck it. I'm crazy in bed but that was too much. And the brother had a small dick. There were absolutely no rewards for all that work the man wanted me to do."

"All the money in the world can't make up for a nightmare at home," Tracee said, eyeing a woman who had just come out of the cigar room. "Now look over there at this woman in the business suit."

"What are you talking about, Tracee?" Kim asked, following her friend's gaze.

"These women have absolutely forgotten who they are. They've replaced their sexuality with blandness. There's nothing to them. They've become sexless, and that's not who we are. Black men have never been attracted to blandness. What these professional women fail to realize is that we're women first. Can you see me in something like that?" Tracee asked, looking in the direction of a woman in a gray suit that look like it had just been dropped on her without any regard to style or fashion.

Kim looked over at the woman then at her friend. "Tracee, where is all that hostility coming from?"

"Let's go into this room," Tracee said, pushing open the door to the sports room.

"This is not bad at all," Kim said as she took a seat on a soft red bench. "But back to my first question. What's been happening with you? Why all that anger toward businesswomen."

Tracee put down her matching Prada handbag next to Kim. "It's Winston."

"What about Winston? You guys have only been dating for about three months. Isn't he the one from Wharton Business School? The one who's 'marrying material.'"

"That's the motherfucker. Do you know he's having an affair on the job? He's fucking one of his managers at his job, and he has the nerve to tell me I can deal with it or leave. Can you believe it?" Tracee asked, squeezing Kim's hand. "So you know what I did."

"Yes, Tracee, you fucked some sense into him."

Both women looked at each other and started to laugh. At the same time a couple poked their head in the door. Tracee held on to Kim by the elbows and looked at the couple who quickly closed the door.

"It works every time," Tracee said. "Of course I fucked the

daylights out of him. Now I'll use his ass to find another contender. I told you I'm not going to marry anyone who's not making high sixes."

"Good luck with that girl."

"Well enough about me. You said you went to see Rashaun at the hospital. Now why did you do a dumb thing like that? I told you to leave that man alone," Tracee said.

"When it comes to Rashaun, I just can't help myself."

"Listen to yourself, Kim. You're one of the best prosecutors in New York. How many high six-figure offers have you turned down? Most men who meet you are willing to be the bitch in the relationship, but what do you do? You keep going after a man who is oblivious to you."

"Rashaun is never oblivious to me. Tracee, you have never loved a man like Rashaun. He is the only man I know who has gone to another level."

"He's at another level because he turned you down. Now, if you can't have him, you're going to kill him. What happened in the hospital? Isn't he in a coma or something?"

Kim leaned back on the bench, her glazed eyes resting on a number sixteen throwback jersey, one of many that lined the walls. "I don't know what came over me when I went into the hospital. It was just what I've done all my life, take advantage of opportunities."

"Kim, what did you do?" The seriousness in Tracee's voice was evident to Kim.

"I gave him a blow job."

"What do you mean, you gave him a blow job?"

"I sucked his dick. I put his penis in my mouth, I—"

"I get the picture, Kim. You're trying to tell me that Rashaun, the 'I'm getting married in the morning', was receptive to a blowjob from you? The same man who embarrassed you at your job."

"I didn't say he welcomed me with open arms, but I'm sure unconsciously he knew what was happening."

Tracee shook her head. "You gave a blowjob to an unconscious man. There is a name for that, Kim, and I'm sure you, being a lawyer and all, know what it is."

"That's not all," Kim said.

"There's more? Do tell me, O fair one."

"I took it with me," Kim said, looking away from Tracee.

"No, you did not. You did not do a Lorena Bobbit on Rashaun." Tracee slammed her hand on the bench and got up. "Didn't she go to prison for cutting her husband's dick off? Besides it was a white dick so no one cared."

"Nothing like that, Tracee. I don't know why I did it but I took his sperm with me. It's home in the freezer," Kim said. "I needed to have him."

"Kim, listen to me," Tracee said, holding Kim's hands. "You are in serious need of help. As a friend I'll try to set up an appointment with one of the best psychiatrists in New York."

"Tracee, stop talking to me as if I belong in the G building at Kings County Hospital. I don't need to see a psychiatrist. I'm quite aware of what I did. There was a moment, and I got lost in it. I might go home and throw that vial I have away. You've done a lot worst with men that you've seen. Do you remember when you went to Jason's house and you put a piece of foil in the microwave? There was a three-alarm fire on the block that night. You were lucky no one got hurt."

Tracee shook her head for the second time. " I can't believe you went there. I understood that I did something that wasn't normal, Kim. I went and got help after that incident. I'm trying to help you before someone gets hurt in this game you're playing with Rashaun. Sometimes in life we have to say that we tried our best but it wasn't meant to be. We have to know when to move on."

Kim stood and put her hands on her friend's shoulders. "Tracee, you're my best friend. I respect your opinion, and I know you want the best for me, but I'm okay. I do not belong in Kings County's G building for crazy people and I'm not about to lose it. I did something that just came about on the spur of the moment. I didn't plan on going to the hospital and extracting sperm from Rashaun. Things got a little crazy, and this is the result. I promise you it won't happen again."

"You promise, Kim?."

"I do, Tracee. Stop worrying so much," Kim said.

"And when you go home, you're going to throw that vial of sperm out the window?"

Kim didn't say anything for a while. "I will."

"I was worried for a second," Tracee said.

"I know. Don't worry, Tracee, Kings County is far away from me."

Tracee snatched up her handbag. "Now, let's go have these men spend."

"Tracee, I can buy my own drinks," Kim said.

"So can I but why deprive the fellas of the honor?" Tracee asked, opening the door.

"Who knows, you might meet someone who will have you saying Rashaun who."

Kim looked up and down the hallway. "I doubt that, not at 40/40. Maybe someone would offer to buy me a forty."

"Yeah, and you could sprinkle some on the ground for the fellas who have passed away," Tracee said as they entered the hallway.

The cold of New York was showing no signs of abating anytime soon. Winter's official last day had passed two weeks ago but it was still freezing. Rashaun had driven from Brooklyn to the big island, Manhattan. The big island that a few years ago everyone in the world was fixated on as two planes smashed into the twin towers. The whole world watched as the two of the tallest buildings in the world received the devil's food. Things were more or less back to normal except for the cops at the entrances to the bridges who looked at everyone as if they had just converted to Islam. Rashaun had told the African parking attendant who shivered in his thin gray jacket and blue pants his name and the attendant motioned to the pier after asking him if he wanted the car washed. The attendant told him it was a courtesy afforded their customers. Rashaun asked him how much it cost to park and he was told fifty dollars, not including tip, but very rarely did guests pay.

Rashaun's host was not waiting for him at the rope gate that led to the entrance to the *Pearl,* a hundred-foot white yacht that stood motionless at the pier. There was a tall white man with white gloves and a thick black coat with a captain's hat on. He bowed, detached the rope and lifted it as Rashaun approached. Rashaun said thank you and pulled on the collar of his coat. He climbed the steps and went onto the boat. He didn't have to open the white door labeled entrance at the top. As was the case with the captain earlier, it opened as he approached.

"Welcome, Mr. Jones," a white man with a wispy mustache dressed in a white shirt and black pants greeted him.

"Thank you," Rashaun said as he was hit by the hot air emanating from some place in the boat.

"Can I have your coat?" Rashaun quickly removed his coat, which had become too hot all of a sudden. He stood on a mat and wondered if he was allowed to step on the soft beige carpet that lay ahead of him.

"Here you are, sir."

Rashaun turned to his right as a beautiful black woman wearing an identical uniform to the man who had opened the door held brand-new slippers on a tray. Rashaun quickly took off his Timberlands and set them neatly to the side. The young woman bent and put the slippers in front of Rashaun, and he stepped into them.

"Follow me," she said.

As she walked ahead of him, Rashaun felt guilty for the thoughts he was having. She definitely wasn't hired based solely on her work ethic.

She led him down a winding stairway, and at the bottom she slid a gold-plated sliding door to the left and waited for Rashaun to enter.

"Thank you," Rashaun said.

She bowed, and Rashaun was impressed by her glittering smile.

"Please sit here," she said, leading Rashaun to a soft leather couch.

Rashaun followed her steps to a bar located about twenty feet to his right.

"Mr. Jones, my name is Lolita, and I'm here to serve you. I'm a qualified bartender and a full-body licensed masseuse. What would you like to drink?"

"Let me have an Incredible Hulk," Rashaun said and leaned back on the couch. The room was decorated with turn-of-thecentury paintings. To his left was a grand table with sittings for twelve people. Presently there were two serving utensils on the table. In addition to the couch where Rashaun was sitting, there were also two on the opposite sides, each looking as if they were recently purchased at Bloomingdale's or a store with similar or higher prices. The paneling in the room was high-gloss mahogany wood. Rashaun was betting that there was nothing fake in the room, including Lolita who had just handed him his drink.

"Can I help you with anything else?" she asked. Again, that smile warmed more than his heart.

"No, thank you," Rashaun said to more than the massage. He shook his head and leaned back on the couch. He inhaled deeply and pondered his path. A few years ago he would have been all over this woman but now his fleeting lust was replaced by a love for home. His thoughts quickly went to Andria and Wisdom and their life.

"Rashaun, you are amazing," Roundtree said.

Rashaun turned to his left just in time to see Roundtree close a nondescript door with no outside handles. "You are full of surprises, Roundtree," Rashaun said standing to secure himself against the fleet-footed Roundtree.

Roundtree was dressed in all white with gold slippers. He didn't look a day older than when Rashaun met him a few years ago.

"Most men would have been throwing seeds at Lolita right now." Roundtree stretched his hand out to greet Rashaun.

"Most men don't have a firstborn and a woman who stood by them waiting at home," Rashaun said, answering Roundtree's firm handshake with his own.

Roundtree smiled. "Especially men with newborns and women at home. I would have been disappointed if you let your palate take you down rocky roads. Lolita does have her positives." Roundtree sat next to Rashaun and crossed his legs.

"It must have cost you quite a penny for this vessel," Rashaun said, looking around the room.

"I don't own this yacht," Roundtree said. "It's owned by the Willoughby Corporation whose white CEO has a mansion on Long Island."

Rashaun smiled and looked at Roundtree.

"You're right, Rashaun. I do own the majority stake in this boat. Unlike these fools out there who took their drug money and gave it to their mother and family members who are on welfare to buy houses and fancy cars, I took mine and invested it in people who have money but want more money. No one will dare question Trump when he pulls up in a two-hundred-foot yacht, but let an unemployed young black man from Brooklyn do the same. Every part of the U.S. Government will be after him. Enough on what makes the U.S. economy incorruptible. How is the family?"

"The family is good," Rashaun said.

"And how does your head feel? Nurse Audry said you were a model patient."

"Roundtree, I don't even want to think about how you knew my private nurse. My head is healing fine. I suffer from terrible migraines. There's no cure for them and the doctor said it might be something I'll have to live with." Rashaun took another sip of his drink.

"There are so many people with hate in their eyes. The life I chose has left me looking over my shoulder because the unseen blow is usually the hardest. Hopefully when the perpetrator of this crime against you is caught, you can look ahead without constantly looking back. Let me tell you, living looking over your shoulder is no picnic. I also want to apologize for the inconvenience that Penguin had on your legal trouble. It was my fault, and as I told you, I was going to take care of it, but it was a thorn in my side, and I'm sure yours, but I guarantee that it won't happen again," Roundtree said, finishing his drink and getting up and going to the bar. "Do you want a refill?"

"Yeah," Rashaun said, following him. "It was a—"

"No need, the smell of the glass gives me all the ingredients."

Rashaun gave Roundtree his glass and went and took a look out through the porthole in the boat. "Where are we?"

"We are anchored just off Fire island."

The phone in the bar rang and Roundtree picked it up. "Are you ready to eat, Rashaun?"

"Yes," Rashaun said.

"Let me give you a tour of the sleeping compartments," Roundtree said, "I know you won't be able to stay today, but the yacht is available to you and your family. I do need some advance notice to prepare the staff."

"All this is not necessary," Rashaun said.

"Rashaun, you saved my life. After I turned thirty-five, I decided I wouldn't spend another day in prison. As a young boy, I spent a few years there, and let me tell you, I laugh when I hear these rappers today glorify spending time behind bars. The funniest thing is that they're the ones most likely to spend their time on their stomachs with Big D on top of them. My reputation usually precedes me before I get to prison, and for all the amenities that provided me I'm still under lockdown. Look at this," Roundtree said, showing Rashaun the master bedroom with a king-size bed and a fifty-inch plasma TV with an assortment of audio equipment. "Do you think I want to trade this in for ten years in a four-by-seven cell? Why do you think the Mafia kills witnesses and spends tons of money bribing jury and judges to stay out of prison? Rashaun, cages are for animals, and I'm no animal."

Roundtree closed the door to the cabin just as a phone located outside the room rang. He picked it up, spoke briefly then hung up.

"I myself have too much to live for to be put in a cell. I have a beautiful woman and a priceless son. Every night when I look at him, I thank God for being so blessed. I hate to be separated from them for a minute, much less years," Rashaun said, stopping in the hallway, his head down.

Roundtree put his hand over Rashaun's shoulder. "Everything will be okay, Rashaun. You just have to be willing to do whatever it takes to get what you want.

What are you willing to do, Rashaun?" Roundtree asked.

"I don't know," Rashaun answered. "Only time will determine that."

"That's the problem with a lot of people. They put too much emphasis on the winds of time. Time heals the heart of a man who was pussy whipped by a hooker. Time heals the cut from a knife that made an opening in the heart, but only action will stop it from happening again or happening at all. Time does not stop a rolling rock from crushing anything in its path. Only smart and decisive action will stop that. Rashaun, you don't need time. You need action."

Rashaun walked ahead of Roundtree. "Roundtree, I do appreciate your assistance. I came to you before and you were able to help me."

"That was nothing."

"Sometimes in life you have to do it your way and this is one of those times. I'll stand in front of the law, justified in knowing what I did I did to protect two of the most important people in my life. And I would tell anyone if I had to do it all over again, I would not change a thing. Now I have reason to go home, now I have a responsibility to someone else. I hope with God's okay I'll be able to live up to that responsibility."

Roundtree pulled back the chair at the table. "I hear you, my brother, but just remember the law isn't always just, and sometimes we have to help it do what it's supposed to do. I have my ways, and if you need me to use them I will be more than happy to. Please don't wait until it's too late because even my ways sometimes can't undo what time has done."

"Thank you," Rashaun said.

Roundtree lifted his hand in the air, and there was bustling in the room as Lolita and the crew brought out seafood appetizers that included shrimp, lobster, salmon, clams and oysters. It was the start of a five-course meal and maybe the strengthening or the parting of an odd, respectable friendship.

Chapter 4

"Any food is better than what they serve in the G building," Tyrone Wheatley said as he dug into the seafood pasta. Tyrone had spent a few months in the G building at Kings County Hospital when his mother found him in his bedroom hanging from his balls. The memory of Judy lying in bed with the sheets full of blood after an exhaustive night of Blackfunk had driven him over the edge. While he was there, he fell in love with a nurse and with the Holy Spirit.

"A friend of mine told me about this place. The food is good and the price is right." Rashaun twirled the linguine with his fork before using his spoon to hold it together.

"Give me great food in a quaint little restaurant anytime," Yvonne Wheatley, Tyrone's sister, stated as she looked to the door. "I told William to meet us here. I wonder if he got lost."

Rashaun sat opposite Yvonne, and Tyrone was seated next to him.

"I don't think he'll be making it this evening," Tyrone said. "We've been here forty-five minutes now, and there's no sign of him."

"He must have gotten tied up at the office," Yvonne said, looking at Rashaun.

"I'm sure he did," Rashaun said, pouring himself a glass of red wine from the carafe.

"He works at Mount Sinai Hospital," Yvonne said, looking at her cell phone.

"We know. You told us that about fifteen minutes ago." Rashaun sipped on the wine.

"I think the signal in here is no good. Let me go outside and see if he left a message," she said, rising from her chair and exiting the restaurant.

Rashaun watched her through the window. She paced in front of the restaurant, constantly looking at the cell phone.

"She's still in love with you," Tyrone said. "I don't think she'll give up on you until you say I do to Andria. I think she's seeing this doctor to show you that she's not home crying over you."

"Your sister is too beautiful a woman to stay home and wait for any man. I'm sure if circumstances were different I would have gone out with her but Andria and Wisdom are my life now," Rashaun said as he saw a man approach Yvonne.

"Maybe you should tell her that, Rashaun. Pastor Jacobs said that sometimes we need to be direct and honest to get our point across," Tyrone said.

"Your sister told me that you joined the Efigy Christian Church," Rashaun said, pushing his empty plate to the middle of the table. "Isn't that the church that puts on a performance with cameras and giant TV screens, and they're broadcast on cable every Sunday?" Rashaun asked.

"Yes, that's the one. You heard of it?" Tyrone asked eagerly.

"I'm glad you found your faith, Tyrone, but I'm not impressed by a church that requires a city spending budget to operate, especially when the pastor peddles his books during the service. If it has helped you, I'm truly thankful," Rashaun said.

"I guess you're not interested in having your wedding there," Tyrone said, sounding a little down.

"If my wedding doesn't take place in my mom's church I might as well start digging my grave," Rashaun said.

"Yeah, I forgot about that," Tyrone said, finishing the last of his seafood.

"I definitely have to bring Courtney to this restaurant."

"Courtney?" Rashaun asked.

"I met her at the hospital. She's a nurse at Kings County. She introduced me to the Lord. Courtney is a good woman," Tyrone said.

"How good is she?" Rashaun asked, smiling shrewdly.

"Nothing like that. Courtney doesn't believe in sex before marriage," Tyrone said. "I think if I had met her before, my life would have been different, but God has given me a second chance, and I plan to serve Him one hundred percent. The next woman I'm intimate with will be my wife and the bearer of my children."

Rashaun signaled for the waiter.

A tall, slim white man with a ponytail came over. He refilled all the water glasses on the table.

Rashaun pointed to the carafe.

"Refill?" the waiter asked.

Rashaun nodded in agreement.

The waiter was about to leave with the carafe when Yvonne and a white man in a dark gray suit approached the table.

"Would you like to see the menu?" the waiter asked.

"No, thank you. I'll have some water," Yvonne's friend said as he stood next to Yvonne.

The waiter turned around and walked back in the direction of the kitchen.

"Rashaun, this is William Horne," Yvonne said.

"Nice to meet you, William," Rashaun said, reaching for the man's outstretched hand.

"My pleasure, Rashaun. Yvonne told me that you're a good friend of the family," William said, reaching over to shake Tyrone's hand also. Unlike Rashaun, Tyrone had remained seated.

"Well Tyrone and I have been friends for a long time. Yvonne said that you're a surgeon at Mount Sinai."

"Yes. I transferred from Washington Hospital in D.C. When Yvonne left Washington, I decided that was not where I wanted to be," William said. "Yvonne told me you have your own law practice in Brooklyn."

The waiter brought the carafe with an extra wineglass.

"Yes, I do," Rashaun said, "but I'm not practicing at the moment.

"How is business in Brooklyn?"

"I can't complain," Rashaun said, pouring himself a glass of wine. "How long have you known Yvonne?"

"We've known each other for more than five years," Yvonne said.

"Even though we've known each other for years, Yvonne and I have only recently started dating. Yvonne is a beautiful woman. After years of trying to date her, she finally called me in Washington and asked me if I wanted to come to New York," William said, sipping on the wine. "Look at her, who can so no to a beautiful woman like that?"

Rashaun smiled.

"William, are you sure you don't want to order something?" Yvonne asked.

"No. I picked up something in the hospital cafeteria late this afternoon so I'm fine. Do you know where I can find the men's room?"

"Go straight to the back and turn to the right," Rashaun said.

"Excuse me," William said and eased back his chair.

Rashaun waited until William had disappeared. He looked over at Yvonne and sipped slowly on his wine.

"What?" she asked.

"I didn't say anything," Rashaun said.

"Guys, should I leave?" Tyrone said.

"To go where? You didn't drive," Rashaun answered.

"How come I'm not with a brother? That's what you want to ask me. How come I'm with a blond-haired, blue-eyed man?" Yvonne asked, her lips curling in anger.

"Are you happy?" Rashaun asked.

"What do you mean, am I happy?" Yvonne answered.

"That's all I want to know," Rashaun said.

"You have no comment on his color? You don't think a sister should be with a black man?" Yvonne asked.

"What I think is irrelevant. All I want for you is happiness, so are you happy?" Rashaun asked.

"I don't believe you. I saw your reaction when I walked in with William."

"And what reaction was that?" Rashaun asked.

"It's the same reaction I get from the brothers when I walk the streets with William: What's a fine sister like that doing with a white boy? You didn't have to express it in words like some other brothers do, but your look says it all." Yvonne poured a glass of wine, gulped it down then poured another. "Let me tell you why I'm with him."

"I didn't ask for an explanation, and I don't think it's necessary." Rashaun said.

"I should have driven," Tyrone said.

"Let me tell you—" Yvonne's reply was cut short by William's return.

"Honey, what's wrong? You are looking a bit upset," William said, taking a seat next to Yvonne.

"Politics will bring the worse out of people these days," Rashaun said.

"Yes. With Bush in the White House, the whole nation is in an uproar." William poured himself another glass of wine.

"I don't think Bush is as bad as everyone is making him out to be. I think he has moral standards. Unlike Clinton and the democrats, he's not trying to appease everyone." Tyrone said, eager to get into the conversation.

"Tyrone, since you came out of the hospital and became a born-again Christian, your whole philosophy has changed. Just because Bush is against gay marriages and some democrats are for them doesn't make him a politician for the people. Look at the problems we are having in Iraq. American lives are being lost everyday. The only reason we're there is to get control of Iraq's oil," Yvonne said, gently playing with William's hair as she looked over at Rashaun.

"Do you think Saddam was a good man? Didn't he spray thousands of his countrymen with chemical weapons? Didn't he commit a number of atrocities on his people? He even went as far as to invade Kuwait," Tyrone countered.

"No one is saying that Saddam is good, but look at all the people who were killed in Africa. The Hutsu and the Tutsi have waged a war between themselves, killing more than a hundred thousand people. America wasn't in a rush to run to the aid of these people. Tyrone, it all has to do with power and wealth. If America can't get something or strategically it's not a good place to put up an Army base, America is not going in," Rashaun said.

"The threat that Saddam posed to the U.S and its allies was real. I'm not concerned that no weapons of mass destruction were found in Iraq. I believe that sooner or later Saddam would have access to a nuclear weapon. While I'm not a republican or a Bush supporter, I think the invasion of Iraq will have a lot of us sleeping better at night," William said.

"Not the parents of the 18-and 20-year-olds in the Army who shake whenever their telephone rings, wondering if their son or daughter has died. There is no reason except greed that hundreds of young men and women are being killed in Iraq. We did not finish with Afghanistan yet, and we're in Iraq. Osama Bin Laden is on an island sipping pina coladas while he makes arrangements for future bombings of Americans. America had no right going into Iraq. The only people who are happy about the invasion are Bush and his oil cronies in Texas who are salivating over Iraqi's oil," Rashaun said before pushing back his chair. "Do you or your parents have oil interest in Iraq, William?"

"Whether they do or not is not the point," William said. "Saddam was a bad man, and he needed to go."

"How many bad men are there in the world? Why choose Iraq to liberate the people from a so-called bad man. Remember, Iraq was once an American ally, and the same Saddam was in power then," Rashaun said.

"Guys, I think we could go on forever about this Iraq situation but I personally don't have the time. I don't get to see William as much as I want, so I have to take advantage it. As always, Rashaun, it was a pleasure seeing you, and I'm sure I'll see you again. Give Wisdom a kiss for me and tell Andria I said hi. Tyrone, I'll see you at home tomorrow," Yvonne said, slipping her coat from the back of the chair and turning around to William who was finishing his wine. "You ready?"

"Yep. Do you want to pick up anything to snack on? I have absolutely nothing in my refrigerator."

"What happened to the chicken I made yesterday?" Yvonne asked.

"I'm afraid I ate it for breakfast this morning," William said, slipping on his coat.

"Well let's stop at the supermarket and pick up a few things," Yvonne said.

"It was a pleasure meeting you, Rashaun," William said, extending his hand.

"Likewise, I'm sure we'll meet again." Rashaun shook William's hand. "Take care of that beautiful lady."

Yvonne glanced at Rashaun as she turned and walked out the restaurant, her hand in William's.

Rashaun signaled the waiter.

"She's still in love with you, Rashaun," Tyrone said again, adjusting his jacket.

"Does it really matter now?" Rashaun asked, signing the check.

Tyrone stood. "I guess not."

Rashaun buttoned up his jacket and slipped on his gloves. "Where are you going?"

"You?" Tyrone asked.

"Home," Rashaun answered.

"Do you mind dropping me at church?" Tyrone asked. "I know it's a little bit out of your way."

"Not a problem," Rashaun answered.

"What time did you meet with Pastor Thompson?" Kim asked

as she reached for a black pen with her initials engraved in gold on the bottom half. It was a gift from Rashaun her second year of law school.

"I spoke with Pastor Devon Thompson yesterday at 6:00 P.M. I told him that we would like him to be a witness in the state versus Rashaun Jones trial for first degree murder," Roger said, sitting opposite Kim as he read from a small notepad.

"His response when you gave him the specifics of his testimony?" Kim asked, flipping the white collar her Jones New York shirt.

Roger adjusted himself on the seat. He looked at Kim then toward the slightly ajar door. "Pastor Thompson said that he wasn't interested in testifying," Roger muttered.

"Did he say why?"

"Yes, he did." Roger still did not look at Kim. "It seems there was an incident that happened a long time ago that was very painful for him," Roger said.

"Painful for him?" Kim said sarcastically. "Did you tell him that I was the DA on the case?"

"Yes. He said he was aware of that. He had followed your career after law school. He said to tell you hello. He also said he was praying for you and Rashaun."

"Did you tell him I was interested in his testimony not his prayers?" Kim rocked back slowly.

"No. I didn't because he seemed very genuine. He is a man of the cloth," Roger said.

"That he is-but men are always flesh first and cloth after," Kim said, a wicked smile crossing her face.

"Did anything happen between you, Rashaun and the pastor?" Roger asked.

"Are you talking to me as a lawyer or as the person fucking

me?" Kim asked, her voice firm. "We already spoke about Rashaun, and you chose to continue in this relationship."

"I guess I'm talking to you as both," Roger said.

"Well, Roger, this is not the place to get personal. When we're at work and in my office, we will only talk about business. Is that clear?" Kim said, maintaining eye contact.

"We weren't being businesslike when we made love in this office a few weeks ago," Roger said, mimicking Kim's monotone voice.

"Roger, let me explain it to you: If you ever want to touch me again, please do not contradict me, especially when my reputation is on the line. For the eight years I have been in this profession, I haven't lost a case. How many cases have you won? Not a single one. So what I advise you to do if you want to continue to work here and enjoy the pleasure of my company on the outside is to listen and learn. Now back to Pastor Thompson." Kim looked over at the cowering Roger. "I know he's is not here for long. Do you know when he's leaving?"

"In two months."

"The case starts in a week. This gives us enough time to convince Pastor Thompson to change his mind about testifying," Kim said, standing for the first time.

"How are we going to do that? Have him testify as a hostile witness?" Roger asked.

"No," Kim said. "There won't be any hostility in Pastor Thompson's testimony."

"He sounded very adamant about refusing to testify."

Kim looked out the window. "So he did. I'm sure you didn't explain the situation the way I will."

"You're going to talk to Pastor Thompson?" Roger asked.

"Obviously you couldn't get the job done," Kim said. "I'm

disappointed in you, Roger, but you're still learning. One day you'll realize that there are many ways to skin a cat, and not all the ways are in the book. If you want to succeed as a lawyer in New York City, you have to find out the other ways."

"Is that all, Ms. Rivers?" Roger asked, gathering his things to leave.

"No, it's not. Sit, Roger," Kim said, maintaining her composure.

Roger sat back down. "Do you need anything else or are there any more insults I have to take from you today?"

"What do you know about Pastor Thompson's personal life?" Kim asked.

"He's happily married with two kids, a boy and a girl. They're staying at Pastor Robin's house in Queens. I have all the information here. Do you need anything else?" Roger asked, putting down a sheet of paper on the desk.

"That will be all. I'm working late tonight, so don't wait for me," Kim said, picking up the paper Roger had left on the desk.

Roger walked out of the office as Kim stood from behind the desk.

"So Devon, you want to play hardball. Pastor or no pastor, you are still a man, and I'll prove it to you," she said, looking out at the people walking on Jay Street.

Rashaun opened the side door at the back of his mother's house. It was the door that he and Andria used when they didn't want to disturb his parents.

"Hi, honey, I'm home," Rashaun said, gently closing the door just in case Wisdom was sleeping.

Andria came out the bedroom wearing a long white T-shirt with a picture of Africa emblazoned on the front.

Rashaun slipped his hand around her waist and kissed her on the cheek. "How is my baby's mother doing today?"

"I see we have jokes," Andria said, reaching up to tap Rashaun on his injury.

"Okay, I'm sorry. I never said I was a comedian but they say the key to a good relationship is laughter. So you can't say I'm not trying my best," Rashaun said, opening the bedroom door. "I see Mom has Wisdom."

"No, Rashaun, your father came to get him. Wisdom is upstairs with him," Andria said.

The transformation on Rashaun's face was fast and troubling. Andria felt him untangling himself from her.

"He what! Excuse me. I'll be back," Rashaun said and headed through the door to the steps that led upstairs to his parents' house.

"Rashaun," Andria shouted.

Rashaun took the stairs two at a time before knocking on the door to his parents' house.

"Come in." Edward Jones, Rashaun's father's voice crackled through the door.

"What are you doing?" Rashaun asked.

"I'm sitting here playing with Wisdom," Edward said, sitting on a black leather recliner with Wisdom comfortably in his arms.

"You don't have a grandson," Rashaun said, his eyes blood red. "The same way this black child was not yours."

"What are you talking about, Rashaun?" His father asked rocking Wisdom who was twisting and turning in his arms.

"I'm talking about you going around telling everyone that this black boy wasn't yours. I'm talking about putting my mother through hell because you thought I did not belong to you. You treating me like shit, taking my brother and sister out and leaving me at home. Taking them to your job and introducing them to your friends while I trembled in my room. The world that I had to deal with was difficult enough. Being the blackest child in every class I attended was enough to deal with." Rashaun rested his hand on the doorknob.

"Rashaun, how many times must I say I'm sorry?" Edward said.

"Sorry? Do you know how many times I contemplated suicide as a young boy? After being treated like I didn't exist in school I would come home and my father would look at me like he wished I were dead. What you fail to understand is that I had no control over the shade of my skin. If I did, I would have asked the Lord to make me light skinned. You hated me for something I had no control over. Do you understand that?" Rashaun said, pounding his fist on the bed.

Wisdom started to cry.

"The first time you came to any of my events was when I graduated from law school, then all of a sudden you had another a son. I said fuck you then and I'm telling it to you again. You don't have a son, and you definitely don't have a grandson!"

Edward looked over at his son. "Rashaun, over the years I have reached out to you but you have turned me down over and over. The Lord says you must give a man a second chance. Is there any way in your heart to forgive me? I hold Wisdom in my arms, and I don't ever want to let him go because I remember the hurt I caused you. Please give me a chance to love him the way I didn't love him. Just give me a chance to be a grandfather to Wisdom."

"No, I can't do that because you never gave me a chance. If it weren't for Mom, I don't think Wisdom would be here right now.

I was never good enough for you. You hated me before you even got to know me. All the time in school I worked so hard for you to congratulate me, but you never did. I came home and put my report card on the table for you to see but you just passed right by it. You would buy Ray and Rachel presents if they got one ninety on their exam while I made one hundreds in everything and you would just ignore me. I so wanted to hear something positive from you but all I saw in your eyes was hate and disdain. I survived, and Wisdom will never go through what you put me through. To me you're dead, and that won't change. My mother remained with you all these years but that's her prerogative. Blood is thicker than water, but it can also be washed down the drain, and I washed your blood down the drain a long time ago. Now give me my fucking child!" Rashaun went around the bed and took Wisdom from his father's arms.

"Son, listen to me—" Edward started to say but the door was shut before he could continue.

Rashaun saw his mother outside the door.

She reached out and touched him on the head. "Rashaun, your father is sorry. He talks to me all the time about you. It's time Rashaun. It's time, to forgive him."

"I can't, Mom. After all these years I still can't," he said as he looked down into Wisdom's soft brown eyes. "When I needed him, he was never there. I grew up without a father, Mom. I wrote him off a long time ago."

"In time, Rashaun, you will forgive him. I know you will. You have Wisdom now, and that's all your father talks about. He loves your son with everything he's got. I don't know if it was because of his relationship with you but Wisdom makes him so happy. I think his friends are getting tired of hearing him talk about the baby. He's also very proud of you. He might not say it to you but he tells me all the time. Your father is a good man. He has his ways but he hasn't forsaken his family. He might not have been there like you wanted him to, but he supported the family. He was the one who put food on the table. There are a lot of people out there who wish their father gave anything at all," Albertina said, playing with Wisdom who was looking up at her.

"Mom, I understand what you're saying but you were one of the few people who knew how my father felt about me. He hated me. He hated me from birth. I never did anything to disappoint him except for my minor skirmishes as a boy. Now you stand here telling me how good my father is."

"Rashaun," she said firmly, "I'm not telling you to go and hold your father's hand and walk down the street with him. What he did to you sometimes hurt me more than it did you, but a lot of time has passed, and he has expressed to me so many times how awful he feels about the way he treated you. All I'm saying is give him a chance to be a part of your life. If not for you, do it for Wisdom. Boy, don't let hate rule your heart. Your father is not young anymore, and time is of the essence."

"I'm taking Wisdom to Andria," Rashaun said. "I'm sorry but I don't have it in me to forgive him."

"Son, I don't think you'll do anything you don't want to do, but do me one favor, just look in your heart for a second chance," Albertina said.

"Andria," Rashaun said, opening the door to the basement.

"I know Andria is waiting. I came in right after you came upstairs. She was concerned but I told her not to worry. You can't live in a house and act like another person under the same roof doesn't exist. Your father is afraid to get in your way. He tries not to be around when you are around because your hate is so strong. Andria and I sat and talked for a while. Tell her I'll be down later to see my grandson and finish up the christening plans." Albertina bent and kissed Wisdom on the cheek. "He looks like you and your father. I know you hate to hear it but there is no mistaking the Jones."

"I'll see you later, Mom," Rashaun said and descended the stairs.

When Rashaun went in the bedroom with Wisdom, Andria was sitting on the bed.

Wisdom started to cry.

"He's hungry," Andria said and took him from Rashaun. "I wish you could breastfeed him."

"You know I would too," Rashaun said.

Andria put Wisdom against her breast and he started sucking immediately. "Do you want to talk?" she asked.

Rashaun came over and slipped his hand around her as he focused on Wisdom. "Not right now," he said.

"Okay," she said and leaned back on his shoulder. " What time are you and the guys going out tomorrow?"

"We're meeting at a bar downtown around 6, but knowing Lance and Pedro 7:30 might be more accurate."

Wisdom stopped feeding, leaving Andria's nipple exposed.

"Don't even think about it, you pervert."

"Hey, daddy needs milk too," Rashaun said, making a sucking noise between his teeth.

"You are not driving tomorrow, are you?" Andria asked, putting a sleeping Wisdom down in the crib.

"His life is so simple. All he does is eat, sleep and shit," Rashaun said, standing over the crib with Andria.

"Well let's hope we get to that point in life—and that means no drinking and driving."

"Andria, you know me better than that. I have too much

to lose for me to drink and drive. There isn't enough time in the world to love you, and I'm definitely not going to cut into the time we do have."

Andria took Rashaun's hand and swung it. She looked down at Wisdom. "We did good, didn't we?" she said.

"You did good, baby. I was just along for the ride."

"I love you," she said.

"Well show it," Rashaun said, leading her out of the room.

"Sir, what are you talking about? The doctor said I can't do that," she said, taking off Rashaun's T-shirt.

Rashaun guided her to the couch. "Well I did some research, and I found that there are some things that we can do."

Rashaun unbuttoned his Levi's and pulled the zipper down.

"How long did it take you to do the research to find that out?" Andria asked, kissing Rashaun on the chest.

Rashaun's eyes fluttered. "I can't recall."

Andria continued to kiss Rashaun, going past his stomach as she pulled his pants down to his ankles. She pulled gently on the hair around his scrotum.

"I like that," Rashaun said as his legs stiffened.

"I know you do." Andria caressed the inside of Rashaun's legs, positioning herself so that she was directly over his erect penis. "I see that you've been missing me."

"More than you know," Rashaun answered. "All thirteen inches of me."

"Oh, you've grown a few inches since the last time we got together," Andria said, stroking Rashaun's penis.

"Well you know what they say after childbirth. The woman—"

"Rashaun, you say another word, and you'll have to go and jerk off in the bathroom."

Rashaun laughed and reached down and kissed Andria on the

lips. “They say a woman is more beautiful than ever after childbirth because through God you were able to bring life onto this earth, therefore, you now have a heavenly pussy.”

“Rashaun, the shit you come up with,” she said, still stroking his penis. “Now what do they say about the woman’s mouth—”

“Well—”

Andria engulfed Rashaun’s penis with her mouth.

“It’s gooooood,” Rashaun said as his left leg stiffened.

Andria licked up and down Rashaun’s penis then engulfed him once more. She continued to suck on his penis while she played with his scrotum.

Rashaun started to experience that old familiar feeling, the rushing of all his blood to his penis. His body started to twitch but Andria held on to his butt as she buried his penis in her mouth.

“Baby, I’m coming,” Rashaun said, holding on to Andria’s hair and pulling her head from side to side.

Andria continued to suck on Rashaun’s penis until he stopped shaking.

Rashaun laid back on the couch, totally exhausted.

Andria stood.

Rashaun started to laugh.

Andria pointed to her hair. “I see you find this funny.”

“Ma’am, are you having a bad hair day?” Rashaun asked.

“Give me your wallet,” Andria said, her hands at her waist.

“Here.” Rashaun handed her his wallet.

“One hundred, one twenty, one forty, one fifty.” She took the money and threw the wallet down on the couch.

“One fifty to do your hair. What happened to seventy-five dollars?” Rashaun asked, sitting up on the couch.

“Seventy-five dollars for my hair and seventy-five for you laughing at me. Maybe I’ll buy something for myself, maybe I’ll give it to a beggar on the street."

"Baby, you know I love you."

Wisdom started to cry.

"There's breast milk in the refrigerator and you know the rest. Bye." Andria went to the closet, took out some clothes then went into the bathroom.

Rashaun pushed himself off the couch, went to the kitchen and washed his hands. He then went to the refrigerator and took out a small bottle of breast milk. He put it in the microwave for a few seconds. He stopped in front the bathroom. "Can Wisdom and I join you in there?"

"Rashaun," Andria shouted.

Chapter 5

"It's cold like a motherfucker out there," Lance Moore, one of Rashaun's friend said, pulling off his black leather gloves, which matched his long wool coat that ended six inches above his Gucci shoes. The short curly hair that bounced up when he took his wool cap off was in sharp contrast to his pale skin and blue eyes. "Even the whores on Eleventh Avenue got on clothes. I'm sure they're discounting the pussy right now. Why did we follow the white people to this uninhabitable climate?"

"That was slavery, Lance. They brought us here, and can you have a conversation without talking about sex?" Tyrone asked, sitting between Rashaun and Pedro McLean another one of Rashaun's friends. Tyrone was the only one without something on his head. Rashaun had a small bandage to the side of his head and Pedro had a red, black and green hat that kept his dreads covered.

"Tyrone, I understand your problem with pussy but don't take away a man's main focus in life. Didn't you hear the saying?" Lance asking, plopping down on the chair.

"What saying, Lance?" Pedro Davis, the only Jamaican in the group, asked, a bottle of Heineken in his right hand. Heineken was the only beer besides Red Stripe that he drank. A long extra-width scarf the same color of his hat rested loosely in his lap. Those were the only overt signs that Pedro was born in a country outside of the United States.

"They say a man came from pussy, and he spends the rest of his life trying to get back inside pussy. Everything a man does, the ultimate goal is to get pussy," Lance said, rubbing his hands together. "I need something to warm me up."

"I'll drink to that." George McLeod was Rashaun's best friend and the best man in Rashaun's wedding, said bringing a purple-colored drink to his mouth.

"George, what the fuck you drinking?" Rashaun asked.

"This is a 'Purple Motherfucker.' I don't know what's in it but it goes down good," George said as he put the drink back down on the table. George was dressed in a gray wool vest with a white shirt underneath finished off with black pants. He wore glasses that appeared way too small for his face. He insisted that the glasses had dropped many wet drawers.

"Anyone spoke to Pete?" Pedro asked.

"Yeah, I did," Rashaun, said. "He said he might get here a little bit late."

"It's 7:20. Did he forget that drinks are free until 7:30?" George asked.

"Not everyone's life revolves around alcohol like you, George," Rashaun said.

"Alcohol and pussy, my friend, alcohol and pussy. The rest of life is just work," George said.

"That's my man," Lance said. "Unlike some people, George knows the basics of life."

"There is more to life than that, Lance, but you obviously aren't ready. I would invite you to church with me but I'm afraid that would be fruitless," Tyrone said, sounding a bit irritated.

"Not necessarily, Tyrone. I heard a lot about church girls. All you have to do is quote them a scripture and pull out your dick," Lance said, rising off his chair. He took another look at Tyrone. "I'm going to get me a drink before I have to start paying. "

"That's a problem for a man who drives a Mercedes Benz S500, a man who has a wife who has money coming out of her ass," Rashaun said, trying to get comfortable on the couch with Tyrone and Pedro. "How does it feel to be stupid rich?"

"I'm sure it's better than being poor and married, but a woman is a woman whether rich or poor. Now, Rashaun, you mentioned my wife and you depressed me. Now I have to order two drinks." Lance headed for the gray and black suits of men a formable foe that encircled the bar like teenagers watching a fight. You'd get there eventually, but no one was in a hurry to let you through.

"That's one troubled soul," Tyrone said as he watched Lance disappear behind the gray suits. "I don't think he'll ever grow up."

"Talking about troubled souls, here comes Pete," Pedro said as he watched Peter Jefferson make his way to the group.

"Sorry, guys, had to go and pick up something for the wife," Peter said. "Soon you'll know what that's like, Rashaun."

Peter was the smallest one in the group. He stood barely five-four, and he weighed less than a hundred and twenty pounds. The parka jacket he pulled off was insufficient in adding any size to his hallow frame.

"Pete, you better get to the bar now because soon you'll have to pay for whatever touches your lips," Pedro said.

"He already pays for whatever touches his lips—and I'm sure that includes pussy. Pete's wife doesn't cook," George said.

"Fuck you, George. That's why your wife threw your ass out," Pete said, putting down his black-and-red scarf over his jacket on a chair next to Lance's coat. "I hope Grenada did something to help your ass, otherwise you're gonna have to do like Halle Berry's husband and go to pussy anonymous."

"I don't think I can take you guys for much longer. God doesn't want me to hear such language. Courtney said that I would need to find some friends in the church. I think she's right," Tyrone said as he adjusted his white turtleneck sweater and leaned forward to pull his coat off the couch.

"Tyrone, relax for a bit. Life is changing. Who knows when we'll get together again? Lance will be back soon. After Pete gets his drink we'll do a little bit of toasting," Rashaun said, tapping Tyrone on the shoulder.

"Yeah, Tyrone, relax yourself," Pedro added.

Lance came back with two drinks.

"I see you're still here," Lance said to Tyrone. "The Lord hasn't moved you off your seat yet, Tyrone."

"Lance, Tyrone has a right to his beliefs," Rashaun said. "We are all here, and all you guys are in my wedding party, so let's try not to insult one another. Tyrone doesn't find it funny."

"Well Tyrone obviously has problems and maybe a bar is not a good place for him." Lance put one drink down and brought the other to his lips. "He is definitely suffering from pussy withdrawal."

Rashaun looked at Tyrone who was getting more and more agitated.

"Can we all get along?" Rashaun asked, trying to break the ice.

"I'm going to drink to that," George said, finishing off his drink.

"As the only single person here—" Pedro shot a glance at the departing George and Lance who had gulped down his first drink— "I congratulate all of you on your beautiful women waiting at home for you. I especially would like to congratulate Rashaun on the birth of his son and his impending marriage."

"Before we start toasting, let's wait for George," Lance said.

"What did I miss?" George asked, putting two drinks down on the table. "Sorry, guys, these are the last two free drinks. The bar is now open for your money."

Pedro stood. "This is a toast to Rashaun's upcoming wedding and the birth of his son, Wisdom."

"And a quick end to that bullshit trial. I'll drink to that," George said as he stood with the rest of the men, touching one another's glasses. "Rashaun, we understand the situation with the attempt on your life, and I'm sure I'm speaking for everyone here when I say, we are there for you whenever you need us."

Rashaun stood. "Thanks, guys. You all have been great, visiting me at the hospital and being there for me. I'm thankful and blessed to call all of you my friends. I would like to propose a toast to Tyrone. Tyrone, at one time I thought we had lost you, but you have endured and overcome. It's great to have you here with us again."

The men toasted and drank.

Tyrone stood. "This toast is for Lance. May he re-examine the commitment he made to his wife and honor and be faithful to her. Let not he be tempted by the wickedness of the flesh. "

"I hope God is still able to move mountains because that's the only way Lance will give up the sins of the flesh," Rashaun said before he brought his drink to his lips.

"Amen," Pedro said, and the men clinked glasses again.

"To Pedro, hoping he will stop meeting women at Weight Watchers. A woman over four hundred pounds is not healthy— she is fat. A woman who eats a whole chicken for dinner with a bottle of diet soda is not on a diet, she has an eating disorder," Lance said, bringing his glass to the middle of the circle for a toast.

"To George, judging from his behavior, it's obvious that his trip to Grenada was a waste of time. He doesn't need a cleansing, he needs a good beating," Peter said, bringing his Hypnotic drink to the middle.

"Thank you, Peter. I know you and your wife had your little situation to deal with—emphasis on little. I hope your dick has grown in size and your wife's vagina has decreased in width, making friction possible in your life." George said, barely able to contain his laughter.

All the men including Peter started laughing.

"If you and your wife have been able to get over that, there is still hope for me. To Peter, a giver of hope," George started another toast.

"Did you guys see some of the white meat that's in this bar?" Lance asked.

"This is my cue to leave," Tyrone said, getting up from between George and Rashaun.

"Alright," Rashaun said, standing and giving Tyrone a handshake and a hug.

Tyrone repeated the gesture around the room until he got to Lance.

"I'll be praying for you," he said as he embraced Lance.

"Do that and also give some of the sisters my number. I would like to pray with them," Lance said, giving Tyrone a few of his business cards.

Tyrone took them and put them in his pocket.

"Tyrone is a changed man, Lance," Rashaun said after Tyrone left.

"That's good for him but we aren't. I still call vagina *pussy* and breasts *tits* and sex *fuck*. This is a bar. He did the right thing leaving."

"He's got a point," George said.

"I'm not denying that he doesn't. I just wanted us to hang out like the old days," Rashaun said, feeling much more relaxed now that he wasn't squeezed in on the couch with Tyrone and Pedro.

"The old days are quickly disappearing. Our next milestone is not thirty-it's forty. We are becoming the old in old days," Lance said. "I'm just thankful for Pfizer. Through Viagra they make it possible for pussy as the sun sets."

"You stupid man, Pfizer did not make that possible with Viagra. The Jamaicans have had that remedy for years now," Pedro said.

"Alright, Pedro, you know the only thing the Jamaicans know how to do is to grow pot. All those sex drinks only hurt your stomach. I have drank a whole lot of sea moss, stay hard, back breaker, and all they do is give me the runs," George said, drinking his last two drinks much slower.

"I tried that Viagra shit. Man, I was fucking nonstop for five hours. This nurse gave it to me. She never did that again," Lance said.

"Lance, do you sleep with your wife?" Rashaun asked.

"Not presently, but I did once and now she's pregnant," Lance said without hesitating.

"And I thought I was bad," Peter said. "At least every now and then I do my little thing."

"So I guess you didn't do the operation because you're still saying *little*," Pedro said.

"If God wanted me to have a big dick he would have given me one," Peter said.

"Amen to small dicks," George said, standing, "Now, let me tell you guys this joke."

"Okay, George, but none of those grandma sick jokes you get off the internet," Rashaun said, looking up at George.

"Nah, nothing like that," George said. "Now answer this. How many feet does a rooster have?"

"A rooster? You mean a fowl," Lance said.

"Yeah a rooster, cockadoodle doo," George said.

"Two legs," Rashaun said.

"How many wings?" George asked.

"Unless it's deformed, two," Peter answered.

"Alright. How many whiskers does a cat have?" George asked

The men looked at one another then at George.

"Who the fuck knows how many whiskers on a cat?" Rashaun said.

"That's right, motherfuckers. You guys know all about cocks but you all don't know shit about pussy," George said and started to laugh.

The men joined in.

Lance toasted George. "That's a good one."

"I heard that in a barbershop. This drunk-ass-looking white boy said it."

"Talking about barbershop, any of you guys seen *Barbershop 2*?" Rashaun asked.

"Nah," Pedro answered, "but knowing Ice Cube, there will be a *barbershop 3, 4,* and so on. I might as well wait and get all ten when he finishes with them."

"You're right, what is he on, the third Friday after last Friday?" Peter said.

"Something like that," Lance said. "The only trilogy that lived up to the hype is *Lord of the Rings, The Return of the King*. There aren't any brothers in it, but it was a damn good movie."

"The only brother who's been getting roles in movies is Denzel and he is way past his prime but his last one *Man on Fire* is on the money," Rashaun said, looking at his watch. "Even Snipes has taken a hiatus. Maybe he'll return with another *Blade Runner*."

"Not *Blade Runner,* Rashaun. It was *Blade* something. *Blade Runner* is that old flick with Harrison Ford," Lance said, looking at two white girls giggling at the bar.

"Guys, I got to go make a phone call." Rashaun stood and inched his way around the table.

"Checking in?" George asked.

"Got to say good night to my little one," Rashaun said, flipping his phone open.

"I'll come with you, Rashaun. I saw some buffet stuff downstairs. I'm going to get some," Peter said.

"Bring us back a plate," Pedro said.

"That's going to look really ghetto me filling two plates with Buffalo wings." Peter secured his jacket on the chair and pulled down his sweater sleeves.

"Who gives a fuck what these white people think about us?" Lance winked at the two girls at the bar. "I'm going to get another drink."

"Be back in a minute," Rashaun said, pulling his jacket on.

Rashaun made his way through the quickly disappearing crowd. It was 8:00 P.M. Peter trailed a step or two behind Rashaun who walked past the two bouncers dressed in black, putting on his gloves as he went out. Peter stopped to talk to the bouncers. The cold wind mixed with nicotine from the group of white men and women shuffling their feet made Rashaun duck his head into his coat. He stood to the left side of the bar on the opposite side of the puffers. He pressed two buttons on the phone then whispered "Home" into the phone.

"Damn, this voice dialing never works when you want it to," he said, sliding his right glove off. He quickly dialed his home number.

He put the phone to his ear as Peter pushed the door open. Rashaun spoke quickly into the phone, watching Peter who had his hands in his pockets twisting from side to side. Rashaun flipped the phone closed.

"You ready to go in, Peter?" Rashaun asked.

"Not yet. I like standing out here. The air feels clean," he said.

Rashaun looked over to where the group was smoking earlier. The only remnants of their existence were cigarette butts on the ground.

"What's up, Pete? There's got to be a reason you're standing outside here shivering in the cold," Rashaun said, putting his hand back into the glove.

"It's my wife," Peter said, looking out at a homeless man pushing a cart with empty cans. "These people are very innovative. Do you see how many cans they are able to carry with one small cart?"

"What does she want, Pete?" Rashaun asked, ignoring the homeless diversion.

"She wants us to have a threesome," Peter said, pulling his hands out of his pockets.

"Yeah, the homeless people are one step away from inventing water," Rashaun said, unable to think of a response to Peter's statement.

"She said we need to try something new," Peter continued.

"A man or a woman?" Rashaun asked, hoping that it would snow. Snow was not always bad.

"A woman. She said she doesn't want to insult my manhood," Peter said, putting his hands back into his pockets.

"And a woman doesn't do that? Sometimes I wonder what the fuck is going through these women's minds. Their reasoning is sometimes totally ridiculous." Rashaun lifted his head as two white women headed into the bar.

"I definitely don't satisfy her in bed, so maybe she's right. Maybe we could try something different," Peter said, starting to twist again.

"I heard about counseling, picking up sex toys and role playing but bringing another person into bed can open up a big can of worms. Don't get me wrong, there is nothing like a threesome. It's ninety-nine percent of our fantasy but we don't usually think about it with our wives," Rashaun said. "I can't tell you not to do it. All I can say to you is be prepared for the aftermath. This could be the best thing for your marriage; it could also end it."

"She said she wouldn't eat the woman or anything like that, so maybe it will work out," Peter said.

"Okay," Rashaun said, looking up into the sky.

"Would you do something like that with Andria, if that's what she wanted?" Peter asked.

"She wouldn't ask," Rashaun said, bringing his coat up to his ears. He didn't feel them but he hoped they were there. They must be because he could hear Peter clearly.

"Let's go in. It's getting cold out here," Peter said.

Rashaun looked at Peter who had turned to open the door. It was freezing before they came outside and it would be freezing for the next few days. Some people took longer to feel the cold; he hoped that Peter didn't take too long.

Kim waited until the beautiful petite woman with the brown hair and a pastel blue dress left with two kids in tow. She was guessing that was Devon's wife and kids because they were the last ones to leave the church. Kim had entered earlier when the service was going on and sat in the back. She had seen Devon to the right of the priest wearing the multicolored frock. The priest who she assumed was the main priest of the church left in a Lexus 430 soon after the service. Kim walked across the street wearing a wide broad- rimmed hat, her winter coat doing nothing to hide the measurements of her well-toned body. She ignored the tooting horn of a passing Land Rover. There was only one car left in the parking lot, a Camry with Maryland license plates. She pushed the door to the church open and was surprised that it yielded to her.

Devon came rushing down the aisle of the church, looking a little bit flustered, still in his priest's uniform. "Miss, the church is closed. Can I help you?"

"Devon, you're in New York now. You know you never leave the door unlocked. Criminals are not afraid of being smitten by the holy one," Kim said, lifting her head up so that Devon could see her face.

"I was wondering when you would come," Devon said, clutching a worn red Bible in his right hand. He was dressed in a long white robe with an extra-long red-checkered scarf around his neck.

"Great to see you, too, Devon. How are the wife and kids?" Kim asked, turning around to lock the door.

"Is that necessary? I didn't think you would be here that long." Devon moved to the left side of the pew as Kim walked down the aisle. He followed her to the pulpit.

“Should I kneel to receive the communion?” Kim asked, a wicked smile coming over her face. She took off her hat and placed it on the pulpit in front of a small stand covered with a red cloth. On either side of the stand equal lengths apart was an off-white candle in a gold holder. On the wall behind the pulpit was a statue of the crucifixion of a white God. Kim’s rainbow-colored hat contrasted sharply with the white cloth covering the pulpit. On either side of the pulpit were two stands about four feet in height, each holding a vase of flowers. Next to them were some benches about six feet in length.

“So how have you been, Devon?” Kim asked, taking a seat on the right bench, exposing her long, shapely legs.

“A lot better after you left.” Devon leaned on the pulpit and looked at the flowers to Kim’s left.

“I see you gave up the law profession and you went from a whore to a priest,” Kim said, making herself comfortable by leaning against the walls.

“God called me and I answered his call. My jealousy of Rashaun drove me to an unspeakable act with you, and I think that made me wake up when I lost my best friend,” Devon said, looking at Kim’s black heels then back at the flowers on the stand.

“Devon, we all make mistakes. Why dwell on them?” Kim asked, crossing her legs. As she did, her coat, which was buttoned midway between her leg and knee fell to the floor.

“Kim, we’re in a church. Do you mind showing some decency in His name?” Devon said, trying to keep his eyes on the upper part of Kim’s body.

“Devon, I don’t think that a man who gave his flesh so that man could live would be offended by my mode of dress.” Kim uncrossed her legs and sat up with her feet about shoulder-width apart.

"Oh God," Devon said as he looked away from her.

"My assistant told me that you refused to testify about the incident in law school," Kim said, looking at the small beads of sweat starting to form on Devon's forehead.

"Kim, Rashaun beat up that guy for you. He was constantly protecting you. Rashaun was your man, and he did what he thought he had to do. The guy even called some of his friends to hurt Rashaun. Now you're asking me to give damaging testimony. I'm sorry, but I think I did enough to hurt Rashaun. I'm hoping one day he'll forgive me."

"Don't hold your breath," Kim said. "Rashaun is not the man you once knew. He took a life, therefore he should be punished for his crime. What we did was wrong, I admit that, but there's a big difference between murder and infidelity. By the way, Devon, where is the Blackfunk tape? The one where you were trying to fuck me to death. We both had one. You know what happened to mine, but I don't know what happened to yours."

"Kim, I would be foolish to do anything with that tape. It could hurt both of us," Devon said, turning around to look at Jesus on the cross. "It's in a safe place."

"I guess that means you won't give it to me," Kim said, standing.

"No, I won't." There was resiliency in Devon's voice.

"Okay. Is that your final answer?" Kim asked, walking over to the pulpit.

She took each of the candles with their respective holders. "I don't suppose you have a match, do you?"

Devon shook his head.

Kim went back and sat down with both candles. She rummaged through her bag before coming out with a box of matches that had 40/40 written on it. "No, Devon, I don't smoke. I took the box for the address," she said, answering Devon's inquiring look.

"What are you doing?" Devon asked, looking at Kim light one of the candles.

"Devon, do you know why there are so many candles in the convent?" Kim asked, taking one and dripping the wax onto the other.

"No, Kim, I don't know why the convent is full of candles," Devon said, shaking his head.

"Most people think that the first dildo was an invention of some sexaholic, which is far from the truth. The dildo with it smoothness and hardness was invented by nuns. They had taken a vow not to be with a man. You see, Devon, you can take away one instrument from a man but when the flesh calls, man gets very creative." Kim molded the unlit candle in the shape of a penis.

"Kim, I think you should leave," Devon said, leaning heavily on the pulpit.

"Are you saying that the nuns did something wrong, Devon?" Kim asked, taking off her coat and putting it behind her bag.

"Oh God," Devon said, looking at Kim who was attired in a red bra and a matching thong. "Get out from His house, Kim. Get out from His house."

"Why, Devon? Are you like the nuns? Is the flesh weak my brother?" Kim asked taking the candle and rubbing it around her neck. "Be strong, my brother. Walk away from the temptations of the flesh."

Devon sank to his knees. "Lord, give me strength."

Kim worked the candle over her breasts as she lay back, one foot on the floor, the other on the bench. She traced the candle down her stomach and ran the head that she had shape like a penis over the front of her panties.

"Kim, I'm happily married with two beautiful children," Devon said, tears coming to his eyes. "Please stop and go away."

"What do you want to do to me, Devon? Come over here and tell me," Kim said, removing her bra. She pushed her bag farther down the bench.

"Please, Kim, don't do this to me. This is the house of the Lord. I'm a changed man. I have never cheated on my wife. Don't make me go against everything I stand for."

"Look, Devon, I'm all wet," Kim said, pulling her panties to one side as she exposed her dripping vagina. She inserted the tip of the candle inside her, leaning back and closing her eyes as she felt it enter.

Devon pounded against the pulpit, his fist held tightly in a ball. "This is a test. I'm not going to give in."

"Come, Devon, don't you remember how warm and tight I am? It's like being with a virgin over and over," she said as she kept sliding the candle in and out of her vagina, her eyes closed.

"Oh." Kim opened her eyes to feel Devon's hands on her shoulder. He was standing there butt naked. His robe and underclothes lay at the foot of the pulpit. His penis stood out hard and strong in front of her. He knelt and grabbed both of Kim's legs and spread them apart. He entered her with the force of a thousand sinners. The bench rocked back and forth as he slammed into her over and over. Her back hit the wall of the church, pushing the bench away from it.

"Please, God, forgive me," he said as he went in and out over and over. He flipped her over and grabbed her by her ponytail.

"Yes, Devon, fuck me," she said, returning her butt to him with the velocity of his thrust.

"I hate you, Kim," he said, unable to control himself anymore. His thrusts increased as his orgasm started.

Kim felt him about to come in her. She braced herself on the wall and pushed back hard onto him, throwing him back to the pulpit. As he slid on the floor, an offering was made in front the pulpit.

"You are not worthy, Devon. You are weak and pitiful," she said, standing over him, putting on her underclothes.

Devon lay flat on the floor in front of the pulpit, looking up at the picture of Jesus painted on the ceiling.

Kim put on her coat and picked up her bag off the floor. She opened the bag and took out a small digital camera. She made some adjustments then knelt next to Devon and held the camera over him.

Devon turned away when he saw himself with Jesus on the cross in the background through the small viewfinder.

"I want the Blackfunk tape delivered to my address tomorrow before 10:00 A.M., and don't even think of making a copy because you have a lot more to lose than I do. I have a career but you have a family and a career. I'll send Roger over to set up the time of your testimony." She put the camera back into her bag and grabbed her hat from the top of the pulpit.

"You are pure evil," Devon said.

Kim gave the laugh of a conqueror.

"Get out of God's house," Devon said, starting to get up off the floor.

"Pastor Devon Thompson, you should know that it's not God's house if the preacher is the devil," she said as she took a knee at the front pew before walking down the aisle toward the exit door.

"Get out!" Devon shouted.

Kim opened the door. "Devon, please don't forget to straighten the statue of Jesus Christ. It's crooked."

Chapter 6

Andria looked down at Wisdom and smiled. He was the best-looking baby boy in the whole world. And today he looked even better in his three-piece white suit that Rashaun had bought for the christening. He was asleep as usual, and she stood there mimicking the way he pulled his lips in.

"Okay, Andria, give my godson a break. You're going to scorch this kid with your eyes the way you're always looking at him," Robin said, putting her coat in the closet. "Your mother and future mother-in-law cooked up a storm."

"Yeah, they didn't want me anywhere close to the kitchen. I don't think Rashaun ever wants to hear about another christening. They had him going to the store every minute. The poor boy must be dead tired," Andria said, adjusting her clothes in the mirror.

"Where is Rashaun?" Robin asked.

"He went to pick up his brother at the airport. I think he should be home soon," Andria said.

"Since I came back from vacation, it seems like I've been running nonstop. I told my husband we need to take another vacation. Did you bring out the barbecue chicken?" Robin asked.

"Oh no. Albertina is going to kill me. Robin, can you?" Andria's eyes drooped noticeably.

"I'll do it, Andria. I see that you're in no mood to leave your child's sight." Robin pulled her jacket on and opened the door.

"Tell Albertina I'll be out in a minute," Andria said, putting a blue-and-white blanket over Wisdom. Andria sat on Rashaun's parents' bed. It was a queen-size bed covered with a beige quilt with imprinted artwork of kings and queens of the British Empire. On the other side of the bed next to an old gray six-foot metal cabinet stood the imposing wicker chair where Rashaun's father spent most of his time. Andria turned around when she heard a knock on the door.

"Auntie Andria, Grandma is looking for you," Sheila Riddick, Rashaun's niece, said, coming up and peering at Wisdom. "Can I pick up Wisdom?"

"No, Sheila. He's too young."

"But I'll be careful."

"Come here," Andria said, beckoning to Sheila.

Sheila came over to her and stood leaning against Andria's left leg.

Andria brushed Sheila's hair back lightly. "Sheila, as soon as Wisdom gets a little older, you'll be able to hold him, but right now he's too young."

"But I won't drop him on his head."

"I know you won't," Andria said, smiling.

"I love my cousin."

"I know you do."

"So can I hold him?"

Andria rolled her eyes. "Okay, let me tell you what I'm going to do. When Uncle Rashaun comes home we'll ask him if you can hold him, okay?" Andria said.

"Okay. Can I kiss him?" Sheila asked, walking back over to Wisdom.

"Yes, you can, but first you have to go and wash your hands," Andria said, happy they had moved on to something more manageable.

"Be right back," Sheila said and jetted out of the room.

Andria looked out the window in time to see a black Mercedes S500 pull up to the driveway. She recognized the car as belonging to Lance. He was the only one of Rashaun's friends she didn't like. The passenger side of the car opened and Lance's pregnant wife stepped out with a small wrapped box.

"I'm back, and I washed my hands." Sheila said, standing over Wisdom.

"Okay," Andria said, closing the curtain and going over to Sheila and Wisdom.

She lifted Wisdom out of his bassinet and sat down with him in her arms.

Sheila almost ran into them as she followed Andria to the bed.

"Okay, now you can have your kiss," Andria said.

Sheila did exactly what Andria expected her to do. First she played with Wisdom's fingers, then she touched his ears then his hair. Once that was done, she took a deep breath, and with a proud smile on her face, she reached down and kissed Wisdom on the cheek. Then she looked at Andria and stood there waiting.

Andria looked back at her. "Okay Sheila, I'll put him back down now."

"I'm waiting for you to turn his cheek so that I can kiss his other one."

"Oh, I'm sorry," Andria said, turning Wisdom's head to the other side.

Sheila kissed the baby's other cheek. "I love you, Wisdom."

"Great, Sheila. Now let's put him down and go and help

grandma." Andria gave Wisdom a kiss on the cheek before putting him down.

"I can't wait to take him to school with me," Sheila said.

"Well that will be a while," Andria said, clipping the white-and-blue baby monitor to her long blue skirt.

"Thanks for picking us up," David Jones, Rashaun's brother said.

A person meeting David would not think Rashaun was his biological brother. He had a pale skin complexion bordering on albino. His nose was flat, and he was about six inches shorter than Rashaun. He sat in the front passenger seat, his large frame absorbed the complete front seat of the ML 320 tilting it more to the passenger side.

"Hey, I appreciate the fact that my little brother and his family flew in from Florida for Wisdom's christening," Rashaun said as he drove out of the Ramada Inn located a short distance from the airport.

"I wouldn't miss this for the world," David said as he looked out the window. "So, my big brother is finally getting married. Mom must be overjoyed. Her favorite son has met a woman he loves more than his mother."

"Not love more than my mother. It's a totally different kind of love."

"Uh-huh. How you and Pops getting along?" David asked.

"Same as usual."

"That's not good. You still haven't forgiven him, have you?"

"I guess you can say that. Where are you going anyway? You

left your wife and kids at a hotel near the airport and you jump in the car with me. You'll be here for the weekend. I'm sure you can go and see your friends tomorrow," Rashaun said, looking over at the white Escalade that seemed to be coming too close for comfort.

"I need for you to drop me off at 34th Street and Brooklyn Avenue. You don't need to pick me up. A home boy of mine is going to lend me one of his cars to drive while I'm in Brooklyn."

"Isn't that where your old girlfriend use to live? What's her name again?"

"Deedra, and who said she's an old girlfriend? We went through some drama after I got married but me and her are still tight."

Rashaun looked over at his brother.

"What, you think this married thing is easy? If it weren't for Deedra I would have been divorced a long time now," David said, shuffling through a small black Kenneth Cole leather bag he had brought with him.

"You never told me about that before," Rashaun said as he came off the Belt Parkway at the Rockaway Parkway, Exit 14.

"And, what's your point. Does it matter to you?" David asked, sounding defensive.

"David, I'm still your big brother, but you're also a man. I can't tell you what to do with your life," Rashaun said.

"I would think that you would be the last one to tell a man about cheating. Brother, I can't forget the days when you had them calling the hot line," David said, a smile coming over his face.

"I guess you're right. I can't tell you what to do with your life, and I won't even try," Rashaun said pulling onto Brooklyn Avenue. "What's Deedra's address?"

"It's 999 East 34th Street off Brooklyn. Thanks, brother. I guess I'll be seeing you and your family in a few hours," Rashaun said as he pulled up in front of the apartment building.

"You know the deal, I'm by an old friend if questions are asked." David said as he got out of the car.

"Yeah, I know the deal," Rashaun said, putting the truck back in drive.

"Thanks, bro." David closed the door and started to walk toward the apartment building with the little bag in his hand.

As Rashaun turned on Foster he started to wonder if infidelity was imbedded in his family genes. As with most things, saying he would never cheat on Andria would be a lie. Only time would tell.

The black sports car held on to the road with the nimbleness of a squirrel racing up a tree. It moved from behind the white BMW 330 with a quick puff of smoke from its exhaust. The BMW driver, a white man in his early thirties, ignored the challenge as the Z raced ahead past Exit 26 eastbound on the Northern State Parkway.

"Roger, do you feel you must challenge every sports car you meet on the highway?" Kim asked, her head resting lightly on the leather headrest.

"Do you have a problem with the way I drive too?" Roger scanned the sides of the road.

"Do I detect a bit of attitude coming from you?" Kim turned her head toward Roger. "You had an attitude last night, and when I asked you about it, you said there was nothing wrong. Now here you are trying to kill us before we get to my parents' house. If you didn't want to come, all you had to say was no."

Roger slowed the car down behind a beige Toyota Camry that had a sign in the window informing motorists that there was a baby on-board. "What happened when you visited Pastor Thompson?"

Kim licked her top lip. "Well, I went to the pastor, and he threw me down on the altar and fucked my brains out. Is that what you want to hear, Roger? Is that what you think of me? Because if that's the case, you can let me out right here," Kim said, unhooking her seat belt.

"I don't know what I think about you, Kim. I've fallen in love with you, and these crazy thoughts get in my head. I know I'm wrong but sometimes I just can't help myself."

Kim reached over and started to gently rub the back of Roger's neck. "Roger, do you know how many men I've brought home to meet my parents? One, Roger. I'm thirty- five years old now, and I've only brought one-man home to my parents and that was a long time ago. Exit 32 is coming up. Make a right when you get off."

Roger pressed a button on the side of his seat, and it became upright. "Do you think your parents will like me?" he asked.

"My father might but my mother won't," Kim said, looking out at the well-manicured lawn of the big houses in Old Westbury.

"So how should I act? I know you told me to be myself but I'm getting a little nervous."

"Turn here," Kim said, pointing to a street with a green sign that read Clam Drive. "Go to the left, and my parents' house is the last one on the block."

"Your parents have done well for themselves," Roger said, pulling up in front of a large white house with multiple windows.

"I told you my father was a judge and my mother inherited so much wealth from her parents that she hasn't held a job since graduating from Harvard with a doctorate in anthropology."

"And you are an only child?" Roger asked, getting out of the car. He peeped his head back in. "Should I come over and open the door for you?"

Kim opened the door and stepped out. "My parents are rich, but they don't live in ancient civilization."

They walked up the newly tiled walkway past the driveway where an old black man was wiping down a spotless Mercedes Benz S600. Next to it was an antique-looking blue Corvette.

"Hi, Cedric." Kim waved at the old man.

"Hello, Kim. Great to see you," Cedric said, putting the cloth down and coming from the garage.

"How are the kids?" Kim asked.

"The kids are not kids anymore. They're all married with kids of their own now. Last week my tenth grandchild was born at St. Mary's Hospital in Brooklyn. How have you been, Kim? Have you made the judgeship yet?"

"Not yet, Cedric. Not yet." Kim said as she waved good-bye and walked up the steps with Roger. She rang the bell and waited.

A small Mexican woman in her late sixties opened the door. Her eyes lit up when she saw Kim. "Miss Kim, you are looking so pretty," she said, hugging Kim tightly and almost pushing Roger down the steps.

"Isabella, this is my friend Roger," Kim said when she was finally left to breathe on her own. "Isabella took care of me from the time I was six months old," Kim told Roger.

"Nice to meet you, Mr. Roger," Isabella said, stretching out her small hand to Roger. "I was so happy when Madam Rivers said you were coming to visit. Kim, I made your favorite, and I made that brownie dessert you love so much."

"Thank you, Isabella. I can't eat too much of that dessert because I'm not as active as I use to be," Kim said, patting her stomach.

"It doesn't matter. What you don't eat you can take with you," Isabella said, leading Kim and Roger into the living room, which was obviously expensive, and size wasn't a determining factor in its building and decoration.

Kim looked around the room as if seeing it for the first time. She had grown up in this home yet she felt like a stranger. The table was set for a party of four, which meant there were place settings on each end and the sides. Twelve chairs surrounded the dining table, which meant that Kim and Roger would be sitting opposite each other, and they would be separated from her parents by at least two chairs. After all these years, not a damn thing had changed. Since graduating from college Kim had steadily withdrawn from her parents. Whether it was a natural growing process or a need to create a loving distance to womanhood she wasn't sure. Kim heard the patter of small feet and looked up and saw her mother, a tiny woman about five-four dressed in a blue pastel frock with elongated diamond earrings.

"Kim, my missing daughter, has resurfaced." As she made her way toward Kim and Roger, Isabella started to walk backward until she disappeared through the swinging doors of the kitchen. Kim kissed her daughter lightly on the cheek.

"Great to see you, too, Mother," Kim said, matching the tone of her mother's voice.

"I see you've brought a friend with you," Mrs. Rivers said, turning to Roger.

"Mom, this is Roger. He recently joined the DA's office," Kim said.

Roger extended his hand to Mrs. Rivers, clasping hers softly.

"How are you, Roger?"

"I'm just fine, Mrs. Rivers. You have a beautiful daughter, and now that I've met you, I see the apple didn't fall far from the tree," Roger said, releasing Mrs. Rivers' hand.

"Do you and your parents live in New York?" Mrs. Rivers asked, turning and walking toward the table.

"No. My parents live in North Carolina. They own a grocery store down there," Roger answered.

"Is it a store chain?"

"No, just one store. My father bought it about forty years ago, and we have all worked in it. It's a beautiful store," Roger said, standing behind the chair Mrs. Rivers had motioned him to.

"A small store in North Carolina, huh," Mrs. Rivers said, looking over at Kim.

"Is there a problem, Mother?" Kim asked.

"Kimberly." The voice was authoritative yet gentle.

Kim turned around to see her father making his way down the stairs dressed in a black shirt with beige pants.

"Daddy," Kim said, moving away from the table and walking toward her father. The smile on her face was a declaration of love. She reached her father at the foot of the stairs, hugging him and planting a big kiss on his cheek. Her father picked her up off the floor and spun her around.

"Sebastien, I'm not taking you to the hospital if you hurt your back," Kim's mother shouted across the room.

"Kimberly, you live in New York and you rarely come and visit us. If I don't come to Manhattan, I don't get to see my priceless daughter," he said, walking to the table holding Kim's hand.

Kim's father was the only one who called her Kimberly. Kim had given up on telling him to call her Kim, which she believed sounded so much more ethnic than Kimberly. During her revolutionary years in college Kim had asked her parents to change her name to an African one as so many of her friends were doing at the time. Her mother was insulted that Kim had even approached them with such a request and suggested that she change colleges. Her father had a lot more empathy and was fortuitous in granting her request, but Mrs. Rivers was so adamant about her feelings toward the matter that the request was splitting the household apart. In the end, Kim decided to retain her name to avoid the destruction of a lifetime union.

After walking Kim over to her seat, Mr. Rivers walked over to Roger.

"Don't get up," he said, extending his hand to grip Roger's in a firm handshake. "Kim said you recently joined the DA's office," Mr. Rivers said, taking a seat at the head of the table.

"Yes. I was fortunate to get an opportunity to work with the famed Brooklyn DA's office, thanks to your daughter," Roger said.

"Our daughter believes in cutting out the road for herself instead of using the fast and free highway." Mrs. Rogers lifted her hand and Isabella came over. "Kim failed to realize sometimes it's not how you get there but the fact that you have arrived. Who cares that you took the bus, car or limo to get there?"

"I do, Mother. It makes a big difference to me." Kim flapped open her cloth napkin. "My record in the DA's office speaks for itself. I bet I will be nominated after this case."

"Isn't that the case with your friend from law school?" Mr. Rivers asked.

"Yes, it is," Kim said. "Can we eat?"

"Rashaun is his name. I remember him. I told you he was no good. It all starts with the family. If the family structure is weak, the children will have problems," Mrs. Rivers said.

"I'm sure you won't let this case stand in the way of your judgeship. Rashaun won't know what hit him when Kimberly Rivers gets through with him. Let's eat. I'm famished," Mr. Rivers said, flapping open his napkin.

"Not before grace," Mrs. Rivers said, bowing her head.

Rashaun looked down at Wisdom sleeping in his arms. He didn't know what else life had in store for him but he knew at that moment he was blessed. Andria had changed Wisdom's clothes. Instead of the white suit he had on earlier, he was now dressed in a light brown shirt with a black pants barely able to fit his tiny waist. There was a party going on a few steps down but Rashaun was oblivious to it. Once more the pride of being a father came upon him. This wasn't his niece or nephew or a friend's child, all of whom he loved dearly. This child was part of his blood—whether he was ugly or beautiful to the outside world. Wisdom belong to him. Rashaun's heart felt heavy as he held on tightly to his son. He realized his love for Wisdom was different from the one for Andria and his mother, the only other two people in the world who made his heart heavy.

Wisdom was somehow an entity. He found himself repeating over and over that he had a child, a living, breathing human being. No matter what became of him, Wisdom would always be his son. It felt like the clash of the Titans where he was going up against a warrior of the ages to claim the right to his son. It was the grandeurs or image that made him put his child's life in front, of his. Over the last few months Rashaun had gotten life insurance and created a fund so that if anything should happen to him,

Wisdom would be well taken care of. He wasn't worried about Andria because he knew she could fend for herself. It was Wisdom who required his attention. Wisdom was a child of pure innocence waiting to hear the sights and sounds of an unknown world. Wisdom would depend on him and Andria to guide him through this treacherous but great world. In Andria, Rashaun had chosen a fighter who felt the same way about Wisdom, and that was very important. He knew that regardless of the faith of their love, Andria would always be there for Wisdom. He knew his mother was right when she spoke to him in the hospital about making choices, choices not for now but for the future. Rashaun's only hope was that he and Andria would be as good a guide for Wisdom as his mother was to him. Rashaun brought Wisdom to his face and kissed him lightly on the cheek.

"I love you," he said, and a tear fell, "and I promise to take care of you."

"Here, Rashaun. Do something useful with yourself instead of kissing the poor child every second." Albertina took a diaper from the green-and-white baby bag and rested it next to Rashaun.

"Got to change you, my man," Rashaun said, resting Wisdom on his lap and pulling down his tiny pants.

"Can I help you, Uncle Rashaun?" Sheila, his niece, came up to him, a determined look in her face.

"Sure you can," Rashaun said. "Hold this for me." He gave her Wisdom's pants.

She took them, folded them in two and put them down next to the baby bag. "What else can I do?"

"Can you get me the A&D ointment?" Rashaun asked, wiping Wisdom with a baby wipe. "It's in a brown-and-white tube on the side of the baby bag."

"Uncle Rashaun, I can read. You don't have to tell me what

color it is," Sheila said, taking out a tube from the side of the bag. She quickly put it back when she saw it was lotion. "Here we are," she said, handing the tube of ointment to Rashaun.

"Thank you, ma'am," Rashaun said, taking the tube and flipping open the small cap. He squeezed some into the center of his palm.

"Can I do that?" Sheila asked.

"No, Sheila. Only adults can do that," Rashaun said.

"Soon I'll be an adult, and I'll be able to do everything," Sheila said.

"Yes, you will, be but don't force it. A lot of responsibilities come with being an adult."

There was a knock, and the bedroom door opened.

"Rashaun, everyone is downstairs asking for you and Wisdom," Andria said. "Are they asking for me too?" Sheila asked.

"Of course they are," Andria replied.

"Sheila, can you carry Wisdom's bag?" Rashaun asked, picking it up.

"I'll see you guys downstairs," Andria said, turning around.

"Of course I can. I'm very strong," Sheila said, taking the bag from Rashaun and putting it on her shoulder.

As Rashaun was about to make his way down the basement stairs, the doorbell rang. He opened the door and Lethal came in carrying a package. Rashaun didn't want to see Lethal today even though he knew that Lethal was outside in a parked car watching the house.

Lethal brought him back to roadblocks that stood in the way of him and his family. Lethal was a reality check. Yes, there was someone out there trying to hurt him and his family, and he didn't know who it was and their reason for choosing him.

"Sheila, go downstairs and tell Andria to come and get

Wisdom," Rashaun said as he looked over at Lethal who kept a box in his hand. Rashaun did not approach Lethal. Instead the men remained a few feet apart as Rashaun waited for Andria to come up.

"There is no return label on the box so I don't think we should rush to open it," Lethal said. "I have someone in the squad who could take a look at it for me."

"Why was it delivered today?" Rashaun asked.

"That's another reason for me not rushing it in. The timing of the delivery concerns me too."

"Give me a minute to talk to Andria, and I'll be right out," Rashaun said, turning around as he heard footsteps coming up the stairs.

Andria opened the door as Lethal closed the outside door. "What's wrong? Aren't you coming downstairs?" She asked.

"Mom told me to get some ice, so I'll run to the store and get it before she takes my head off," Rashaun said as he handed Wisdom over to Andria.

"Okay. I'll see you in a few minutes," Andria said.

Rashaun reached over and kissed her on the cheek then headed for the door.

"Aren't you going to put on your coat?" Andria asked.

"I think all the excitement is making me lose it," Rashaun said, walking back.

"It's freezing out there."

"Yeah, you're right," Rashaun said, slipping on his coat. "Do you need anything from the store?"

"Only you," Andria said.

"You already have me," Rashaun said.

"And I intend to keep you," Andria said as she turned and opened the door to the basement.

"Be back in a few," Rashaun said as he made sure Andria had closed the door before he opened the outside door. Rashaun walked up and down the street and waited for a black Navigator to pass before he walked over to Lethal's Chrysler 300 M. Rashaun opened the passenger door and sat down.

"It could be nothing," Lethal said as he pulled the car out from behind a black Pathfinder.

"Yeah, but it's better safe than sorry," Rashaun said as he glanced back at the box on the backseat. He buckled his seat belt and looked at the lights in the basement. No, he didn't want anything happening to the people in that house.

"I called my man in the bomb squad. He said to bring it right over," Lethal said.

"He's working on a Sunday?" Rashaun asked.

"With the nation on orange alert, these guys barely get to go home for an hour. A person would call them if someone left a bag of groceries in front of their door."

"A man shouldn't have to live like that," Rashaun said.

"Yeah, but the operative word is *live*. We are alive, Rashaun, and we should be very thankful."

"Yeah, I thank Him everyday."

"Your case starts next week, right?" Lethal asked.

Rashaun looked out at the cars jetting by on Kings Highway. At a bus stop he saw two teenagers hugging each other. He wondered if they understood what lay ahead in life. "It's the opening part of the trial. My lawyer will do his opening statement."

"How do you feel?"

"Like I feel everyday, like I have everything to lose," Rashaun said, glancing back at the package on the seat.

"I hear you," Lethal said.

Rashaun looked up into the sky and hoped that not only Lethal heard him.

"Oh, what an evening," Kim said, taking off her dress and resting it on the bed.

"I think that was the longest dinner I've ever attended. Your parents are stories in themselves. I nearly shit in my pants when your father asked what my intentions were." Roger took his shirt off and put it on a hanger in the closet.

"Imagine living with that for seventeen years. I was so happy to go away to college. I think if I had stayed home to attend school, I would have been an instant dropout." Kim unhooked her bra and dropped it on the fluffy beige chair on the side of the bed. She went over to the mirrored doors of her armoire and flipped the hair from her face. "I need a shower really bad."

"I think I'll join you in a minute," Roger said, heading to the kitchen in his white Calvin Klein boxer shorts.

Kim opened the bathroom door and stepped on the dark blue marbled tiles. She stopped in front of the mirror to take one last look at her wrinkle-free face. She pulled opened a drawer and removed a white plastic shower cap. She twisted her hair then took a few hairpins she had left in the drawer earlier that week and pinned her hair up then slipped the shower cap over her head. She took off her panties and hung them on a white Faberware hook next to the shower door. Another hook held a large purple towel. Kim stood back as she adjusted the water. It took her a few minutes to get it just right before she stepped under the steaming spray.

She felt good as the water ran from her face down to her toes. She washed her face with her hands before reaching for the lavender body wash. She put a few drops in her hand and stepped back a few inches before starting to rub the body wash over her skin, starting with the back of her neck. As her hand passed her shoulders and went to her breasts she gave a soft sigh. As she cupped her breasts, her mouth opened ever so slightly as the water ran down her face. She continued to play with her breasts as the water streamed between her hands onto her breasts.

"Kim," Roger said, coming into the steamy shower, "where are you?"

"Use your sense of touch, and you'll find me," she said, leaning against the wall, her right leg outstretched.

Roger's hand settled on the tip of her toes. He bent down to suck on them as he moved under the shower, bringing her foot down with him. As he started to kiss her toes and move up her legs, Kim let out a small groan.

"You were great with my parents today," she said.

"Thank you. I'm glad you were impressed."

"So impressed that I—" She took Roger gently by the face and brought him up from under the shower. She ran her hand from his head all the way down his back to the crack of his ass.

"I was that good," he said as Kim took the body wash and started to lather him up. She worked the soap around his neck then she went to his chest as the soap followed the water then her tongue, making her way down his body. Kim rubbed against him. She pushed him against the wall and spread his legs apart. With her breasts and pelvic area resting against his chest she worked the soap down his upper body to his penis. When it was erect and jutting out almost against the wall, Kim worked the soap and her hands over Roger's penis to the moans emanating from his mouth.

Slowly Kim started to glide lower and lower down Roger's body, her tongue flickering with the accuracy of a hungry lizard. Her head settled just over the crack of his ass. She removed one hand from his penis and brought it to his butt. She nudged the right cheek apart with her right hand and again her tongue continued down his butt. Roger started to move back and forth. As he did Kim pulled on his penis then flicked her tongue around his ass hole. She continued downward, the shower cap on her head lay useless in the water below. Kim's hair clung to her head and the side of her face. As she went under Roger she moved her hands to his butt, taking hold of it as she started to suck on his scrotum. Kim and the steaming water kept up their work on Roger's shaking body. Gradually she came up, licking along the underside of Roger's penis. She worked her way up to the tip of his penis, and with one gulp, she took him completely in her mouth. It was an amazing feat.

"For goodness' sake, what else can a man ask for?"

It was a question Kim was about to answer, she released his penis from her mouth and stood in front of Roger. She pushed him backward and aligned his penis to enter her.

"Will you marry me?" He managed to say. He came so violently that he scratched Kim's back as he barely stopped himself from being knocked unconscious on the bathroom wall.

"What did you ask me?" Kim asked, running her hand through Roger's hair.

"I asked you to marry me."

"And you're serious?" She asked.

"What man wouldn't be?" He asked, the water beating down on his face.

Kim stood over him, the water running down her breasts over

her stomach, and dripping off the hairs of her vagina onto Roger's face.

"Ask me again in a few months. I think at that time the next phase of my life will begin. Right now I have to get ready for a trial next week," she said, stepping out of the shower, leaving Roger on the bathroom floor. The hot water had run out, and now the cold water came down in torrents. Roger didn't move because he didn't have the strength.

Kim walked into Roger's bedroom, her hair matted on her head, the only foreign object touching her body was the rug on the floor. She had quickly dried her skin before exiting the bathroom. She picked up her dress off the floor and draped it over the chair. She took one of two pillows at the foot of the bed and rested it at the top. She pulled the flat multicolored sheet to the side then laid down. She felt cold so she got up and took a blanket from the linen closet. Roger was a good man, she thought, as she pulled the blanket over her head. He was a smart and promising lawyer, and she got along very well with him. Her father told her that he liked him, and she knew the only man who would make her mother happy was a brain surgeon or a judge.

Roger genuinely loved her—after all, why else would he put up with her shit? She knew she had problems. She could be a bitch most times, and at others she just wasn't the nicest person in the world, but Roger held on to the few times when she could be lighthearted and happy. She covered her head to stop the next thought that was coming into it. But she couldn't.

Rashaun. Why did she have to think about him? She was sure he was somewhere with his woman and child and she wasn't even on his mind. Well, maybe he did think about her because she stood between him and metal bars. She didn't want him to think about her like that. She wanted him to think about her the way she thought about him. How long would it take him to realize that she was his soul mate? Would she have to make the penitentiary drive some sense into him? She didn't want to send him to prison, but she couldn't live with the fact that she would no longer be a part of his life. "Rashaun," she mumbled as a warm body joined her under the covers. She reached out to hug the person, and he reciprocated. Her eyes felt heavy, and it was then the dream began.

She was standing in the middle of the ocean, naked except for a black veil over her face. In the distance she could see two vessels approaching—one black, the other white. As the vessels came closer, the water around her started to rise. She started shouting for the vessels to stay away, but they kept coming, one on each side of her. She lifted the veil to see who was commanding the boats but there was no one on board. The water had reached her neck and was about to cover her face when she heard a baby crying. It was a loud, shrieking cry, and the water around her turned black. As it covered her head she reached up for something she saw floating by. She grabbed it and pulled it toward her. It was then that she screamed because she held a lifeless baby girl, naked like she was. She tried to push the baby away but she couldn't. Slowly she started to sink lower and lower with the lifeless baby cradled in her arms.

"Kim, wake up. Kim, wake up," she heard Roger say, and she bolted upright.

"What happened?" She asked, looking around the room.

"You were having a nightmare," Roger said, hugging her.

Kim was still in shock. "But I never have nightmares," Roger brushed the hair aside from Kim's face. "My mother says that people have nightmares when their minds are on two things. It is the subconscience way of trying to work it out so that the person can be at peace."

"But, Roger, my whole life has been like that. I've always lived a battle between my two worlds," Kim said.

"Well maybe your mind can't live like that anymore. Maybe it's looking for peace," Roger said, gradually bringing Kim's head down onto the pillow.

"Thank you for being here," she said as her eyes began to close.

"I'm in for the long haul," he said. "I don't expect it to be easy but I think you're worth it."

Kim didn't hear the last part of his statement because she needed rest.

"Go back to sleep, Rashaun," Andria said as she got off the bed. "I'll take care of Wisdom."

"Are you sure, baby? I know you're tired." Rashaun started to ease off the bed.

"Go back to sleep, Rashaun. I'll take care of him. You have a big day tomorrow. You need to be more alert than me." Andria walked back to the bed and slipped her hand around Rashaun. She bent down and kissed him lightly on the lips. "I'll take Wisdom out into the living room for a few minutes. I'll wake you when I come back into the room."

Andria walked over to the crib and lifted the wailing Wisdom. He looked up at her and continued the assault on her ears. It was obvious that just holding him was not going to do the job. Andria opened her nightgown and extracted her breast from the nursing bra. She lifted Wisdom higher so that his mouth was right next to her nipple. In a second Andria felt a tinge as Wisdom bit down on her nipple then the room became absolutely quiet. She closed the door softly so as not to wake up Rashaun who had fallen back to sleep. She was guided to the rocking chair in the living room by a small white oval nightlight plugged into an outlet a few inches away from the couch.

She sat back on the chair and started to rock slowly as Wisdom sucked on her breast. It had been a long and draining day. Even though she didn't have to do any of the cooking, being the host for the party was major work. As usual her friends, Robin, Hilda and Paula helped tremendously.

She missed Sharon who couldn't make the trip because she to had gotten pregnant by accident. It was an accident because Sharon was HIV positive but her boyfriend wasn't. Condoms were supposed to be ninety percent reliable but the ten percent left room for Sharon to become pregnant. Her boyfriend did not get HIV, but the result was an unplanned pregnancy. This might have been a good case for pro-abortionists except that Sharon and her boyfriend, Chris, decided to go ahead with the pregnancy. As a result, Sharon had to increase her medication to include something that would stop the transfer of HIV from mother to child. Sharon's doctor had assured her that if she kept up the medication, there was very little chance of passing the virus on to the baby.

Chris proposed to Sharon but she turned him down. Sharon wanted to be certain that her baby wasn't born with the killer disease. Andria felt for Sharon. She knew what she had to go through when she was pregnant with Wisdom; she could only vaguely imagine what Sharon had to deal with daily. Sharon, however, promised Andria that she would not miss the wedding even though she turned down the invitation to be a bridesmaid.

Andria kept rocking Wisdom, even though her nipple had slipped out of his mouth and he was fast asleep. It was one in the morning, and Andria was wide-awake. God had been both good and bad to her—well, if she listened to her mother, the good things came from God and the bad from Lucifer. Andria was very thankful to have Rashaun and Wisdom in her life, but with that also came complications. Rashaun had spoken to her after he had left the christening only to return three hours later. Upon his return he didn't want to talk to her about where he had been and she did not force the issue. She waited through the well wishes and the hopes and dreams bestowed upon Wisdom. She waited through the constant doting of Rashaun's brother, David, over his wife. They were so deeply in love. Andria wondered if she and Rashaun would be like that after five years. She out waited Sheila who took every opportunity to be next to Wisdom, being his protector whenever someone came too close to him. After the house had emptied and the final good-byes were said, she and Rashaun left Albertina and went downstairs. It was then after much persistence that Rashaun told her what happened.

Rashaun and Lethal had taken a suspicious-looking box over to be inspected by the police. It turned out that there wasn't a bomb or anything in there but a haunting message, typed on a white piece of paper attached to the charred remains of a baby doll was the note, YOU WILL SUFFER THE WAY I HAVE. The stress on Rashaun's face seemed to be making him age at a tremendous pace. He tried to act lighthearted around her but she could see it in his eyes. Rashaun was worried. He had made a will and explained everything to her. He didn't know what he did in his past that had resulted in such hate but he didn't want his enemies to get to him through her and Wisdom. He didn't want her to come to the courthouse; neither did he want her to go out unnecessarily. He spoke to her about leaving his beloved Big Apple after the trial and heading some place. When he said that, she knew that hope to him was hanging by a string in the wind. The Rashaun she knew would not leave New York to go down South, up North or West or anywhere. He had told her that he would live and die in Brooklyn.

But now she understood that he wasn't thinking about himself anymore. If he was, she knew he would stay in New York and let the deck of cards fall where they may. No, Rashaun was thinking about her and Wisdom, and to that end, he was willing to make sacrifices. Besides loving New York, Rashaun also liked being close to his mother, and she knew that it would tear him up inside to leave her. Most women would be jealous of Rashaun's relationship with his mother, but Andria wasn't like most women. She understood his relationship. Rashaun saw his mother as a savior. He understood that it was okay to give birth but motherhood was more than giving birth. The same could be said about fatherhood. He put her first in his life because in essence she was first, and she had put him first. For someone to come along after more than thirty years and say "I'm first" would be cheating. Andria understood that even more clearly now that she had Wisdom. To her, Wisdom was her main love—not to take anything away from Rashaun or her own mother, but Wisdom was the one for whom she was responsible. She intended to be there for his wants and his needs. Only time would tell how Wisdom related to her.

Rashaun, on the other hand, believed that his mother would need him, as her age became a weakness. He wanted to be her strength when that happened, and for that Andria applauded him. To that end, she didn't want Rashaun to leave New York. Hopefully he wouldn't have to. She knew that brighter days were coming; they had to be. It was just that it was so damn cloudy outside.

Chapter 7

"Members of the jury, you will now hear opening statements by the prosecutor," said Judge Bob Hilton, a white man approximately seventy years old with matted white hair. He spoke with a southern twang reminiscent of Sheriff Roscoe of the archaic *Dukes of Hazzard* TV show. He showed as much interest in the case as the bottles of pills he took to keep his droopy eyes open.

The chair Rashaun sat on listening to the judge was made of hard plastic, which had faded to an off blue. In any other environment this chair would have gone the way of the recycle bin, maybe reappearing as part of a plastic bowl for dog food, but this was not any ordinary environment. Rashaun was sitting in this chair in the Brooklyn Supreme Court because he was on trial for murder. It was a crime punishable by twenty-five years in prison.

Rashaun's face held no emotion but his legs were wobbling and the chair was doing its job of keeping him in position. Rashaun was dressed in a light gray suit with thin black lines. The black Perrini shoes, an Italian product, felt snug on his feet. Next to him was his lawyer, Bob Yelram, wearing a dark pinstripe blue suit. The brown folder at the far right end of the table, which contained the defense of Rashaun's life, remained closed. There was very little attention focused on the defense table because standing in front of the jury was one of Brooklyn's top district attorneys, a person who had been written about in every major newspaper in the metro area. The fact that she had lost only one case in her eight years as a prosecutor was a commendable feat, but that wasn't the reason all eyes were focused on her. The fact that this was a murder trial and one life was lost and another one hung in the balance wasn't important. Murder trials happened very frequently in Brooklyn—it wasn't a major event. The fact that it was one black man killing another made it even less newsworthy. No, all eyes were on Kim Rivers because she was absolutely beautiful.

As was her trademark, Kim was dressed in a sexy black-laced Gucci suit that was tight fitted on the top but flared at the bottom. Her attire was completed with black Manolo Blahnik four-inch pumps. "Your honor, ladies and gentlemen of the jury, we live in an imperfect society. Everyday the newspapers and television news shows are full of crime and evil deeds. The approximate death per second from homicide in this country might never be known because it happens so frequently. Law enforcement has difficulty keeping up with the numbers. I have been working with the prosecution for countless years, and every time a murder crosses my desk I become very angry. Guns and their use are destroying our beloved city. They make it unsafe for everyone. I want you to ask yourself, how would you feel if you came home to find a loved one, maybe a spouse, child, parent or friend lying in a pool of blood with numerous bullets in his body. One shot to the stomach, maybe you operate and save the person, providing no vital organs were hit. Two shots—one to the stomach another to the pelvic area—maybe there is a chance the person might live. Don't get me wrong here, I'm not saying that shooting anyone is okay," Kim said, walking up to the front of the jury.

"No, I'm telling you that with the above scenarios a person

might survive but the defendant, Rashaun Jones, shot the victim fifteen times." Kim held up both her hands. "That's more times than we can count with both sets of fingers. Now if you shoot someone one or two times, there is a possibility that person could live, but emptying a gun on someone from a short distance means death. Rashaun Jones had one thing on his mind the evening he came home to find his live-in girlfriend in the arms of her ex-lover. He was a hurt man. His ego was pulverized. A man in his apartment with his pregnant girlfriend. Forensic evidence will also show that the victim was in a very compromising position with the defendant's girlfriend. Were they embraced in a passionate kiss? What about the child that his girlfriend was carrying? Was it his? There were probably a lot of questions going through the defendant's mind. Rashaun Jones' manhood was stripped bare. What could he do? Walk away and live with that image for the rest of his life?"

"The prosecution will show that Rashaun Jones lost his temper and became overcome by jealousy and anger. Mr. Jones was so angry that he shot the defendant without even thinking about the consequences of his action. As a result, he didn't only kill the defendant; he also shot his girlfriend who was pregnant. Of course that could be a mistake or maybe not, shooting your pregnant girlfriend and her ex-boyfriend, is too much of a coincidence. Mr. Jones, in his action, showed a ruthlessness and total disregard for human life." Kim started to walk back to the prosecution table. She stopped in the middle. "As you sit and listen to the evidence in this case, I want you to understand one thing: The defendant is on trial for a murder but could it be that he not only intended to kill his fiancée's ex-boyfriend but also his fiancée and his unborn child. Maybe he didn't believe that the child was his. Thank you."

"Thank you, Ms. Rivers," Judge Hilton said. "We will take a thirty-minute break, and we will hear opening statements from the defense."

Rashaun got up off the chair with his legs still wobbly. Kim did not make eye contact with him in her opening statement and he did not look over to the prosecution table. Today was not a good one for him. He expected part of the opening statement from her—it was the logical move—but what disturbed him most was her last remark. He had tried very hard to avoid thinking of his actions as reckless and careless, but what he had avoided thinking about Kim had brought to the forefront. Two of the people he loved the most in the world could have been dead.

"She is a masterpiece, isn't she?" Yelram said, gathering the folder and dumping it in his brown leather bag. "She's trying to change our defense. By her last statement concerning the shot that wounded Andria, Kim is telling the jury that you don't care who gets hurt. This is her attempt to try and derail our defense, which was what you did what you had to do to protect your family from grave danger."

Rashaun followed Yelram out the room, getting a view of Kim's back as he walked out.

"I think this is her attempt to rattle me," Rashaun said as he walked toward his mother who was standing in the middle of the walkway.

"There is no question that you'll have to testify now. She made sure of that. The only person who could show that you weren't trying to hurt Andria is you. Did Andria have any dealings with Paul before the incident?"

"Yeah. I think they met a few times," Rashaun said. "Hi, Mom." Rashaun kissed his mother and hugged her.

"We have to talk some more about that. If Rivers finds that out, it won't be good," Yelram said. "Anyone else witness their meeting?"

"I think her girlfriend Robin did," Rashaun answered. "How are you holding up, son?" Albertina asked.

"I'm okay, Mom," Rashaun said. "Have you spoken to Andria?"

"I spoke to her a few minutes ago. She said everything was alright. She's more concerned with how you're doing," Albertina said as she walked out with Rashaun and Yelram.

"I'm going to give her a call," Rashaun said.

"Your father said he'll come by later," Albertina said, walking on the right side of Rashaun while Yelram occupied his left.

"Uh-huh," Rashaun muttered without missing a stride. "The phone signal is weak in here so I'll step out for a few minutes and make the call."

Kim and Roger sat in the office, each with a salad and a cup of fountain soda.

"I didn't know that you were going to imply that the defendant might have been trying to kill his girlfriend and their child," Roger said, picking the blue cheese out of his salad.

"I would have returned the salad," Kim said, looking over at him in annoyance.

"Too much trouble, and we don't have enough time."

"Then you shouldn't eat it. You're allergic to blue cheese. I can't have you swelling up at the prosecution table."

"I'll be fine. I got all of it out."

"I hope so. For your sake."

Roger replaced the cover on the salad. "Do you think it's a good idea to accuse the defendant of trying to kill his fiancée and child?"

"I know you don't." Kim chewed slowly on a piece of lettuce then drank some of the fountain Diet Pepsi. Her face reflected her disgust for the drink.

"Why don't you return the drink?" Roger asked, a slight smile breaking through.

"Because I got what I expected. You should know, just because you swallow it doesn't mean you have to like it. By implying that Rashaun was trying to kill his girlfriend and unborn child, I guarantee that Rashaun will take the stand in his defense."

"Do you believe he was trying to kill his fiancée and child?"

"Nope." She stood. "It's time to get back."

Roger followed suit. "So you're playing a game?"

"Roger, the quicker you realize it, the better off you'll be. Life is a game. And with the game of life, it's not how you play it but the results that count." Kim walked away from the table with Roger in tow.

Yelram stood and walked straight to the jury. He stopped six feet in front of them. He parted his legs until they were shoulder-width apart.

Rashaun sat alone at the defense table, his eyes fixated on Yelram and the jury.

"Your honor, ladies and gentlemen of the jury, today begins the trial of a man who did the only thing that he could do. The defendant, Rashaun Jones, is on trial for saving his woman and their child. Rashaun is not on trial for meeting a man on the street and shooting him in an attempt to rob him. He is not on trial because he came home and found a man in bed with his woman and killed him. Rashaun is not on trial because of some drug deal gone bad. No, Rashaun is on trial because he was trying to protect his woman and their unborn child from eminent danger from his fiancée's deranged ex-boyfriend.

"How many times have we heard the stories of the ex-boyfriend coming back and killing the girlfriend and whoever is standing in his way? It didn't happen like that this time. Rashaun Jones should not be on trial here. Instead he should be given a medal for preventing a tragedy. The defense will show that Rashaun acted in the only way possible to save his woman and child. He did what you or I would do if the situation were reversed. He protected his family: A madman entered his house and threatened the life of his woman and their unborn child. Rashaun took the threat very seriously, the same way you or I would."

Yelram did not move. Instead he inhaled deeply then exhaled slowly. "I want you to look at this man, sitting at the defense table. To this man, his woman and their child mean everything. To this man, life is nothing without his family. To this man, protecting his family could be self-sacrificial if necessary. At the end of the trial I want you to do one thing for this man: I want you to send him home to his future wife and their son. Thank you."

Yelram moved for the first time since his opening remarks. He turned around and walked back to sit next to Rashaun.

For the first time since sitting down for the trial, Rashaun felt all eyes on him. When Kim spoke he knew the jury was watching him but he didn't feel the rest of the courtroom attention was on him, but as Yelram spoke and directed the jury's attention to him,Rashaun felt he was the center of attention by everyone in the room. He had never felt like this in his life. He had never known how the defendant sitting next to him felt as he tried to save them from the bars of time. It wasn't a good feeling. This wasn't the right time. He had too much going for him. A few years ago, maybe he would worry about this effect on his mother, his family and friends, but life had changed over the past few years, and this focus on him wasn't good.

"I think we're done for the day," Yelram said as he sat down.

"It's a good thing because I don't know how much more of this I can take today," Rashaun said.

"I don't think the judge is up to anything else either," Yelram said, looking over at the judge who had started to nod off.

"Ladies and gentlemen, we will reconvene at 9:15 A.M. tomorrow. Thank you for your time and patience. Court is dismissed," Judge Hilton said, bringing his gavel down and bringing the court attendees to their feet.

Andria sat down with Wisdom in her arms. She looked over at Rashaun who was finishing up half a chicken, and rice and peas. She had cooked early because she didn't want the detectives coming when they were eating. She had eaten a leg and had a little of the rice and peas before picking up Wisdom who had stated to cry. She nursed him briefly and now he lay in her arms with those bright eyes looking up at her. Rashaun had come home a few minutes earlier. He had kissed her on the lips, gone into the bathroom, washed his hands then picked up a sleeping Wisdom.

"You told me how the first part went but then you didn't say

Rashaun put his fork down. “It was only the opening statements. Kim said I tried to kill Paul, you and Wisdom. I didn’t expect her to say that but I understand why she did it.”

“I hate that bitch,” Andria said, her lips curled and eyebrow raised as her face reflected her anger toward Kim.

Rashaun got up from the table, taking the empty plate and finishing the glass of water. “It was a good move,” he said.

“How is that?”

“Anytime you can guarantee that the defendant takes the stand in a case, you’ve won a little battle,” he said.

“But you were going to testify.”

“Yeah, I know that, and you and Yelram knew that but Kim could only take a 50/50 guess on that. What she did gives her a ninety-nine percent chance that I’ll have to testify.”

Andria stood with Wisdom and followed Rashaun to the kitchen. “I’m not worried. I have confidence in you.”

Rashaun soaped the plate with Palmolive dishwashing liquid. “Well in some cases, depending on putting the defendant on the stand can help clear the defendant but in most cases it’s usually detrimental to the case. A good lawyer can make a defendant hang himself during cross-examination. One wrong answer can make the defendant look like a liar and therefore appear guilty in the eyes of the jury.”

“Like I said before.”

The doorbell chimed.

Rashaun looked at the clock. “I guess they’re here.”

Andria went in the room with Wisdom.

Rashaun headed to the door. He opened it and the detectives stepped in.

Andria came back without Wisdom, her hair in a Bob Marley cloth wrap. She joined Rashaun and the detectives at the table that Rashaun had recently vacated after his meal.

"We have some developments in your case," Detective Sanchez of the ninth Precinct said. "Let me not get you guys excited. We did not find the other man in the car the night you guys got attacked."

Andria's face turned gloomy.

Rashaun remained emotionless.

"However, we were able to find out some information about the other perpetrator," Detective Sanchez continued.

"What is it?" Rashaun asked, his eyes distant.

The second officer, Detective Monk spoke this time. He was a black man with blue-rimmed glasses on a hard square face. "The perpetrator wasn't Hispanic as we previously assumed. We found out that he was a white man without any distinguishing features. The only eyewitness—a black man who was jogging by when the incident occurred—said the other man was definitely white."

"Did he know his approximate age?" Rashaun asked.

"They said he was between thirty and forty years old," Detective Sanchez said.

"Mr. Jones, we were hoping that you might know someone in that age range who you have defended or who was a victim of one of the defendants you were able to free."

"I worked for one of the most expensive law firms in Manhattan. Most of our Caucasian clients were between that age group. Victims range from children to seniors above seventy. It could be a victim's father, uncle, friend the possibilities are endless," Rashaun said, sounding frustrated.

"Did any of these people threaten you?" Detective Monk asked.

"Not anymore than normal. I got 'you are going to burn in

hell,' 'your time is coming' and 'I'm going to get you.' All these are common as a defense attorney."

"Do you have any files on these people, so that we can try to contact them?" Detective Sanchez asked.

Wisdom started to cry. Andria excused herself from the table.

Detective Sanchez and Detective Monk stood briefly to give Andria the courtesy of an exit.

"The little man is up, huh?" Detective Monk said, a faint smile appearing on his face. "They are adorable at this young age."

"Do you guys need to talk to me?" Andria asked.

"I don't think so. We looked at your social work clientele, and we don't see the danger coming from them," Detective Sanchez said.

"Can I offer you all something to drink?" Andria asked.

"No, thank you. We made a stop at the Arch Diner on the corner of Ralph and Flatlands Avenue." Monk said touching his stomach for emphasis.

"We'll just finish up with your fiancé here, and we'll be out of your hair," Detective Sanchez said as Andria left the room.

The interaction between Andria and the detectives gave Rashaun the time to think about his clients. He knew getting any paperwork from his previous employer would be close to impossible. With the exception of Roundtree, most of his clients were Caucasian with the occasional Asian and Indian. Roundtree was one of four African Americans he had defended.

"So, Mr. Jones, with the additional information we've given you, can you think of anyone who would try to hurt you or your fiancée?" Detective Monk asked.

"I thought about it but no one stands out as overtly threatening. Were you able to get any information from the package with the note I dropped off?"

The two detectives looked at each other.

"What package?" Detective Sanchez asked.

"I dropped it off at the precinct last Monday. I told the sergeant to make sure you guys received it," Rashaun said.

"When did you receive the package?" Detective Monk asked, looking a little perturbed.

"Sunday. It was my son's christening," Rashaun said.

Again both detectives looked at each other.

"How many people knew you were having a christening?" Detective Sanchez asked, jotting down something on his pad.

"Andria, myself, her mother and my mother did most of the invites." Rashaun said.

"We'll need for you to get a list of all the people who were invited and when the invitations were sent. It could be a coincidence, but the way this case is going, I believe the person or people involved know a lot about you, or they've been watching you. We have to leave right now but we'll look into the package you received," Detective Monk said as he stood.

"Thank you for your time," Detective Sanchez said, shaking Rashaun's hand. "We will be in touch."

After the detectives left, Rashaun sat the table. He knew without the detective telling him that the stalker was keeping very close tabs on his and Andria's movements. He also knew that the person was being patient and deliberate. Rashaun pounded his knuckles on the table. He looked around the room. With the exception of the utensils in the kitchen, there were no weapons in the house. Once more he felt afraid. His life and his family's life weren't in his hands. He knew that life and death remained with the Eternal Father, but he also believed that a man had to protect his own. In the room were his woman and child, and somewhere there was someone planning their demise. If he had his gun, he wouldn't feel so useless, even though it had him battling for his freedom, but that was okay. At least he was able to save Andria and Wisdom. What was he going to do when the next attack came? How was he going to protect his family?

"Rashaun, come to bed," Andria said, standing in the doorway.

Rashaun lifted his head off the table. "What time is it?"

"It doesn't matter. You're tired." Andria replied.

"I need to think some more."

"You'll do your thinking later, but for now I want you to lie in bed next to your woman and child," Andria said.

Rashaun got up from the table. He looked at Andria, and he realized why he loved her so much. Besides being beautiful, she always knew the right thing to say.

Chapter 8

"Lance is a whore. I don't want to walk down the aisle with him," Paula said, sitting with her legs tucked under her.

Andria walked in from the kitchen, a bowl of potato salad in her hands. Robin followed her carrying a bucket of fried chicken. They laid the food in the middle of the table next to the rice and peas, nuts and salad.

"Paula, who cares what kind of person Lance is? You're not going to marry him," Robin said, exhaustion in her voice.

"Lance being a whore is his wife's problem, not yours," Hilda said, grabbing a handful of nuts.

"Well, why don't you walk down the aisle with him?" Paula said, becoming agitated.

"I didn't make the arrangements. Andria is the one who made them." Hilda said.

Andria returned the stares from Paula and Hilda but remained silent. She had no intention of changing any of the wedding plans. She had already spent enough time pairing the women with the men, and she was still missing one bridesmaid.

Robin sat next to Paula, and Andria joined Hilda on the sofa.

"I really don't see any argument here. We're not being in the wedding because of Lance. We're in the wedding to support Andria. It really shouldn't matter who you pair up with," Robin said, sipping on a glass of water.

"Would you have preferred if I put you with Tyrone?" Andria asked.

"Hell no. That boy has been a religious fanatic since he came out from Kings County. I'm surprised Rashaun has him in the wedding party," Paula said. "On second thought, let me stay with Lance. At least he is gorgeous."

"Well that's settled." Hilda moved the nuts to the side to reach for a plate.

"Okay, the wedding party will be this: Robin and George are best woman and best man, Paula will be partnered with Lance, Hilda with Pedro, Sharon with Peter, and I'm one person short. I need someone to put with Tyrone," Andria said, looking around the room.

"How about a friend from your job?" Paula asked.

"That's no good because everyone else will want to know why they weren't selected," Andria said, wiping her right eyebrow with a napkin. "I don't want to create unnecessary tension. And also there isn't anyone I was that close to at work because I hadn't been on the job that long."

"What about family members? A cousin or something," Hilda said.

"I haven't really been in touch with the rest of my family. I think because of what happened when I was a child, my mother and I were more or less ostracized. When my grandmother was around I used to see my cousins and nieces but that was a long time ago. They treated my mother like a disease because she killed my father. Therefore, I honestly haven't kept up with anyone, and I doubt my mother talks to any of them."

"That's a bummer," Paula added.

"Well, Andria, if push comes to shove, I have a cousin. Her name is Michelle. They call her the wedding planner. She could be in the wedding, and everyone would think that you and her are the best of friends," Robin said.

"Well as long as she doesn't steal the groom like J-Lo did in the movie," Andria said, filling her plate with rice and peas.

"I doubt that will happen. Do you see how Rashaun looks at Andria?" Robin said, winking at Andria.

"You're right. He looks at her like she's the most beautiful woman in the world," Paula said.

"You guys just stop that," Andria said, her cheeks becoming red. "Rashaun does not look at me like that."

Robin stretched out her right hand to Andria. "Girl, we're not mad at you. Rashaun loves you to death."

"And you're getting married. You're gonna need all that love. Trust me," Hilda said. "Getting married is the easy part. Staying married is a whole other story."

"If we ever get married," Andria said, a far-away look in her eyes.

"Oh, you guys are getting married. Whether it's on Rikers Island at city hall or the church on St. Marks Avenue, Rashaun will not let you go," Robin said.

"Sometimes I just don't know. We're having so many problems," Andria said. "I'm constantly looking over my shoulder for fear of an attack. Rashaun is fighting to stay out of prison."

"Yeah, but your problems aren't internal, they're external. Problems like these, we have no control over them. Look at my husband and me, the fool. He left our three kids and me for a woman with four kids. Now he wants to come back because all that great loving he used to get from her when he was with me he doesn't get it anymore. Now our problems are in the relationship. The woman he cheated on me with is a contributing external factor but we basically have to get us right. You and Rashaun have only external factors affecting your relationship. The attack and the trial have nothing to do with your love for each other."

"Hilda, have you been going to counseling? You sound like a counselor." Paula looked at Hilda in amazement.

"Yeah, Hilda, you really broke it down," Robin concurred.

Andria remained silent, staring into space. She didn't hear a word Hilda had said because her mind was focused on whether she would actually get married. She was supposed to be planning for the best day in her life. She had dreamed about it all her life, and now that it was about to happen, she was afraid. "I'm sorry, girls. Excuse me for a minute," Andria said, getting up from the table. "I'll be right back."

"Rashaun's trial is really bothering her," Paula said, putting down her food.

"The shit that's been happening to her will bother anyone. Not knowing when and where someone will attack you, living in total fear for yourself and your family, getting ready to marry a man who might spend the rest of his life in prison I'm surprised she's holding up so great," Hilda said, glancing back at the bathroom where Andria had run.

Robin got up from her chair. "I'll go and see her now. Guys, put on the movie."

"Call us if you need us," Paula said as she took the *Underworld* DVD from its case.

Robin knocked lightly on the door. "Andria, can I come in?"

"Robin, I'll be out in a minute," Andria said in a tearful tone.

Robin knocked again. "I'm coming in," she said as she heard the bathroom door unlock.

Andria was staring into the mirror, her eyes bloodshot. "This seems like déjà vu."

"But it's not. The last time I had to come into the bathroom after you, I almost had to break the door down. You were with an asshole who cared only about himself. I'm here now to tell you that the man you're with loves you like crazy. And even though things seems topsy turvy now, I guarantee you that better days are coming. You've just got to believe. Andria, you've been very strong so far. I won't let you give up now. Baby, don't break down now," Robin said, wiping the tears from Andria's face.

"Robin, I see it in his face. Rashaun is stressed. He doesn't like to show it to me but I don't think he's confident that he'll get off. It seems like he's carrying the whole world on his shoulders. Before we had Wisdom, Rashaun was always saying 'we'll do this and that.' We are supposed to go on vacations all over the world, Wisdom is supposed to receive the best education possible, but he doesn't talk like that anymore. Instead it's like he's making arrangements for us to survive in his absence, and that scares me."

"Andria, I don't think Rashaun believes you guys won't be together. I think what he's doing is making arrangements so that just in case things don't fall into place, you guys are protected. It's something we should all do. Tomorrow is not promised to anyone, and with our country run by an idiot who knows where the next attack will be coming from? Rashaun is doing the right thing. It's something my husband and I did a long time ago. Sometimes it takes a terrible incident to wake people up. I think this is what happened here. Just be strong for you and him. When his hope is waning, step in with yours to bring him up. You do the best that you can, and the rest leave in the hands of the Creator," Robin said.

Andria turned around from the mirror. "I hope the girls—"

"Don't even think about your friends because they might have their ways but they will stand by you 110 percent. Now let's go out there and listen to Paula gripe about men and Hilda talk about her no-good husband," Robin said, smiling.

A faint smile broke across Andria's face. She hugged Robin. "You're always here for me."

"Hey, I remember when you were here for me too. This is not a one-way street. Because of you, I have a family to go home to," Robin said, slipping her arm around Andria's waist.

"Thanks, Robin," Andria said, opening the door.

"Let's get out there before Paula eats all the potato salad." Robin followed Andria out of the bathroom.

"While you guys were in the bathroom, Sharon called. Andria, she said she wants to talk to you. She wanted to know what caused you to pick out those ugly bridesmaids dresses," Hilda said.

"You guys think the bridesmaids dresses are ugly?" Andria asked, reclaiming her seat next to Hilda.

"I'm not going to say anything except that Cyndi Lauper wore better clothes in her videos," Paula said, restocking on the potato salad and fried chicken.

"Who else thinks the bridesmaids dresses are ugly?" Andria asked.

"I'm not saying anything," Hilda said, turning away from Andria.

"Okay, I get the picture. Now, what can we do about the bridesmaids dresses?" Andria put her food down and picked up a pen and a napkin.

"Well we could start with the frills," Paula said. "That's what my mother use to wear."

"Let me go and get some paper. This looks like it will take a while," Andria said, getting up off the chair. "Robin, don't touch my chicken."

"Who does the catering for this place?" Tracee asked, chewing on a colorless piece of chicken. "I could go to the Chinese restaurant and get better chicken than this."

"Tracee, what do you expect? This is a business meeting. The catering most likely was done by one of the top chefs in the hotel. The secret to eating in these places is to load up on the salad and fruit bar. Look at me. I did not even touch mine," Kim said, popping a steamed shrimp into the cocktail sauce in front of her.

"This is some nasty food," Roger said, pushing his chicken to one side and hesitantly putting his fork into the potato salad.

"Well, we didn't come here for the food," Kim said, looking around the room at the rest of the patrons digging into the chicken. "Look around you. Everyone else is enjoying the food."

"Kim, everyone else with the exception of a few dots of color is white," Tracee said.

"Exactly. This food was not catered for us. Some down-home cooking in here would send most of the patrons cowering to the exit. This is not our kind of party but Patrick Dempsey invited me, so I'm here." Kim picked up a glass of water and drank half of it.

"Well thanks for inviting us," Tracee said, rolling her eyes. "There aren't even any decent men in here to flirt with."

"Why are you looking at me like that?" Kim asked.

"Who, me? I'm not looking at you. I'm looking for a sugar daddy," Tracee responded.

"Tracee, I wasn't talking to you. I was talking to Roger," Kim said.

"You look gorgeous in anything you wear. Today, you look absolutely gorgeous," Roger said still staring at Kim, who was wearing a black business suit and a blue blouse.

"Roger, put your tongue back in your mouth. You're creating puddles on the table," Tracee said, barely glancing at Roger.

"Here comes Patrick," Kim said as a tall white man who judging by his complexion spent an enormous amount of time in the sun maneuvered his way toward the table.

"What does he do, Kim?" Tracee asked, looking approvingly at the approaching man.

"He's a judge," Kim answered.

"This chicken is excellent," Tracee said loud enough for their guest to hear.

"Kimberly," Patrick said, reaching down and kissing Kim on the cheek. "I'm sorry I'm a little late but there was some kind of explosion on Sixth Avenue." "Patrick, this is Roger McLean and Tracee Waters," Kim said.

Patrick shook Roger and Tracee's hands. The eye contact between Patrick and Roger was brief but Tracee seemed to have garnered Patrick's attention with her approving smile.

"Okay, Kim. I'll see you in a few minutes," Patrick said and took one last look at Tracee before he left the table.

"Tracee, you are pitiful. Poor white man, he doesn't know what he is getting into," Kim said, looking over at Tracee who hadn't taken her eyes off Patrick. "He's married."

"And in this day and age thats suppose to mean?" Tracee asked, finally bringing her attention back to the table.

"I guess whatever you want it to mean," Kim said.

"Exactly. If things work out, I could dump this other loser I told you about. I want to get a hookup like Ingrid," Tracee said, picking at the potato salad.

"And what kind of hookup does she have?" Roger asked.

"She's seeing this old white man who comes by once a month for her services," Tracee said.

"Tracee, that's prostitution," Kim said, raising her voice enough to show her displeasure but keeping it low enough as not to draw attention.

"The only services Ingrid does for the old man is to strip naked and jerk him off. She doesn't blow him, there is no penetration—a strip and a jerk, that's it," Tracee said, putting down her fork. "And for that he pays for an apartment in midtown Manhattan for her, and he gives her five hundred dollars every two weeks."

"Does Ingrid have a man?" Roger asked.

"Yeah. Her man lives there with her. They're saving to buy a house in Queens. He works, and she's a teacher in the Bronx. This has been going on for the past five years. The old man said he left her a good bit of money in his will so they're waiting for him to croak. Now tell me that is not a good setup," Tracee said, looking around.

"Forget about doing that with this one. Patrick has a reputation of being the reincarnation of John Homes, that dead porn star who had the biggest dick in the industry. They say Patrick beat him by a few inches," Kim said.

"How do you know?" Roger asked a little too quickly.

"Roger, you know Clara Mcquire?"

"That little light skin paralegal girl in the office with the braids?" Roger asked.

"Well, little Ms. Mcquire has a reputation for trying big dicks. Tell her a man has a big dick, and she'll find some way to confirm it. She confirmed it by staying home for two days after she came back from the Bahamas with Patrick."

"Little Clara?" Roger asked.

"Book covers only get your attention. The real story has nothing to do with the cover," Kim said.

"Thanks, Kim. Now, what am I suppose to do?" Tracee asked.

"Learn to take care of yourself," Kim said.

"That's too hard. Is there anyone in here little Clara hasn't tested? Some women like pain. I don't go for that," Tracee said, turning her attention to a man not more than four feet tall who was sitting next to a white lady with chalky makeup. "What about him?"

"Tracee, stop it. Patrick has made his way to the podium," Kim said, focusing on Patrick.

"Ladies and gentlemen, I hope you all have had a good meal. Please forgive me for getting here late but New York traffic beat me again. Let me get right to the point of why I invited you here this evening. Today, you will have the opportunity to meet not only one of the most beautiful prosecuting attorneys but the next district court judge," Patrick said, stopping briefly to drink some water.

"Kim, you didn't tell me," Tracee said, looking over at Kim astounded.

"I didn't know," Kim said, her mouth opened in surprise. "I thought I was here to get another award."

"You are trying to tell us that you had no idea that Patrick was going to nominate you for civil court judge?" Roger asked.

"I swear to you I had no idea. If I did, you know I would have invited my father. He will go absolutely ballistic when I tell him this," Kim said.

"Ms. Rivers has demonstrated exemplary service as one of Brooklyn's finest DAs. Her record of conviction is second to none. She has made the Brooklyn's DA's office one of the most respected in the nation, and she has done it with a hands-on approach. Even as we speak Ms. Rivers is the lead prosecutor in a very difficult case. As always, we are more than certain that she will get her man. Well, I could stand here and ramble on and on but let me have you meet the next district judge, Ms. Kimberly Rivers."

Kim stood to join the occupants in the room who were on their feet cheering loudly. She pushed her chair back and made her way to join Patrick at the podium. Once she arrived, she shook Patrick's hand one more time before stepping up to the mike.

"This is so much of a surprise," Kim said, her feet trembling with nervous energy. "It was my dream that one day I would be a judge in Kings County, Brooklyn. I've worked hard, and I'm overjoyed that I've been rewarded with the nomination. I wish to thank everyone for their support, and I hope ten years from now I can stand here and you can clap because I have exceeded expectations. I will not bore you with a long speech because I wasn't prepared to make one. All I'm going to say is thank you and God bless." Kim stepped down from the podium.

"And she is humble too," Patrick said, stepping up to the podium and bringing scattered laughter into the room.

"How does it feel to be nominated for judgeship?" Roger asked as Kim sat down.

"Besides butterflies fluttering in my stomach, it feels like destiny. If you guys will excuse me, I have to go call my father," Kim said, getting up one more time.

"Go on, girl. It's your world," Tracee said.

"Now I definitely need to teach Rashaun a lesson," Kim said.

"I hope you can," Tracee said, knowing Kim understood she was talking about more than the case.

"With my help, she will," Roger said, as Kim walked away from the table.

"Officer Sandra Reid, do you see the man who was in the apartment on that evening of the murder?" Kim asked.

"Yes," Officer Reid said, looking over at Rashaun. Officer Reid was a small woman, no more than a hundred and twenty pounds on a good day. She was wearing her police uniform, which added an extra ten pounds.

"Can you identify that man for the jury?" Kim asked.

"He is sitting at the defense table dressed in a light beige suit," Officer Reid answered.

"Let the record show that the witness identified the defendant, Rashaun Jones," Kim said, walking toward the jury box.

"Officer Reid, what exactly happened when you entered the apartment, identified previously as belonging to the defendant?"

Officer Reid turned to face the jury. "I was answering a 1030 in progress—"

"What exactly is a 1030?"

"Code 1030 is multiple gunshots at a location."

"Did you rush into the apartment?"

"No. I identified myself, and after getting no response, my partner kicked the door in."

"What happened next?"

"I went through the busted door and I saw the defendant with a woman in his arms."

"And what did the defendant say?"

"He said to get an ambulance."

"Were those his exact words?"

"No, his exact words were 'Ger her a fucking ambulance.' "

"And your response was?"

"I told him to calm down while my partner called for an ambulance. I took that time to look around the room for a weapon."

"And did you find one?"

"Yes. I found a nine millimeter a few feet away from the defendant."

"Can you tell the court the approximate distance between where you found the gun and where the defendant was standing?"

"I would say about five feet."

"Who else was in the room?"

"There was a figure crumpled on the floor."

"How far from the defendant was that figure?"

"I would say approximately three feet."

"Did the defendant say anything else to you?"

Again Officer Reid turned to the jury, "he said 'I shot her by accident.' "

"What else happened in the room?"

"My partner asked the defendant to put the woman down, and he refused, so I kept my gun on him while my partner went over and searched him. We didn't find any weapons on the defendant. My partner checked the figure on the floor. It was a man and he had no pulse."

"Where was the defendant at that time?"

"He was still standing in the middle of the room holding the woman we assumed was pregnant by her raised stomach."

"Did you ask the defendant what happened?"

"Yes."

"And his response."

" 'I killed the motherfucker.' "

"Those were his exact words?"

"Yes."

"He didn't say he shot the motherfucker?" Kim asked, walking over to the witness.

"No, his exact words were 'I killed the motherfucker.' "

"What happened next?"

"Emergency personnel arrived on the scene and ran over to the defendant. Only then did he release the woman. We arrested the defendant and led him out of the building."

"Was there anyone else in the apartment?"

"No."

"Did you notice any signs of a break-in or broken glass associated with burglary."

"No."

"Did the defendant do anything else?"

"He tried to follow the EMT with the woman. But my partner and I held him until some more officers came on the scene."

"Did the defendant say anything else after that?"

"No. We read him his rights, and we arrested him."

"Thank you, Officer Reid."

"Does the defense want to redirect?" the judge asked.

Yelram stood. "Not at this time, your honor."

"Officer Reid, you are excuse. Ms. Rivers, please call your next witness," the judge said.

"The prosecution calls crime scene investigator Pierre Lamark to the stand." Kim went back to her table while Pierre walked up to the stand. She stood and walked back to the stand after the witness was sworn in.

"Officer Lamark, how long have you been an investigator for the New York City police department?" Kim asked.

Pierre Lamark had a dark, round face and sunken eyes. He couldn't be more than forty years old. "I have worked for NYPD for more than ten years, the last seven with CSI," Officer Lamark replied in a high-pitched woman's voice.

There was some giggling in the court as he spoke.

Kim ignored the giggles. "Were you the principle investigator at the aforementioned crime scene?"

"Yes."

"When you got to the scene, were you able to establish the location where the shots were fired from?"

"Yes."

"What was the distance between the victim and the defendant?"

"He was standing fourteen feet away from the victim."

"You are positive?"

"Yes."

"Officer Lamark, can you step down for a minute so that you can demonstrate exactly where the defendant was and where the victim was found?" Kim asked as she stepped away from the witness stand.

"This will not be exact but it will give an approximate distance," Officer Lamark said, stepping down from the witness stand.

"Would this make it an exact measurement?" Kim asked, brandishing a measuring tape.

"Definitely." Officer Lamark said, walking toward Kim.

Kim handed him the metallic tape measure. She then went and stood a few feet away from the jury box. "Officer Lamark, can you measure fourteen feet from where I'm standing and please stay at that position when you are finish."

Officer Lamark brought the tape and measured fourteen feet from Kim. "The defendant was here when he fired at the victim," he said.

"Can you raise your hand in a shooting gesture?" Kim asked.

Officer Lamark lifted his hand and pointed at Kim.

"Ladies and gentlemen, this is the very short distance the defendant was from the victim. As you can see, with the added hand distance the defendant whose arm's length we can assume is a few inches more than Officer Lamark's shot the victim fifteen times," Kim said. "The defendant saw the effects of each and every bullet. Officer. Lamark, can you explain the effect that a bullet from a nine millimeter gun has on a person at close range?"

"A gun fired from this close a range pushes a person back a few inches. The impact of the bullet creates a jolt of energy that would move an immobile force."

"Based on your expertise, can you demonstrate?"

"Objection, your honor, this is not an acting class, and Officer Lamark will only be guessing," Yelram said.

"Objection overruled. Go ahead, Officer Lamark," the judge said.

"The force of a bullet from that close a distance, if the intended target was in a standing position..." Officer Lamark moved his hands forward then backward to demonstrate.

"Which the victim in this case was," Kim added.

"...Would push the target at least six inches back, depending on the location of the body where the bullet entered."

"Let's put the location as the upper torso," Kim said.

"Well, definitely, the victim would be pushed back a few inches, like this." Officer Lamark said, jumping back a few inches.

"How many bullets would it take to render a person useless to themselves?"

"Maybe three if the bullets entered the upper torso."

"And in this case, all the bullets did. What about the threat to someone else?"

Officer Lamark smiled. "Most people watch movies, and they see a person being shot ten or twelve times and keep on attacking. In real life, it is very different. Most victims don't get up after the first shot, much less absorb ten or twelve shots."

"So basically when someone shoots someone ten to fifteen times, they are in most cases shooting at a lifeless corpse or an immobile object?"

"Yes, that has been my experience."

"In the case here, how many shots did it take for the victim to become a corpse or immobile."

"Based on the impact of the bullets, I would say after thc second shot the victim was immobile, and the third and forth shots cemented his fate."

"By that you mean killed him?"

"Yes."

"So based on your testimony, the defendant shot at least eleven times into a lifeless body."

"Yes."

"And after the first two shots, the victim was immobile. Could he have hurt someone standing next to him?"

"He couldn't hurt a fly."

"In your years working in the CSI department of the NYPD, what is usually the reason for shooting someone fifteen times?"

"Objection, your honor. The prosecution is leading the witness."

"Question withdrawn. No more questions, your honor," Kim said, walking to her chair.

"Defense, cross examine?" the judge asked looking at Yelram.

"Yes, your honor," Yelram said, rising from his chair.

"Officer Lamark, you are a police officer?"

"Yes, I am."

"How many shootings by officers have there been in the last six months in New York City?"

"I cannot recollect."

"Your honor, relevance?" Kim asked, rising from her chair. "The New York City police department is not on trial."

"Your honor, I will show the correlation in a minute," Yelram said, walking up to Officer Lamark.

"Go ahead," the judge said.

Yelram went back to the defense table and opened a manila folder. "There have been four shootings by the NYPD in the last six months. The average number of shots fired was eighteen. Let's not talk about the forty-two shots fired by the three officers in the Bronx that killed a man who was reaching for his wallet. The average distance of the shots fired was seven feet. Now Officer Lamark, what does that say about the NYPD? Are they terrible shots or are they pumping bullets into corpses?" Yelram asked.

"I cannot comment on the department. Most of our officers are well trained, and they do their job to the best of their ability," Officer Lamark said, looking at the judge.

"Another thing, Officer Lamark, you stated that a bullet has the tendency of pushing the victim backward. As a reflexive action, doesn't the human body have a tendency of coming forward once it is thrown back? Is it safe to say that the victim also came forward once he was shot?"

"Well maybe for the first three shots but after that the victim was thrown backward."

"So it could appear that the victim was coming forward?"

"Well..."

"Yes or no. Officer Lamark," Yelram said.

"Your honor?" Officer Lamark said, appealing to the judge.

"Please answer the question, officer Lamark," the judge said.

"Yes, he could have come forward," Officer Lamark replied.

"So the victim could have been coming forward with his hands flailing."

"That might have been possible," Officer Lamark said, sounding disgusted.

"No more questions, your honor."

"Officer Lamark, you can step down now. Thank you for your testimony," the judge said.

Chapter 9

"The dildo must have been at least sixteen inches long, and the diameter had to be half of that," Peter said, banging on the hard gray dashboard of the truck for emphasis. "I have never been so humiliated in my life."

"At least you tried," Rashaun said, knowing that his words were of little comfort.

"Rashaun, I didn't know the human vagina could take such a big object. And don't tell me that a baby comes from there so it can, because as you and I well know, half of the women who have babies usually rip their vaginas." Peter made a turn on Remsen Avenue with the U-Haul truck. "And that wasn't all. I thought that I could eat pussy, so I went down on the my wife for about half an hour then I did my wife's friend for about the same time, give or take a few minutes because she had this sweet-smelling pussy. I have never had pussy like that before. It was a cross between strawberries and peaches. It was really nice. Then the women started to eat each other, and I swear they did it for about two hours."

"So what were you doing during that time?" Rashaun asked.

"I fucked my wife and came. They continued to eat each other like I wasn't even there. I swear my wife forgot that I was in the room. I felt like I was a receiver standing in the end zone shouting that I was open and no one was paying any attention to me. They just kept going at each other. You guys laugh at me about the size of my dick, but I swear if anyone of you were there, the women would have ignored you. Her girlfriend even had a strap on, and she gave it to me, and my wife asked me to put it on." Peter looked over at Rashaun in disbelief. "Can you believe it, a strap-on? And if you thought the dildo was big, I didn't think they made those things in those sizes."

"I hope you walked out then," Rashaun said, taking his attention away from his cell phone. He was waiting for a call from Andria who had gone to see the pediatrician with Wisdom who was experiencing his second cold. The doctor told them it was normal but they could bring him in anyway.

"No."

"What were you doing?"

"What else could I do? I turned on the TV, and I watched porn. Direct TV was having a three-for-one sale." Peter made a right on J Street.

"Do you know that ninety percent of the heterosexual men out there wish they were in your shoes? It's the ultimate male fantasy," Rashaun said, reaching between the seats for his weightlifting belt.

"They can have it. Any woman who tells me she doesn't mind eating pussy, I'm running away from her as fast as I can." Peter pulled up in front of a driveway with a white Escalade parked behind a blue Jetta.

"Whose Escalade?" Rashaun asked, getting out of the truck.

"I guess her friend moved in already," Peter said, his eyes blood red.

"Are you okay?" Rashaun asked.

"What time did the guys tell you they were coming over to help?" Peter asked.

"They said they'll meet us over here, but as you can see they're not here. I didn't expect them to be. They'll most likely come when we're almost finished," Rashaun said.

"Thanks, Rashaun."

"It's nothing, Peter," Rashaun said.

"I don't know. I was willing to increase my penis size for this woman, and I'm not out the house yet, and she's got another pussy in there." Peter stood in front of the door. His hand was over the bell but not touching it.

"Peter, you don't have to do this now," Rashaun said, standing impatiently behind him. "We can come back later."

Peter rang the bell. "Now is as good a time as later. We tried to make it work, and we couldn't. Now it's time for us to move on. My wife has."

The door opened, and Peter's wife was standing in the doorway. "Hi, Peter. Felicia came by to drop off some videos. Hello, Rashaun. How is the family?"

"The family is good," Rashaun said, peering into the house.

"And the trial?"

"Time will tell with that. I'm sorry that you and Peter didn't make it," Rashaun said.

"Sometimes its best two people go their separate ways. We don't have any kids, so that's a good thing. Peter is a good man. I hope whoever gets him realizes that," she said, looking at Peter.

"You packed all my clothes?" Peter asked. His voice seemed to have passed through sand paper.

"Yeah, they're in the spare room." Peter's wife stepped aside so that Peter could enter.

Peter entered and Rashaun stood on the steps.

"Rashaun, I don't think Peter can carry all the stuff by himself," Peter's wife said, smiling at Rashaun.

"Yeah. Yeah, right." Rashaun followed Peter. As they passed through the living room, Rashaun saw the door to the bathroom open. He started walking slower, looking to see who was coming out.

"Karen, we have to change the colors in the bathroom." The woman walked out of the bathroom and stopped when she saw Rashaun. Peter had already gone into the bedroom. "Hello."

"Hello. I'm Rashaun, a friend of Peter's."

"Nice meeting you, Rashaun. I'm Felicia. Do you know where Karen is?"

"I think she's outside," Rashaun said, turning around to enter the bedroom.

"Okay." Felicia said, heading to the front door.

Rashaun went into the room where Peter was sitting on a big brown cardboard box. "She's a little bit heavy but her face is cute."

Peter got up off the box. "Let's do this," he said.

"How big you said the dildo was again?" Rashaun asked.

"You are an asshole," Peter said, smiling.

"Sometimes a little bit of humor helps you handle life better," Rashaun said, lifting a box labeled Perishables.

"Hey, I really appreciate you coming and helping me."

"I needed a break from that. This gives me a good breather. Your stuff is light compared to what I'm dealing with." Rashaun lifted the box onto his shoulder. "Shouldn't we be moving the big stuff first?"

"The only big thing we need to take is the TV, and for that we need the rest of the guys. I'm not taking the bed, and the furniture is hers."

"Alright," Rashaun said and added. "That four-poster bed is very nice. All you got to do is change the mattress, and it's like new."

"Thanks, but no thanks."

"Well let me go put his in the truck before I collapse in here." Rashaun walked out into the living room, looking around to see if he saw the two women. He didn't see them until he got out in the driveway. Karen was standing outside the door of the Escalade. She stepped back when she saw Rashaun and waved goodbye to Felicia who reversed out of the driveway. Rashaun dumped the box into the truck and jumped down.

"Your friend is very close-minded, you know?" Karen said, standing there in a tight purple sweat suit.

"Aren't you cold?" Rashaun asked, not wishing to go in the direction she was taking the conversation.

"I'm okay. Rashaun, we tried, but sexually we're not there," Karen said.

"Karen, I don't think I need to hear this," Rashaun said, turning around to head back to the house.

"Rashaun, why are you acting like this? I know Peter told you everything about us, but sometimes you need to listen to both sides of the story," Karen said, looking down at the cracked driveway.

"What can I say?" Rashaun asked, looking at a blue car approaching.

Karen shook her head. "I tried to explain to Peter that it wasn't his fault. I've always been ashamed of my body. I stopped having sex before I met Peter. It wasn't because I was saving myself or anything like that. The boyfriend I had before really did a number on my self-esteem. Do you know what it feels like for someone to tell you that you are too big down there?"

Instead of answering her, Rashaun turned away. He didn't have any answers. He also knew that he had said some pretty hurtful things to women in the past without any regard to their feelings.

"When it's true, it hurts in the bones. And he wasn't the first one to tell me. Do you know what it's like for people to find out something like that about themselves? Your whole life changes, and you almost give up on love. I was at that point in my life when I met Peter. As you and I know, he hasn't been around."

"You got that right," Rashaun said, taking a seat inside the truck, his feet swinging freely.

"Maybe I should have told him, I don't know, but I wanted it to last. Rashaun, I'm not a lesbian. Felicia wants a lot more from me than I can give, but what she's done is make me feel special. I was beginning to feel like a freak. I still love Peter, and regardless of what happens between us, I don't want him to question that," Karen said, looking at the approaching Mercedes Benz.

Rashaun's attention was drawn to it, too, because he was trying to make out the license plate. It was Lance's car.

"Here come the fellows," Rashaun said, happy to end the conversation. He was starting to feel weasy inside. Their conversation had put Karen in a completely new light.

"Rashaun, please keep what I told you between us," Karen said, turning to go into the house.

Rashaun walked down to the car as Lance opened the door. George exited from the passenger side followed by Pedro from the back.

"Peter is finally leaving the lake," Lance said, a grin on his face.

"I thought you guys would never show up," Rashaun said, ignoring Lance's comment.

"Where is Peter anyway?" George asked.

"He's inside getting his stuff together," Rashaun said.

"Maybe he's making one last hit," George said.

"Well, he would have to stop on the down stroke because I've got a date later, and I'm not planning on spending the whole day here," Lance said, walking to the house. "Besides, when Peter gets together with his wife, there is no feelings involved. They'll be glad for the interruption."

Rashaun didn't say anything. He continued his stride with the boys into the house. He was hoping not to run into Karen again, even if that was close to being impossible. He wasn't feeling too good about himself because he had made a mockery of someone's pain and suffering.

Andria wasn't hoping for the impossible. All she was hoping for was to have her wedding go smoothly and live happily ever after with the man she loved. As she drove with Lethal, Albertina and Wisdom, Andria was wondering if any of the things she hoped for would actually come true. First she had to deal with the girls and the dresses. It was a small problem but irritating nonetheless. Now she was on her way to meet the caterer Albertina had recommended. The view from the back of the car consisted of a shiny black horsehair wig that Albertina insisted was human hair and a cap with a Yankees insignia on Lethal's head. As always Wisdom was asleep, which occurred exactly five minutes into the ride. Andria pulled out the sheet with the wedding menu printed on a flowery designed paper. Andria wasn't West Indian but she enjoyed almost all their food, which was a good thing considering Rashaun's taste. During the few months she had lived with Albertina, she had learned how to make stew peas, curry goat, chicken and beef; how to steam and stew fish and make the number one West Indian food rice and peas. Of course she had perfected the fried plantain, including how to pick the best ones out in the supermarket. She could now go and open her own West Indian restaurant like she had seen people do on nearly every block in Brooklyn.

"Andria, you'll like the caterer," Albertina said in her lowest possible voice.

"I hope he doesn't spoil the wedding," Andria said, her right hand still clutching the menu. "I think people remember lousy food more than anything at the wedding."

"Yeah, I know what you mean," Albertina said. "I went to my nephew's wedding in Westbury, Long Island, and the food was a disaster. I think they had this white company cater the wedding. The chicken was white, and talking about no seasoning. I think the only seasoning they used was salt, and plenty of it. Now tell me how you can have food like that for black people? There were about ten white people in the reception. Granted it was his boss and family but the rest of us didn't have to suffer for that. I stopped at McDonald's on my way back because I was so hungry."

"Albertina, you know I have no problem with West Indian food but some of the guests will be Americans."

"Girl, please, tell me what West Indian restaurant doesn't have the sign West Indian and American food, and I'm sure they're not talking about white meat chicken. West Indians and Americans have always enjoyed the same food. In the sixties and seventies, there was this stupid competition among them but I don't think the problem is there anymore. Go into any soul food restaurant, and you can see West Indians sitting and eating, and the Americans know more about jerk than me."

"You're right, Albertina. I love me some jerk pork," Lethal said, keeping his eyes on the road.

"Well I'll see in a few minutes," Andria said, feeling a little bit relieved.

They pulled up in front a restaurant with a big rainbow sign that read West Indian and American Kitchen. Lethal got out first then opened the door for Albertina then Andria. As he opened the car doors, his eyes swept the parking area. It wasn't a parking lot but more of a big sidewalk with white paint lines separating the spaces.

Andria walked quickly into the door that read Restaurant Entrance; a few feet away was a take-out entrance. There were a few people inside the take-out area. Once they stepped into the restaurant, a waiter in black pants and white shirt greeted them.

"Hello, and welcome to West Indian and American Kitchen." His accent was almost American.

"We're here to see Stephon," Albertina said, looking behind the waiter. The restaurant was empty except for an elderly black couple with two bowls of soup.

"Hold on," the waiter said and pulled out his cell phone.

There was a loud beep followed by a "Stephon, some people are here to see you." "I'm coming right up. Please seat them and prepare the table," Stephon answered.

"Follow me," the waiter said and directed them to a table set for six.

The waiter pulled the seats out for them and waited while everyone was seated. "Give me a minute," he said and walked to a side table that had a few jugs with water. He brought one back to their table and filled each glass. "Stephon will be right out."

"This is a nice little restaurant," Andria said, looking around the room. There was a vase with fresh flowers on each table; the cloth napkins were multicolored with drawings of the different West Indian islands along with their favorite foods.

"Arthur and I come here on special occasions. It's the only restaurant he would eat from," Albertina said.

"I had some of their take-out before. It was pretty good," Lethal said. "This is my first time in the restaurant."

Andria saw a black man with a jovial Santa smile approaching the table. If she were a betting woman, she would put a hundred on him being Stephon Ingram, the cook and owner of the restaurant.

"Mrs. Jones, it's great to see you again," he said, bending and hugging Albertina. "How is your husband these days?"

"Arthur is good. I told you about my future daughter in-law," Albertina said, turning to Andria who was feeding Wisdom.

"And your new grandson," Stephon said, turning his jovial mood over to Andria.

"Congratulations, Andria, on your wedding and your son. I haven't met your future husband, but if he's anything like his parents, you just hit the jackpot."

"Andria, I forgot to tell you Stephon has a sweet mouth," Albertina said, smiling.

"Albertina raves about your restaurant so I came to check it out," Andria said, wiping a trickle of milk that had escape Wisdom's mouth.

"Thanks, Albertina," Stephon said. "Well Andria, Albertina said that you had concerns about my American cooking."

"Well..." Andria started.

"Not a problem. I've prepared a dinner free of charge to show you my down-south side. I was born in Jamaica but I'm an international chef. All you have to do is sit down and relax. The waiter will bring out the appetizers followed by the main course,"

Stephon said, motioning to the waiter to join them.

"Reggie, take care of our guests' drinks and set up the table. You won't need the menu because this is a special meal on the house," Stephon said. "Ladies and gent, enjoy the meal. I'll be back after dinner."

Reggie took their drink orders and went to the fridge located just before the door to the kitchen.

"Albertina, you didn't tell me that Stephon had prepared a meal for us," Andria said, putting Wisdom back into the car seat, which she had strapped to one of the unused chairs.

"Now that's a man with confidence in his food," Lethal said.

"Better yet, that's a man who's about to receive a ten thousand dollar check for a wedding. He ain't stupid," Albertina said.

"Albertina, you sound just like Rashaun," Andria said.

"That's my son," she said proudly.

Chapter 10

Rashaun walked up the stairs of the courtroom. He looked at the line for lawyers and then the one for everyone else. He didn't go through the one for lawyers; instead he waited patiently outside in the line that extended all the way outside the courthouse. What a difference a year made. He pulled his black wool coat tighter to ward off the wind that had found its way in the courthouse. In front of him was a young man with a long diamond earring drooping from his right ear. He was talking to a white man with a Honaker on his head.

"You got to get me off this one, Joshua. I'm looking at twenty-five. I nearly died doing five in 1995. I don't think I could make it with twenty-five," the young man said, shuffling his feet nervously.

"Ahmed, they caught you with five bags of cocaine. The undercover cop bought a bag from you on Franklin Avenue," Joshua said.

"I swear to you I was holding it for a friend of mine. He told me to give one to this guy when he came up to me, so I did," the young man said, going from his toes to his heels in an attempt to fight the cold. "This winter is killing me."

"I think the winter is the least of your worries," his lawyer said, stepping forward.

"Hi, Rashaun," Tyrone's sister, Yvonne said, coming up beside him.

"What you doing here?" Rashaun asked.

"Well I don't start working at Brookdale Hospital until next month so I decided to come hang out at the courthouse," she said, handing Rashaun one of two cups she had in her hands.

"Miss, there is a line," a small white woman with smudgy brown glasses said to Yvonne.

"I know there is a line. This is my boyfriend. I told him to hold a space for me while I went and got us chocolate," Yvonne said with an attitude.

"These people," the woman said, turning up her straight nose at Yvonne.

"She's with me," Rashaun said to the woman who turned away from them.

"How are you holding up?" Yvonne asked.

"I'm doing good," Rashaun said as he inched forward with the line.

"Well I'm going to be here if you need someone else to talk to," Yvonne said, sipping from her paper cup.

"Thanks, but I'm sure you have better things to do with your time," Rashaun said.

"Rashaun, after all that you've done for Tyrone, I think it's only fair that I support you. Besides, there's a lot of drama going in the court."

"What do you mean by that?" Rashaun asked.

"Well, I think the DA still has the hots for you, but she also wants to kill you. What did you do to that girl?"

"Nothing."

"Come on, Rashaun, the way you guys go at each other."

"What do you mean go at each other?"

"Well, someone has to be Stevie Wonder to miss you two," Yvonne, said.

"I guess you're not."

"Maybe I'm emotional but I'm not blind. Are you sure you're ready to get married, Rashaun?" Yvonne asked. "There are a lot of women out there who think you're the bomb," Yvonne said as they were ordered by the security guard to go through separate metal detectors.

Rashaun's belt caused the metal detector to beep, so he had to get a full-body search. When he was finished, Yvonne was by the wall waiting for him.

"I hate those things," Rashaun said as they began to walk through the court.

"They're a necessity," Yvonne said. "You want to have lunch later?"

"If you don't mind sitting with me and Yelram and talking about the case," Rashaun said.

"I'll see you guys at lunchtime," Yvonne said as they entered the courtroom.

"Look at him," Kim said, looking in the direction of the defense table. "He's sitting there with this smug look on his face."

"What are you talking about, Kim?" Roger asked, his white shirt and pastel yellow tie contrasting heavily with his black business suit.

"Rashaun. First he walks in late with a woman as if he's some kind of superstar. He sits down and expects everything to start."

"Kim, he's the defendant. The proceeding usually starts when he's here. Besides, did you see the line at the security stop? We were able to walk through without waiting, but I saw a lot of people waiting out in the cold," Roger said, placing three folders on the table. "I hope your witness was able to get here on time."

"Dr. Boston is sitting a few rows back," Kim said.

Roger stood from his chair and looked back into the courtroom audience. "I guess you got your man," he said.

"Money can buy any professional," Kim said, sitting down and picking up one of the three folders Roger had put on the table. She shuffled through the papers in the folder, rearranging their order.

The judge who seemed to have taken Prozac started the proceedings with a cheerful good morning. Kim continued rearranging her paperwork until she heard the judge mention the prosecution.

"Your honor, the prosecution would like to call Dr. Johnny Boston to the stand," Kim said, looking back to where a white man with a dark gray suit was sitting.

Kim stayed at her desk while the bailiff swore the witness in.

"Dr. Boston, what is your profession?" Kim asked.

Dr. Boston straightened his back in the chair. "I'm a psychoanalyst."

"Can you elaborate?"

"Well, what we do is try to determine why people do what they do. It is sometimes helpful in treating certain neurotic illnesses and explaining a specific behavior."

"Dr. Boston, are you familiar with case #1333359, the state of New York versus Rashaun Jones?"

"Yes, I am."

"As you well know the defendant has been charged with first-degree murder. He shot the victim fifteen times and his girlfriend once. Can you tell the court, in your professional opinion, what state of mind was the defendant?"

"I did not get the opportunity to talk to Mr. Jones," Dr. Boston said.

"Let the record show that the defendant refused to talk to Dr. Boston," Kim stated. "Continue, Dr. Boston."

"The defendant was obviously very angry. The fact that he shot the victim and his girlfriend could mean that he was also angry at his girlfriend."

"So you think the defendant might have been trying to kill his girlfriend also?"

"Based on the facts in the case, one could imply that if he didn't want to kill her he might have been trying to hurt her."

"As you know, the defendant's girlfriend was pregnant with what might or might not be his child. Do you think the defendant was trying to hurt the child also?"

"Definitely."

Kim sat down. "Thank you, Dr. Boston."

The judge leaned forward and said, "Mr. Yelram."

Yelram remained seated. "Dr. Boston, how many criminal evaluations do you make without talking to the accused?"

"In my line of work, it is sometimes difficult to get the accused to talk to you. Sixty percent of my evaluations are made without actually talking to the defendant."

"And why is that?"

"They think that we're working with the police or the DA's office," Dr. Boston replied, shifting nervously in his chair. "Our professional code makes it illegal for us to give false testimony. We give objective evaluations."

"Thank you, Dr. Boston," Yelram said.

"Why are you in such a good mood?" Roger asked Kim who was dancing in circles around him.

"Because the case is going exactly the way I want it. Roger, it's all about getting the right people on the stand. We have one more witness to call then the defense gets to call their witnesses." Kim sipped from her apple martini.

"You are positive that you can break Rashaun down? What about his girlfriend, Andria?" Roger asked, walking to their table, which was located on the edge of the tiny dance floor.

Kim sat in his lap. "I have known Rashaun for a long time. Our next witness will shake him up, and when I'm finished with his girlfriend, he'll want to kill me. Rashaun has a temper."

"Yes, but he is a lawyer."

"No, Roger, when Rashaun takes the stand he won't be a lawyer. He'll be like every other criminal in Brooklyn trying to avoid doing time behind bars. Rashaun is full of pride, and that's a good thing, but sometimes pride makes you do foolish things. Rikers is full of men doing twenty-five because of their pride."

"I hope you're right."

"I'm right, and I want to fuck."

Roger looked around the room to see if anyone heard Kim's last remark.

"Relax, Roger. It's 3:00 P.M. The two couples in the back of the room are too old to pay attention to anyone but themselves. The bathroom is right over there." Kim turned her head in the direction of a dark hallway. "Men and women are right next to each other, so it won't draw any suspicions."

"You're serious," Roger said, watching as Kim drained the last of the martini.

"Sometimes I like it hard and quick. Let's do it today before we get like the couple over there." Again Kim turned her head in the direction of the old couple.

"Give me a minute," Roger said.

"A minute is too quick. I want five minutes, the average time a man spends in the bathroom."

"Where do you get all these facts from?"

"Don't worry about it. Do you have rubbers?"

Roger looked at her.

Kim looked back. "Just because I'm horny doesn't mean I'm stupid," Kim said, gathering her coat and purse.

"Knock three times if you really want me," Roger sang as he went away.

"Just be ready," Kim said to him. Kim raised a fifty-dollar bill up in the air for the bartender to see then she put it down on the table. "Be right back."

The bartender continued to wipe a glass he had in his hand.

The attire for a ride to the airport was a pair of jeans and whatever top she could find in the second drawer. Andria had on a pair of blue Guess jeans and a sweater she had picked up at Express. Rashaun who was in the back with Wisdom was sporting a black Calvin Klein jeans and a sweatshirt Andria had picked up for him from Structure. He was in the backseat trying to teach Wisdom the ABC's even though Wisdom was barely able to recognize his parents. Kennedy Airport was continually going through renovations, which meant that she had to pay close attention to the billboards that had the airline terminal numbers.

"Look out, Andria," Rashaun said as he saw an encroaching blue minivan.

Andria sped up a little and moved into the far right lane. "I didn't see him coming," she said, shaking her head.

"What's wrong, Andria?" Rashaun asked as Wisdom fell asleep.

"I'm nervous, and I don't know why," Andria said, her eyes scanning the road.

"It's your friend Sharon. What is there to be nervous about?" Rashaun asked, wondering if it was the car ride or his teaching that had put Wisdom to sleep.

"But I didn't have Wisdom."

Rashaun leaned back in the car and looked at Andria through the rearview mirror. She was serious, and her face looked troubled. "Andria, you don't have to let her hold him."

"How would that look, Rashaun? What am I going to say, don't hold him because you're HIV positive. She's my friend, I can't do that," Andria said, taking the exit for Jet Blue. "She flew all the way from Atlanta to be in my wedding and she's pregnant."

"I don't know what to tell you, Andria, except to do whatever you think is best. You know that I'll be behind you a hundred percent," Rashaun said.

"So you don't mind Sharon holding Wisdom?"

"Of course I do. I'd be lying if I told you I didn't, but I look at it this way: You meet a lot of people every day. Who knows who is HIV positive? We don't live in a vacuum, and neither does Wisdom. I say you take precautions but you don't get paranoid. I don't think Sharon will try to hurt Wisdom."

"I don't think she will either but I'm still concerned." As Andria pulled up behind a brown Dodge Sable her cell phone started to ring. She put the car in park. "You're picking up your luggage now. Okay come out and meet me in the passenger pickup section. I'm driving Rashaun's car. Yes, I have Wisdom with me. He's in the back with Rashaun, sleeping as usual. Okay, I will see you in a minute." Andria put the phone back in her bag.

"You have excellent timing," Rashaun said. "I'm going to go and help her with the bags."

"Okay. I'll be right here."

"If you have to move, just go around, and we'll wait for you here," Rashaun said.

Andria sat in the car looking at the security guard directing traffic. She was hoping he didn't come and ask her to move. When she saw him walking down the line she looked to the terminal for Sharon and Rashaun. She smiled when she saw Rashaun pushing the cart with Sharon beside him.

"Miss, you can't stay here, you have to move," the security guard said as he peered into the car.

Andria rolled down the window. "They're right over there," Andria said, pointing to Rashaun and Sharon. "I'll be gone in a minute."

"Okay, ma'am, but don't let me come back and see you here," the security guard said, walking away.

"Thank you," Andria said before letting the window up. New York was going through an unbelievable cold spell.

Andria pressed the trunk-release button as Rashaun approached the car. She rolled the window down as Sharon made a beeline toward the driver door.

"Hey, girl. How was your flight?" Andria asked, kissing Sharon on the cheek.

"Besides getting kicked constantly in my stomach, the flight was fine," Sharon said. "Where's Wisdom?"

"He's fast asleep in the back. Do you want to hold him?" she asked as Rashaun was getting into the backseat. Rashaun hesitated between the doors as he waited for Sharon's response.

"No, girl, you know how I feel about my condition. I don't like to be too close to kids. It's enough I'm a wreck with this one I'm carrying. If you don't mind, I'll admire the cute one from a distance," Sharon said, getting into the car.

"Are you sure?" Andria said, looking back at Rashaun who was taking out a bottle with water for Wisdom who had just woke up.

"Andria, he is absolutely beautiful," Sharon said.

"Yep," Rashaun said. "Honey, tell her how everyone says he looks like me."

"Rashaun, we're not going through that again," Andria said, pulling the car out from behind a silver jeep that had just parked in front of them.

"It's the truth. Wisdom is the spitting image of me," Rashaun said, putting the bottle into Wisdom's mouth.

"The only thing Wisdom got from you is that appetite of his," Andria said as she merged onto the JFK Expressway.

"You guys are fun together," Sharon said, sipping from a bottle of Alpine spring water.

"Sometimes in life when your troubles seem to be overflowing, a little bit of humor goes a long way," Rashaun said as the car slowed down in front of the new shopping center recently opened off the Belt Parkway in Brooklyn. He had made plans with Andria to go to the Olive Garden but time hadn't permitted them to do so.

"Rashaun, you remember what you promised me," Andria said as the traffic eased up as they passed the shopping center.

"Yeah, baby, I do. We'll go to the Olive Garden after the wedding," Rashaun said.

Andria didn't say anything; instead she looked over to the

other side of the parkway that was open land covered by a white tarp. Rumor had it there were going to be houses there in the future. Major construction seemed to be going on all over Brooklyn. Her wish was simple: She wanted to see the outcome of the development with her family maybe they might even buy a house over there. A tear fell as she signaled for the Rockaway exit.

"Andria, I didn't come all the way from Atlanta to be ignored," Sharon said. "What's happening with the case, and did they catch the guy who attacked you all?"

Rashaun groaned.

"Congratulations, honey. I knew it was just a matter of time," Kim's father said, planting a kiss on his daughter's cheek. "I'm so proud of you."

"And you're not mad that I didn't use you as mom suggested I do." Kim took a seat opposite her father.

"Kimberly, from the time you were born, you have made me proud. I don't really care if you're a judge or a teacher." Mr. Rivers looked directly at his daughter. "I'm sure you're not aware of it, but I've been attending your current trial. I usually come late, and I leave before it's over."

Kim's mouth dropped open. "Daddy, why didn't you tell me?"

"Because I didn't want to make you self-conscious. I remember when we use to come to your school activities, and it use to make you so nervous. It wasn't until we stopped telling you that we were coming that you started to shine." Mr. Rivers took Kim's hand in his. "Even though I think that your tactics are similar to your mother's, I still appreciate the fact that you got the nomination on your own."

Kim smiled. "So, Dad, you're telling me that I'm more like Mom. I always thought that I followed in your footsteps."

"You did, but you did it your mom's way. You have her arrogance and determination, and you were blessed with her beauty."

"I think there is a compliment somewhere in there, Daddy," Kim said, sipping on a glass of red wine.

"My daughter, my love, all I have is yours, and never forget that," Mr. Rivers said, still holding on to Kim's hands. "Whatever you do, I'll always be proud of you, and I will always stand by you. I might not agree with it but I'll always be in your corner."

Kim looked away from her father. "Daddy, what's on your mind?"

"I remember when I could read your mind, now you're doing it to me," Mr. Rivers said.

"I'm right, aren't I?" Kim stated.

"Yes. It concerns your present case. I remember Rashaun when you guys were dating in law school. He was your competition, your best friend, and at that time you called him your soul mate. I appreciate the fact that you brought Roger over to the house. It pleased your mother even though very fleetingly. As you know, her position on color hasn't changed."

"I know, dad. She said the same thing about Rashaun."

"Your mother wants the best for you."

"I know she just wants a light shade, preferably a judge or surgeon."

"Well, we're not here to talk about your mother. I want to talk about Rashaun and why you're trying to kill the one you love."

"Daddy, Rashaun and I were over a long time ago. I admit I was in love with him, but that's history."

"Kimberly, stop that. You're not talking to a stranger. It's clear that you still harbor feelings for Rashaun. I don't care about that. I hope in time you'll move on. What I'm concerned about is that it's binding you. When hate and love clash, there is usually an explosion. I don't want you to get hurt in that explosion."

It was Kim's turn to hold her father's hand, and she gripped it tightly. "Daddy, I won't sit here and tell you that what you're saying isn't true. I have a lot riding on this case, including my heart, but whatever the outcome, just be certain your daughter will survive. And in saying that, I have to do it my way, so I would appreciate it if you don't come to the courthouse for the rest of the case. I think it's going to get ugly—actually, I'm positive it's going to get ugly."

"I'll abide by your wishes, but just be careful. You don't want to throw away the river for the pond."

"Yes, Daddy, there are always a lot more fish in the river than the pond."

"And?" Mr. Rivers said, looking at his daughter.

"The pond could dry up but the river keeps flowing."

They both laughed as a middle-age woman passed by and saw them holding hands, giving them both a scornful look.

Chapter 11

"I tried but it's not working," George said, agitation straining his voice.

"Well you know what you have to do," Rashaun said, watching his friend down his second iced tea.

"Why did God have to make me this way?" George asked. "I love them both so much, and I don't know if I can live without them."

"I don't know what to say," Rashaun said. "I have to give you credit. You tried your best to be faithful to your wife. But when the cleansing didn't work, I knew that it was a matter of time before we had this conversation. I agree with you, Joanna deserves a lot more."

"Did I give it my best?" George asked, his disposition remaining the same.

"George, you'll be able to maintain your relationship with your son," Rashaun said.

"They all say that in the beginning, but things change very rapidly once they don't get their way. You're a lawyer, and I watch those stupid judge shows," George said, motioning the waitress over.

"George, you won't find any answers there," Rashaun said, pointing to the drink.

"Answers are for questions. I'm looking for solace," George said. "Can I have another one, gorgeous."

"Keep the tab on the card?" The waitress asked.

"Yes," Rashaun said.

"Women. They come in all flavors, and I want to try them all," George said, looking at the waitress' butt as she walked off.

"And you're crying about the price you have to pay," Rashuan said.

"Rashaun, I don't want to just fuck them. I want to experience them. I want to go places with them. I want to live the life."

"I remember the last time you tried living the life with a woman."

"Yeah Debra. She was good while it lasted but I stayed with her too long. By then she wanted to put the handcuffs on, and they can be so vengeful. You tell a guy it's over and most sane men walk away. You say the same thing to a woman, and they either try to kill you or go into a deep depression," George said, shaking his head. "It's fucking unbelievable."

"I don't think you'll have that problem with Joanne. I think you might have a problem with her and another man."

"You think so?" George asked, putting his hand under his chin.

"Yeah, especially if he becomes a permanent fixture in the house. You know that means he'll be hanging out with your son, and you don't want him to shun your son either."

"Fuck, shit gets complicated." George motioned to the waitress as he downed the remainder of his drink.

"That it does, my friend." Rashaun continued to sip on his drink.

"You think I should stay with her?" George asked.

"No. Don't make life's complications keep you in a place

you don't want be. I'm sure you'll be able to handle it when it comes up. You're not a one-woman kind of guy, and there isn't anything wrong with that. You're a good father, and I'm sure you'll continue to be that."

"You think you are?" George looked directly at Rashaun.

"I sometimes ask myself that question. All I have to say is that I'll give it a shot because I want to be with Andria for the rest of my life." Rashaun smiled. "I sound like a fucking postcard."

"Rashaun, if any man could be faithful, I think you can. And that feeling of wanting to be with a woman for the rest of my life, that was the reason I married Joanne, but this is many years later, and I've met a few women I felt the same way about. Shit, I'm just gonna live. Hopefully Joanne doesn't punish me for walking away," George said, picking up the drink the waitress had dropped off. "And if she does, I know one of the best lawyers in Brooklyn. He'll fight for me."

"Hopefully, he gets a chance to fight for himself first," Rashaun said.

"Don't worry about that. Everything will work out, and if you see that it's not working out, just go over and give Kim some good dick. I bet you she will drop the charges like Bush drops bombs in Iraq. Give her some shock and awe."

"Just as long as I don't end up in the same situation as Bush did with Iraq. Sometimes life is a lot more complicated than just dropping a load." Rashaun stared blankly into the glass. "Anyway, I got to go home and rehearse for next week."

"You have to rehearse your testimony?"

"Yes, George, I have to rehearse my testimony. Your words are beginning to slur. It's time to take your ass home."

"Yeah, you're right. My head doesn't feel so good," George said, holding on to the chair as he started to get up.

"Hold on, George. I'm going to pay the bill then I'll come back and get you," Rashaun said, getting up from his chair. "Don't get up."

"Alright. Let me finish my drink," George said. The rest of liquid in his glass disappeared in his mouth, and his head hit the table the same time as the empty glass.

Rashaun shook his head. George was a heavy motherfucker.

"She fainted?" Andria asked in disbelief.

"That's what Paula said." Robin put the blue 2003 Ford Windstar in park.

"What is Sharon doing over here?" Andria asked, trying to look through the heavily tinted glass. The dark tint went around the restaurant.

"Haven't you heard about this place?" Robin asked in disbelief.

"No. I've never been in the loop, and my life lately doesn't give me the opportunity to check out the happening places in Brooklyn." Andria closed the door of the van and joined Robin in front of the club. "Did someone call an ambulance?"

"I don't think so. There was a doctor eating in the restaurant. He was able to revive her. I think it was dehydration."

"Robin, I don't think that Sharon would let herself get dehydrated," Andria said, following Robin up to the door.

Robin opened the door, and Andria stepped into the dimly lit room.

"Surprise!"

"What?" Andria blinked as the lights were turned up in the room. Her face had become pale, and tears were running down her face. She slapped Robin on the shoulder as she looked around the room.

"Did we get you or not?" Robin asked, trying her best to stop laughing.

Sharon was standing in front the buffet-style serving containers. Paula and Hilda were to the left, each with a drink in their hands. Albertina was on the right holding a glass of wine with a smile on her face. Andria's mother was seated next to Albertina. There was a host of other women in the room, including Ms. Brown from Andria's job. The music started as the women circled Andria.

"Even my mother was in on this," Andria said, looking at her mother who had gotten up from the chair and come over to her.

"I'm not too old to surprise you," Andria's mother said, holding a glass of wine.

Andria looked over at Albertina, knowing that Albertina was the one who gave her mother the drink.

Albertina looked away innocently.

Andria's mother took her hand, and as she did so a path was cleared that led straight to a white decorated chair with boxes upon boxes around it. Robin put a glass of sparkling apple cider in Andria's hand as she took a seat in the white chair.

"Not so fast," Paula said. She took Andria away from her mother and put her in the middle of the dance floor. The music became louder as Andria stood by herself in the middle of the floor. The women circled Andria, holding hands.

Andria look bewildered, wondering what was coming next. Jay-Z's song "Dirt off Your Shoulder" came on and the women, including Albertina and Andria's mother brushed the shoulder of the woman next to them. It was then that Andria saw the first head pop out from between Paula and Ms. Brown. A slithering masculine body followed the head. Andria covered her eyes as the man came into view. She turned around to look at Robin, and another male dancer was emerging from between her and the secretary from Andria's old job. As her eyes circled the room, she saw another dancer appearing from between Albertina and her mother. The dancers encircled her and they started a slow, gyrating dance that massaged her body all around. She felt tense but in an odd way relaxed. Andria covered her eyes as the dancers continued to move with her as the masterpiece.

Andria held up her hands because she didn't want to touch the dancers. Their bodies were slick with sweat as they gyrated on her to the music. She laughed because she didn't know what to do. She looked over at her friends who seemed to be egging the dancers on. Her mother and Albertina were useless because they were clapping along with the rest of the people in the room. It was her time, she had to let go and enjoy the moment. Andria closed her eyes and slowly started to move her feet. She reached over and grabbed a dancer by the neck, pulling him to her. She moved her waist with the rhythm of the music and the men's bodies. She was going to put on a show and enjoy herself.

The women had stopped clapping to stare at Andria.

Andria let go of the first dancer and stretched out her hands, and the two dancers held on to each hand. She started to move back and forth to the rhythm of the music. She closed her eyes and wondered if she was making a fool of herself, but when she heard the clapping she knew the fun had just begun. It was her night, and nothing was going to stop her from having a good time.

Chapter 12

This was one of the rare occasions Kim had the intention of having a good time in court. As she walked through the corridor, her leather bag in her hand, she couldn't wait for this week to come. Today her final witness was going to testify. Pastor Devon Thompson was going to take the stand.

"Are you sure he's going to show?" Roger asked as he sat down next to Kim at the prosecution table.

"I guarantee it," Kim said, smoothing out her pants as she sat down.

"You're right. He's three rows back," Roger said, "and he is wearing his robe."

"I like Pastor Thompson. He does what he's told," Kim said, shooting a look over at the defense table.

"He looks calm, doesn't he?" Roger asked, following the direction of Kim's gaze.

"Not for long. Mr. Jones won't be calm for too long," Kim said as she sat back as the judge made his introductions. "He doesn't realize that the next witness use to be his best friend in law school. At that time he was known as Henry Dean, not Pastor Devon Thompson."

Rashaun looked over at Kim and noticed that she had this over confident air about her. It was a look he hadn't really seen in the trial. He knew she was looking forward to cross-examining him and Andria but that was not going to happen today.

"Are you sure you don't know the next witness?" Yelram asked.

"I'm not a very religious man, Yelram, but I would remember a priest," Rashaun said.

"Well let's play it by ear," Yelram said, taking his pen out as Kim called the pastor to the stand.

"Fuck," Rashaun said as he saw Devon walking to the stand.

"You look like you've seen a ghost. Who is he?" Yelram asked.

"I know him. He was my best friend through college and part of law school. He obviously has changed his name and profession."

"Can he hurt you?" Yelram whispered as Devon was sworn in.

"Yes."

Kim saw the look on Rashaun's face when Devon walked toward the witness stand. She smiled, knowing that she had caught him and the defense completely off guard.

"Pastor Thompson, can you tell us how you know the defendant?" Kim asked.

"The defendant and I were friends for a number of years."

"How many years?"

"About seven."

"So we could say that you know the defendant very well."

"Yes, you can say that."

"Are you aware of the charges against the defendant?"

"Yes."

"Pastor Thompson, we discussed an incident that happened while you and the defendant were in law school. It was very disturbing, but I think it epitomizes the defendant. Let's go back to it. Now remember that you are under oath, which I'm not concerned with because you are a man of God." Kim could hardly suppress a giggle. "Let's go back to that time. You and the defendant had gone to meet the defendant's girlfriend at her dorm room."

"Yes."

"What happened then?"

"Well when we got there, a guy was in the room with Rashaun's girlfriend."

"What did the defendant do?"

"He asked the guy what he was doing in his girlfriend's room."

"I'm sure he didn't ask that nicely."

There was giggling in the courtroom.

"No, he didn't, but I will not repeat what he said."

"What was the guy's response?"

"He told Rashaun he wasn't leaving, and he could go have sex with himself."

"I'm sure the defendant didn't react too kindly to those remarks."

"No, he didn't," Devon, said.

"Can you tell the court what happened then?"

Devon cradled his head between his thumb and forefinger. "Rashaun jumped the guy so fast it took everyone by surprise. Before I could stop it, Rashaun had beaten the guy to a bloody mess."

"I'd like to submit exhibit C, the police report from the

incident. What happened next?"

"The police arrested Rashaun and charged him with aggravated assault."

"What became of the case?" Kim asked.

"The plaintiff dropped the charges."

"Did you know the defendant to have such a deadly temper?"

"Yes, but Rashaun is a very good person. It's just that sometimes he has a tendency to lose it."

"Did you think the defendant would repeat those actions again?"

"If pushed, yes."

"No more questions, your honor."

Yelram stood, a solemn look on his face. "No questions, your honor."

"Pastor Thompson, you are dismissed."

Rashaun's face was expressionless as he looked at Devon as he exited the courtroom. He was surprised that the hate he had felt for him had dissipated. Devon was the man who had sent his life into a downward spiral. He had no intentions of hugging him to make up, but forgiveness with time had taken place. His mother always told him that everything in life happens for a reason. Now he knew the reason why Blackfunk had entered his life. It was to save him from Kim, a woman he knew for certain was going to ruin him.

Chapter 13

"I'll bring him to his knees, I promise you that," Kim said, the notes from the court case in front of her.

"You're really looking forward to questioning Rashaun and his girlfriend aren't you?" Roger lay on the bed, his eyes locked on the TV.

"I'll bring out all his insecurities. This will be a cleansing for Rashaun."

"And his girlfriend."

"I'll show her for the dumb bitch she is," Kim said, tucking her left leg under her thigh.

"Do you honestly think Rashaun will break down? After all, he is a lawyer."

"Yes, but on the stand he won't be a lawyer. He'll be like any other man fighting for his life." Kim twirled a pencil.

"The jury might be sympathetic to his plight," Roger said.

"No, they won't," Kim said. "You know what, all this talk about the trial is getting me wet. Come over here, Roger."

"I'm watching CNN. You know the president is fucking up again. I bet you if Monica Lewinsky took care of Bush the way she took care of Clinton, the U.S. economy would be moving right now," Roger said from the bed.

"Crawl from the bed to over here," Kim said, making a half circle to face Roger on the bed.

"You're serious?" Roger sat up.

"I want you to eat me until I have at least three orgasms." Kim stretched out her long legs on the chair, easing her panties off. She moved forward so that she sat with her butt on the edge of the chair. She kept her bra and white shirt on.

Roger started to take off his boxers.

"No, leave them on."

He pulled them back up and swung his legs to get off the bed.

"No, not like that. I want you to come off the bed on your hands, like a tiger."

Roger obeyed.

"Now crawl, slowly," Kim said, waving him on with her pencil.

Kim threw her head back as Roger crawled toward her. "Don't touch my legs or any other part of my body. I want to feel only your tongue on my pussy."

Kim began to open her legs wider. Only an inch or two of her butt was on the edge of the chair. She saw Roger stick his tongue out, and its warmth sent a tremor down her spine. "Yes, lick the outside," she said, feeling her juices flowing onto his tongue and over her anus.

Roger darted his tongue the way she had taught him to. He licked the outside of her vagina then he brought his tongue up to her protruding clit as Kim began to moan. He brought his hand toward her vagina.

Kim opened her legs until they were almost parallel with each other.

Roger spread her vagina, exposing the soft pinkness of her womanhood. His tongue reached deep inside of her and darted in and out, going from her depths to her protruding clitoris. He shoved his tongue into her, reached around and grabbed her butt as he buried his head inside her vagina.

Kim felt each of Roger's fingertips dig into her butt as his tongue reached beyond the pinkness of her vagina. She grabbed his head with both her hands, and together they tried to fit his head into her womanhood. As they started the rebirth, Kim felt her body begin to convulse, and as she did she heard Roger's muffled cries. She didn't know if he was suffocating, and she didn't care. Her orgasm was coming like a twister, ripping both of them apart. She was completely off the chair, her hands pulling on Roger's head as he pulled her deeper into him. As her orgasm came, she managed one burst of energy, pushing Roger's head back as she squirted into his face. The chair scraped on the rug as her body sank down.

"This has never happened to me before," she said, her eyes still closed as she sat in a daze.

Roger didn't respond.

She opened her eyes to see Roger's convulsions as he threw life away. His sperm lay dormant on her legs, the rug and her yellow pencil.

"There ain't a woman alive who could make me be faithful," Lance said as he pulled the Benz out of Rashaun's parents' house.

"Fidelity is not about vagina and penis. It's more mental than that," Rashaun said, sliding a CD into the car stereo.

"Fidelity is fool's gold. Once you get it, it turns to dust. We're dust, Rashaun, that's what we are. We're walking dust. Do you think God cares how much pussy we stick our dicks in? Once we're dust, the body doesn't count. Religion uses sex to scare us. You killed a man, and I fucked ten thousand women who the Lord will take into his house?"

Rashaun looked over at Lance. "You're not cheering me up."

"Okay, Rashaun, you're about to go on lockdown and that's of your own choosing. Marriage has nothing to do with outside pussy," Lance said.

"I know you can attest to that," Rashaun said.

"You have never fucked a Chinese girl, have you?"

"No."

"You're about to die and you get the opportunity to, would you?" Lance asked.

Rashaun leaned his head to the side. "A last wish kind of a thing?"

"If that's the way you want to put it."

"I guess I would."

Lance pulled into an all-you-can-eat Chinese buffet-style restaurant.

"Lance, you know I don't eat Chinese food anymore," Rashaun said as Lance straightened the car between the white parking lines.

"You can have iced tea besides Chinese, West Indian, Italian or American. Food is food. I didn't pick the restaurant. George did. You said you didn't want a bachelor party."

"Yeah, but that doesn't mean I want to watch you guys eat in a restaurant."

"George is the one planning this thing. You can shout at him. I would have picked The Waterclub."

"Wait till I get hold of that motherfucker," Rashaun said, jerking the restaurant door open.

Rashaun walked in and quickly scanned the restaurant for the rest of the boys. He had a bone to pick with George. The restaurant was of course crowded with people who didn't need to be going to an all-you-can-eat restaurant.

"Follow me," Lance said, stepping in front of Rashaun.

Rashaun followed him to the back of the restaurant. A Chinese man in his late fifties with slightly graying and balding hair stood in front of a door that read Employees Only.

Lance whispered something to him, and the man stepped aside and opened the door.

"What the fuck is this?" Rashaun asked, standing away from Lance.

The man patted Rashaun on his back as he went in. "Good time. Have good time."

Rashaun followed Lance down dimly lit stairs. At the bottom, another man opened the door for them.

The first person Rashaun saw when he went into the large open room was George surrounded by two Asian women.

George pointed downward at the girls' butts. "They are genetically altered, they got butts."

"Welcome to your bachelor party," Lance said. "Imagine that this is your last day on Earth."

Pete was sitting in a wicker chair with a Chinese girl in his lap. Next to him in a bigger chair was Pedro with two of the fattest Asian women Rashaun had ever seen. The music was eighties disco, and there were about twelve other Asian women dressed only in G-strings. It was obvious that breasts weren't a big commodity in Asia because only one had at least an A cup.

Rashaun stood where Lance had left him. Six of the Asian women came to him.

"They're all yours," George said, sucking the girl's raisin-size tits. "Don't look at this as infidelity, look at it as the end of an era. After this there won't be any reason for you to leave home."

Pete came up to Rashaun and tapped him on the shoulder. "We know you had a hell of a time in court. We can't help you there. No matter what, we know you're going to marry the woman of your dreams. Life is to be lived, live it. You never had one Asian Tonight we give you six. Enjoy."

The music became louder as the lights in the room dimmed. Lance and the rest of the fellows started to disappear down another long dark corridor. The ladies started to take off his clothes, their soft skin exciting him beyond belief. He tried to look around to see what was being dragged on the floor. He didn't see a bed but the women gently laid him down on one. *Is it all over?* he thought. What if he got convicted? Twenty-five years behind bars would drive a man to a horrific end. As the women got him undressed and started to apply subtle kisses on his body, Rashaun thought about Andria and his family. He inhaled and made one big push.

Chapter 14

"The defense calls Ms. Andria Jackson to the stand." Yelram stood as Andria made her way to the front of the court.

Rashaun was hoping this day would never come, but he also knew that it would. As he sat down he could feel sweat running down his skin. Even though he had rehearsed the answers with Andria the night before, he knew people said a lot of things when he went up on the stand. He remembered a defendant confessing to a murder under cross-examination. He tried not to look at Andria as she took the witness stand. After Devon had gone up there and hung him out to dry he didn't want Andria tightening the noose around his neck. He moved his trembling hands from the table to his lap.

Yelram walked up to Andria. "Would you like some water, Ms. Jackson?"

"No, I'm fine. Thank you," Andria answered, adjusting herself in the seat.

Rashaun relaxed a little. Andria wasn't as nervous as he thought she would be.

"Ms. Jackson, Paul Edwards, your ex-boyfriend came to visit you at your apartment on the evening of March 10. Why did he visit you?" Yelram asked.

"He said he was leaving New York, and he wanted to say good-bye," Andria answered.

"Were you pregnant at the time?"

"Yes."

"Was it strange that Paul would want to say good-bye to you?"

"No. While I didn't think it was appropriate for him to visit me in my apartment, I didn't see any harm in it."

Yelram stopped pacing. "So you opened the door immediately?"

Andria paused for a second and looked over at Rashaun. "No, I told him that I wasn't interested in saying goodbye to him. He could leave."

"Did he leave?"

"No. He insisted on seeing me. He said he didn't think he would ever come back to New York City. He sounded very sincere."

"What happened next?"

"I opened the door and let him in."

"Was he in a good mood, sad, angry?"

"His attitude changed when I let him in the apartment."

"How?"

"He wanted to hold me, and he started talking a lot of nonsense."

"What exactly did he say?"

"He said he couldn't live without me."

"What did you say to him?"

"I told him to leave."

"Did he?"

"No."

"What happened next?"

"I tried to call the police?"

"Did you succeed?"

"No. He took the phone from me and slammed it down."

"How did you feel then?"

"I became very scared. Paul had this look in his eyes as if he was going to kill me."

"What happened next?"

"He started to talk about how he was attacked at his mother's apartment. He pulled his pants down to show me. I wouldn't look so he grabbed me by the neck and forced me."

"Paul had you by the neck, and he was trying to unzip his pants? You were scared? What happened next?"

"I screamed for help."

"And what happened next?"

"Rashaun came into the room with a gun in his hand."

"Did he say anything to Paul?"

Andria's eyes started to water. " He told Paul to let me go."

"What did Paul do?"

"Paul jerked my head harder toward him, and he told Rashaun to go fuck himself."

"Did Paul say anything else?"

"Yes. He said he was already dead, and if he was going to die I was going with him."

"What happened next?"

"He jerked me one more time, slamming the side of my body into his. It was then that the shooting started."

"Were you conscious when the shooting started?"

"Yes."

"What happened after the first shot?"

"After the first shot, Paul pulled me into him, causing my head to bounce into his. I don't know what happened after that."

"Were you afraid for your life?"

"I think if Rashaun didn't come when he did, I don't think Paul would have left without me."

"You think he would have forced you to go with him?"

"Either that or worse. The look in his eyes was very frightening."

"You were shot accidentally by the defendant during the incident. Do you dislike him for that?"

"No. I think if he hadn't done what he did I might have been dead right now. Rashaun saved our lives."

"Meaning you and your child?"

"Yes."

"Do you wish that anything had happened differently that evening?"

"Yes. I wish I hadn't opened the door."

"Thank you, Ms. Jackson."

"You wish you hadn't open the door. I guess everyone here could say the same thing, including your boyfriend," Kim said, rising from her chair. "Why did you open the door?"

"Because Paul sounded like he really wanted to say good-bye to me," Andria responded.

"So you let your ex-boyfriend into an apartment you were currently sharing with the defendant? What did you think would happen if your boyfriend came home and found you there with your ex-boyfriend?"

"I didn't think that Paul would be staying long enough for Rashaun to find him there."

"Had you spoken to Paul in, let's say the last few weeks before the incident?"

"Yes."

Kim walked up to the witness stand and stood within inches of Andria. "Were you friends?"

"I wouldn't call it that."

"Were you enemies?"

"No."

"Did you sleep with him?"

"Who do you think I am? I'm not a whore like you," Andria responded, her voice rising.

"Your honor, the prosecution is badgering the witness," Yelram shouted.

"Ms. Rivers." The judge looked over at Kim.

Kim stepped back.

"Was the reason that Paul was at your apartment because he wanted to find out about the baby?"

Rashaun stood.

"Mr. Yelram, please control your client," the judge said.

Yelram pulled Rashaun back down into his seat.

"Ms. Rivers?"

"Your honor, I am establishing motive here."

"Continue, but watch your language," the judge said.

"Had you slept with the victim a few months before the incident?"

Andria was shaking. "No."

"Then why did he visit you at the hospital?"

"He wanted to wish me luck on my thyroid operation."

"Was the defendant trying to kill you and the victim because of infidelity?" Kim asked, once more coming up to the witness stand and standing inches away from Andria.

"No."

"Was he making a claim to your son?" Kim asked, coming even closer.

"Your honor?" Yelram shouted.

"No," Andria answered, her voice shaking.

"Is the victim the father of your child?"

The slap echoed in the courtroom. Andria was in tears as Kim went to the floor.

Blood spurted from Kim's mouth.

The courtroom was silent as Kim picked herself up off the floor.

"Arrest the witness," the judge ordered.

Kim got up off the floor, putting her hands out to stop the court officers. They stopped and looked at the judge.

"Ms. Rivers, do you want to press charges?" the judge asked.

"No, your honor. Give me a minute to finish cross-examining the witness."

Andria looked over to Rashaun pleadingly.

Rashaun smiled.

Kim walked from the defense table to the witness stand.

"Ms. Jackson, do you think that the defendant was trying to kill you when he shot at you and the defendant?"

"Objection, your honor. It's not a known fact that Mr. Jones shot at the victim and Ms. Jackson."

"Let me rephrase. Do you think the defendant was trying to kill you when he shot in the direction of you and the victim?"

Andria's hands were back in her lap. "No. Rashaun wouldn't do anything to hurt me or the baby."

"Yet you were shot with the sixteenth bullet," Kim said. "If he wasn't trying to kill you, why the last shot?"

"Rashaun would never hurt us. He would never," Andria said, tears beginning to fall.

"No more questions, your honor." Kim walked back to the table.

"Andria wasn't shot with the sixteenth bullet," Roger said as Kim sat down.

"I know," Kim said, putting away her pad. "You don't play by the rules if you want to win."

Chapter 15

"Are you ready for this?" George asked, leaning against the church railing.

"Yes, I want my family," Rashaun answered as he stood in front of the church door.

"You know it's not too late. Now, don't get me wrong. I love Andria, and I think she'll make you a good wife, but it's all about you. Marriage isn't easy. I believe you are one of the few of us who can actually make this thing work. All bullshit aside, I'm rooting for you," George said.

Rashaun opened the door slightly and closed it back. "George, I've never been looking for perfection. I can't because I'm not perfect. Andria has my heart. When I think about growing old, sitting in my rocking chair, watching the sunset in some waste-land in Florida, the only woman I think about doing it with is Andria. You know I've had my share of women, maybe a little more than a man should, but all this is behind me now. I've put my dirt aside. The only time I'll touch it again is when it's being thrown over my coffin."

"We're going in different directions. I've left my wife for patches, and you're cultivating the land." George reached out and gripped Rashaun's hand. "Let it last forever. It's a beautiful thing."

Rashaun watched as Lethal got out of the car and started to

make his way up the stairs. Once more, impending danger was brought back to his reality. "I hope I'll get the chance to do that."

Lethal walked up the church steps and met Rashaun midway.

"What's up, Lethal?" Rashaun asked, extending his right hand.

"You said you didn't need me today but I thought I'd come and make sure everything is okay. The detectives said they found the hotel where the man had stayed but he had checked out. He used an alias and paid in cash. He doesn't own a car," Lethal said, looking at the cars parked in front of the church.

"Do they have a description?" Rashaun asked.

"That's the problem. They said he had long blond hair. The opposite of the description that was given when you and Andria were attacked."

"That means he's being cautious. He's also very determined."

"I don't think he'll leave until he completes what he came here to do."

Rashaun looked back at the church. George was waiting for him at the front.

"Don't worry, Rashaun. I'll be out here," Lethal said, walking back down to his car.

"Stop worrying," Robin said to Andria.

"It's not only about this, Robin. Rashaun has been acting strange lately," Andria said, looking at the church door.

"Andria, look at all that's going on. Rashaun has a lot on his mind, but I'll bet you anything that Rashaun will be here," Robin said.

"Robin, I messed up in court. I think if Rashaun gets convicted, it will be my fault. I totally blew it," Andria said, sitting down in the front pew. "Rashaun insists that we're getting married regardless of what happens, but I don't think I want to marry a man I sent to jail."

Robin sat down next to Andria. "Andria, I spoke to Rashaun after your testimony. He didn't believe you did anything wrong. I think he was more upset with the prosecutor for tricking you."

"Not as upset as I was when I found out. At first I felt bad for slapping her, but now I think I should have punched her instead. She's a nasty woman," Andria said.

Robin laughed. "Andria, you're the only person I know who uses phrases like '*nasty woman.' Bitch, whore, slut* I would understand, but nasty woman. It's a good thing we are in a church because I could have told you some things you could have said to Kim."

"Well here comes Marilyn. I'm sure she has had enough of us. I think she might tell us to go home," Andria said.

"Please, she's getting paid regardless. Rehearsal is part of her fee, I think wedding planners are overpaid anyway. How much are you guys paying her to coordinate this wedding?" Robin asked.

"Five thousand dollars," Andria replied.

Robin stood and stared at Andria. "For that kind of money, I would have a taxi pick you guys up and bring you to the rehearsal. I would also do it for a quarter of the price."

"Robin, do you honestly think I would have hired a wedding planner under normal circumstances? And don't tell me that you would have had time to plan this," Andria said.

"Okay, you got me there. Well, here comes the grass eater," Robin said.

"Ms. Jackson, I would like to get this rehearsal started. It seems that everyone is here except the groom and the best man. Is there a problem?" Marilyn asked with her prep school accent.

Before Andria could answer, Albertina joined them. "Andria, is your cell phone off?" She asked.

Andria rummaged through her bag and brought out her cell phone. "I missed three calls," she said.

"And one is your future husband who's been outside with George for the last thirty minutes waiting for a call from you," Albertina said.

"Well, I'm going to get the rest of the group together," Marilyn said and walked away.

"Did she go to military school?" Albertina asked, watching Marilyn walk away. "She's been driving everyone crazy. I think she needs to spend some time at McDonald's with a diet soda."

"Diet soda?" Andria looked puzzle.

"Albertina, you have to bring your daughter-in-law to present-day America. Yes, Andria. Diet soda is what fat people order with their Big Mac and super-size fries at McDonald's."

"And I'm suppose to know that? How many times have I gone to McDonald's?" Andria asked.

"Well, Wisdom will have you living there," Robin replied.

"Not if his father and I have anything to say about it," Andria said.

"Well here comes Daddy now," Albertina said, turning to watch Rashaun walk up the aisle. "He's walking as if it's his wedding day."

"Yeah, very slowly—the black man jitters," Robin added.

"You are not funny, Robin," Andria said.

"Lighten up, Andria," Robin said, turning to Andria.

"I don't think she will until after the wedding," Albertina said, looking at Andria.

"You got that right, Albertina. Now let's hope nothing happens at the rehearsal," Andria said as they began to walk to the rest of the wedding party.

"Are you going to blow up the church?" Tracee sat on the edge of Kim's bed.

"There is no need for such harsh action," Kim said, pulling out a black-and-white outfit from her closet.

"Well, if I'm not mistaken, the wedding is in two weeks." Tracee picked up the outfit and held it up.

"There won't be any wedding, I can guarantee that," Kim said. "Maybe I should wear black, after all there will be a burial on Monday."

Tracee stood holding the outfit against her. "It would look better on me."

Kim took the outfit from Tracee. "I guess that means I would look great in it. You don't think it's cut a little low?"

"Why? you intend to bend down in front of him?" Tracee asked. "Because if you do, I think you should concentrate on a miniskirt and bending over. Black men are not into tits."

"Whatever it takes," Kim said as she put back the outfit.

"What's Roger gonna say about all that?" Tracee asked.

"This has nothing to do with Roger. I'll deal with the Roger issue after the case," Kim said, slipping on a tight-fitting black skirt.

"You have him like that?" Tracee started undressing. "I think I'll borrow the first one."

Kim looked over at Tracee. "Is that why you're here?"

"No, but I have a luncheon to go to with Graham, and I want to look sexy but not ghetto sexy. And Kim, you've mastered that look, so I'm borrowing from the expert," Tracee said, buttoning up Kim's blouse.

"Is this too over the top?" Kim asked.

"Not for your intended purpose. Even a married man won't help but salivate over you." Tracee joined Kim at the mirror.

"I hope he likes it," Kim said.

"You're really trying to stop this wedding, aren't you?"

"In more ways than one. I'm going to crush him then build him back up," Kim said.

"He won't know what hit him." Tracee turned to the right, admiring herself in the mirror.

The phone rang.

"Tracee, pick it up for me?" Kim said, shuffling through her closet.

Tracee jumped on the bed and picked up Kim's cordless phone. "It's love puppy."

"Tell him I'll meet him at Jezebels," Kim said, pulling out a white see-through blouse from her closet.

Tracee hung up the phone and rejoined Kim in front of the mirror. "You and your men."

"What about you?" Kim asked.

"Love don't live here anymore. It's all about business. If you can't produce the green, keep walking," Tracee said, waving good-bye.

"You really are a dirty whore," Kim said.

"Better that than a woman in love with her ex. I still don't understand what makes Rashaun so special. I would fuck him but I wouldn't go after him."

Kim smiled because she honestly didn't know the answer to the question. She only knew that Rashaun had carved out a part of her heart, and she wanted him to be with her for the rest of her life, but first she had to break him down.

Chapter 16

"The defense calls Mr. Rashaun Jones to the stand," Yelram said, standing up at the table.

Rashaun and Yelram walked up to the witness stand. Rashaun sat in the witness chair while Yelram stood next to him.

The bailiff swore Rashaun in.

"Rashaun, let me first congratulate you on the birth of your son," Yelram said, walking up to Rashaun.

"Thank you," Rashaun said, twisting off the cap of the bottled water in front of him.

"How many pounds did he weigh?"

"He was seven pounds, eight ounces."

"Were you hoping for a boy?"

"No. I just wanted a healthy baby, and I was blessed with one."

"So Mom and baby are both doing well?"

"Well you saw Mom, so I would say she is doing well."

"Well, let's get through these proceedings so that you can go back home and be a father to your son," Yelram said.

"I do miss him," Rashaun said, sipping some water.

"Rashaun, I'm going to direct your attention to the evening of March 6. At approximately 7:30 P.M., where were you?" Yelram asked, walking in front of the witness stand.

"I was just getting home," Rashaun replied.

"An apartment in Brooklyn that you share with your fiancée?"

"Yes," Rashaun replied, easing back into the witness chair.

"Is that the time you normally get home?"

"Yes, unless I have a meeting or an errand to run, I'm usually home between 7 and 8. That evening I made one minor stop, and I got home at my usual time," Rashaun said looking over at Kim.

Kim smiled at him.

"What happened when you got home?"

"When I opened the door, I heard a man talking then I heard Andria, my fiancée, scream."

"What did you do when you heard the scream?"

"I grabbed the gun from the top shelf over the door."

"Why did you do that?"

"Because I heard my fiancée scream after hearing an angry, unrecognizable male voice. I thought I was interrupting a burglary."

"So you took the gun to protect your fiancée."

"Yes. I didn't know what was going on in the room."

"What did you see when you got into the room?"

"I saw Paul holding Andria by her neck as if he wanted to choke her."

"Did you do anything?"

"I walked up closer to them."

"What did Paul do then?"

"He pulled Andria closer to him and threatened her and the baby."

"Did you stop?"

"Yes, I did." Rashaun again sipped from the bottle.

"Did you say anything else to Paul?"

"Yes, I did. I told him to let her go but it seemed to have only angered him more. He jerked Andria's head one more time, and that was when I fired the gun."

"Were you trying to kill Paul?" Yelram asked.

"No. I was trying to stop him from hurting Andria."

"Have you fired a nine millimeter gun before?"

"Only when I went to the shooting range with my cop friends."

"Did you know how many shots you had fired at Paul?"

"I don't know, the rest was a blur. All I remember was pulling the trigger and hoping that I didn't shoot Andria. I didn't want to hurt Andria or my child."

"What happened next?"

"After the gunshots, I saw Andria and Paul on the ground."

Rashaun's eyes became glassy. He squeezed them tight then opened them back up. He looked down at the water in the bottle.

"Do you need a minute?"

"No, I'm okay. It's just that when I saw Andria on the ground I thought she was dead. My life would have been over then."

"Rashaun, if you had a second chance would you do the same thing?"

Rashaun sat upright. "I would do anything in the world

to protect my woman and child regardless of my own personal health."

"Thank you, Rashaun."

Kim stood and walked toward the witness stand. She looked through Rashaun.

"Mr. Jones, I would also like to congratulate you on your firstborn."

Rashaun nodded. He knew she was bullshitting him.

"Mr. Jones, have you ever met the deceased, Paul Edwards, before?"

"Yes, I did briefly at the hospital. Andria was having an operation."

"Did you know that you were going to meet Paul at the hospital?"

"No."

"So, you were surprise?"

"I met him for the first time then. Before I had only heard about him."

"Was your fiancée seeing Paul at the same time she was seeing you?"

"No."

"How do you know that?"

"I know the kind of person she is."

"And she would not be unfaithful?"

"No, she wouldn't."

"How did you feel when you found Paul at home with your pregnant fiancée?"

"Angry."

"Why?"

"Because he was hurting her," Rashaun answered.

"Why was he hurting her?"

"I don't know."

Kim walked to the prosecution table then turned around. "Mr. Jones, is the child that your girlfriend had is yours?"

"Yes," Rashaun replied.

"Did you do a DNA test?"

"No."

"So you are not a hundred percent positive that the child is yours."

"Yes, I am."

"Mr. Jones, I don't think the child is yours," Kim said,

walking back up to the witness stand. “I think you came home and found Paul in a loving embrace with your fiancée. He told you that he had impregnated your girlfriend and you went crazy. How could she? Rashaun, you found out that your fiancée was having an affair with her ex-boyfriend. He was fucking her and everyone knew it. The world was laughing at you.”

Rashaun started to sweat. He started clenching and unclenching his fist.

“Your honor,” Yelram shouted.

“The same way people had laughed at you before, the same way they laughed at you when you walked in the room and found your girlfriend talking to another guy in her bedroom at college. As per Pastor Thompson’s testimony, you got angry and you nearly beat the guy to death. Rashaun, all your women have cheated on you, haven’t they? Poor Rashaun, he can’t keep his woman. Everyone screws Rashaun’s women because he’s lousy in bed.”

“No,” Rashuan shouted, rising from the chair. ”She is not a bitch like you.”

“Yes, Rashaun. She played you, so you shot them both, didn’t you?”

“No, I didn’t, but I should have shot you,” Rashaun shouted then became very quiet. “Andria is nothing like you. Andria is a good girl. She wouldn’t do that to me. He was trying to hurt her so I shot him. Her getting shot was an accident.”

“No more questions, your honor,” Kim said softly and walked back to the prosecution table.

Chapter 17

The car door felt like it was made of pure lead as Rashaun mustered his strength to close it. He stood on rubbery legs from a sleepless and stressful night. He had spoken to his mother and Andria then he went and laid in bed, getting up periodically to look at Wisdom. Once more he was about to lose it all, and who knew where that would take him this time? His mother told him to have faith, and Andria was as optimistic as usual, but they were not lawyers. They did not know the extent of his outburst at the trial. He had sealed his own fate. After talking to Yelram about his past relationship with Kim, Yelram told him that it might be grounds for an appeal but it wouldn't get him acquitted. Rashaun couldn't wait for Yelram to pull a rabbit out of a hat because he had too much riding on the trial. He made his last-hope phone call at 8:00 A.M.

The Canarsie Pier was almost deserted on a Friday morning. Rashaun knew all this was going to change by midday because the pier fishermen would come out with their eleven-foot poles to try and catch one of the blue fish or striped bass that called the pier home. There were a few stragglers on the pair—an elderly couple looking out at the water and an old man feeding the birds. Like her presence in the courtroom, Kim stood out as she leaned against the rustic black barrier of the pier. Unlike her appearance in court she was dressed in a light gray sweat suit. Her long black hair blew steadily away from her face with the gentle breeze.

Rashaun tried to clear a lump that had appeared in his throat by swallowing hard as he approached Kim on her right side.

"Hello, Kim," he said, amazed that the words actually came out of his mouth.

"Hi, Rashaun," Kim said, sounding the complete opposite of how Rashaun was feeling.

"Thanks for choosing to meet me," Rashaun said, happy for the support of the barrier.

"Rashaun, you know that if you call me I'll come," Kim said, turning around to look directly at him.

"Well you won," he said, looking straight into her eyes.

"It's not over yet," Kim said, knowing that it was. "A not-guilty verdict could still be rendered."

"If I was talking to a client who didn't know better, I would say the same thing, but you and I know that it's over, so let's talk. I don't want to go to jail. Under normal circumstances I would say fuck it and go to the end. I wouldn't be here talking to you, but this isn't a normal circumstance. I'm not the carefree Rashaun of old. I have a woman and a child who mean everything to me," Rashaun said, looking out at a green-and-white boat with the name *Black Steel* printed at the back.

"Rashaun, I know we've had our bad times, but we've also had great times together. I don't want to see you in prison. I don't like seeing you hurt, but you gave me no other choice," Kim said.

"Please, Kim, don't go there. We've come full circle. Let's stay within this reality. Right now, you're in a position to hurt me, and I'm humbling myself coming here and asking you not to do it. So tell me what you want," Rashaun said fighting back tears. He was begging but he wasn't going to let Kim see him cry.

"I want us," Kim said, running her right hand over his bald head. "It's all I ever wanted."

Rashaun's blood was boiling but he didn't remove Kim's hand from his head. "What?"

"You're what I need in my life. It'll work out for both of us, and I know in time we can be what we used to be," Kim said as she caressed Rashaun's neck. She took his hand and looped it around her neck as she pulled herself against him.

Rashaun stood still, allowing her to have her way with him.

"That's impossible," he said.

"Nothing is impossible, Rashaun. You just have to want it badly enough," Kim said, nestling her head against Rashaun's chest as she, too, watched *Black Steel* out on the water.

"I'll have to give up everything," Rashaun said. "And can you guarantee me that I'll get off?"

"You're about to lose everything and your freedom. Rashaun, you're defenseless. And I don't think you have to worry about me changing the outcome of the trial. I have my ways. Rashaun, I'm your last hope, " Kim answered as she rocked back and forth in his arms. "We could leave New York and go to DC and open our own law firm—Jones and Rivers, Attorneys at Law—just like we said we were going to do when we were in law school. You remember?" Kim said, looking up at Rashaun.

"I can't remember that far back, Kim," Rashaun lied. "What will stop me from leaving you and returning to my family?"

"Me," Kim said, looking into his eyes and smiling.

"My son?" Rashaun said.

"Rashaun, I want you to be happy. I won't stop you from coming to New York and seeing your son. Maybe we can add a daughter so Wisdom will have a playmate," Kim said, her voice relaying her excitement. “Can you imagine us having a child? I can’t wait.”

Rashaun looked out into the ocean, his eyes leaving the man with the small boat. This was his end. Rashaun felt like he was drowning in the big blue ocean and the only savior was going to take him from a watery death to a fiery hell.

“I’ll need some time to think about it,” he said, detangling himself from Kim, her soft strawberry perfumed scent lingering on him.

“You know how much time you have, unless your lawyer can come up with a miracle he has to wrap it up. I have the key to open the door or close it,” she said, slipping her hand in his.

“I believe you,” he said, looking around.

“Don’t worry about me. I’ll call my ride in a minute,” Kim said as she watched Rashaun walk back to the SUV. When he had gone through the gate she took out her cell phone. “Hello, Roger,” she said as *Black Steel* left a big wave in its wake.

It was seven-thirty in the morning, and Kim sat in her living room alternating her attention between the war over in Iraq and her cordless phone. She didn’t want to do what she was about to do, but the decision was his. The buzzer frightened her because she wasn’t expecting it. She threw a white shirt on and went to the door. She looked through the peephole and saw Albertina. She shook her head, knowing that Rashaun told his mother almost everything. Albertina never liked her but she also knew that Albertina would do anything for Rashaun. She hoped that she wasn’t there to beg her to keep Rashaun in the Big Apple because this was one time Momma would have to say good-bye.

"Good morning, Mrs. Jones," Kim said, afraid to greet Albertina informally.

"Hello, Kim. I thought you would be packed by now after Rashaun told me about your ultimatum," Albertina said, walking into the living room and taking a seat on the sofa. Albertina was wearing a flowered dress with a light jacket that signaled the change to springtime weather in New York.

Kim closed the door slowly. "Great to see you, Mrs. Jones. Can you tell me the nature of your visit?"

"Are you going to offer me some champagne or some red wine? I know it's early in the morning, but I have a wedding to go to next week, and I want to start celebrating early," Albertina said.

"I only have orange juice but I'm about to go and get ready for work," Kim said leaning against a couch.

"Kim, you're going to work late today because something just came up in the trial," Albertina said, her face impassive as she looked directly at Kim.

"What? Like hell I am," Kim said, walking to the door. "Get out!"

"Kim, get back over here," Albertina said sternly.

Kim stopped midway to the door and turned around. "Excuse me?"

Albertina got up off the couch. "Have a seat. You will need it more than me," she said motioning for Kim to sit down on the couch she had just vacated.

Kim walked over to the couch but remained standing.

Albertina walked up to the television. "Rashaun said that you've been nominated for a judgeship."

"Yes, I have" Kim, said proudly. "But I would give it up in a minute to be with Rashaun."

"Yes you'll decline it but not to be with my son." Albertina said.

"Like hell I will," Kim asked.

"Because you're leaving the city right after the dismissal of all charges against my son," Albertina said. "I see you're up to date on the latest technology and you have a VCR and DVD player."

"What do you want, Albertina?" Kim said, irritation and nervousness pronounced in her voice.

"We're going to watch a movie," Albertina said, taking out a videocassette from her bag.

"Oh no!" Kim said, both hands going to her face.

"You missed your calling, Kim. You should have been a porn star," Albertina said, pressing the play button on the VCR. "I think you're more suited for the extreme ones though because I don't see how anyone but a depraved mind could get turned on by all that blood."

Kim couldn't bear to watch it. It seemed like another world. She and Devon, the priest, having sex. She didn't know what had gotten into her. Devon was fucking her hard, almost ripping into her. And when she started bleeding he had taken her blood and used it as lubricant before sticking his dick in her ass. She had never had anal sex after that. "Please turn it off," Kim said, looking away from the TV.

"Are you sure?" Albertina asked. "Because it gets better. Well maybe not, I don't think anything could top that last anal scene. This is pure BLACKFUNK. I hope your parents never see this but that's all up to you."

"Turn the fucking thing off," Kim shouted, getting up.

Albertina turned the tape off and ejected it. She put it back in her purse.

"Now listen to me. First, I want you to go to court and whatever excuse you choose to come up with, I don't care, but I want the case against Rashaun dropped. After you come from court, I want you to jump on a plane and leave New York City. I don't care how much it costs. I don't care about the repercussions to your career. Once you get where you're going I want to receive a postcard informing me about your location. I promise you I won't do anything with that tape unless I have to," Albertina said, walking toward the door.

"You know this is blackmail," Kim said. "You can go to jail for that."

Albertina stopped at the door. "Look very closely at me, Kim. Do you think jail could stop me from doing something for my son?"

Kim opened the door.

"Make sure this is our last meeting," Albertina said.

Yelram had told Rashaun to come to the office because of some new developments in the case. Rashaun was eager to meet with Yelram because he was about to tell him that he was leaving New York City. He was taking Kim up on the offer. He believed it would be the best for Andria and Wisdom. With him out of the picture, Andria and Wisdom would be out of danger, and he would still get an opportunity to see Wisdom.

"Good morning," Yelram said, a cheerful look on his face.

“There is nothing good about mornings anymore,” Rashaun said, sitting down.

“It’s over, Rashaun,” Yelram said, smiling. “We are meeting with the judge to ask for a dismissal.”

“What happened?” Rashaun asked, getting up and looking at Yelram in disbelief. “What did you do?”

“Absolutely nothing. I think your ex got religion. She called me in the office and said she had a witness who said that Paul was on his way to Andria to hurt her,” Yelram said.

“Who’s the witness?” Rashaun asked.

“Paul’s mother,” Yelram said.

“Thank you, Lord,” Rashaun said, looking up into the ceiling.

“And listen to this, Rashaun. I don’t think that Kim had any intention of letting you go to prison. I think she was playing a game with you,” Yelram said. “This woman is a piece of work. I don’t know why she wanted to make you squirm like that. What can she possibly hope to gain from it?”

“Believe me, Yelram. Kim always has something to gain. Thanks a million, I have to go home and tell Andria and Mom,” Rashaun said, heading to the door.

“Don’t forget we have to deal with the illegal gun charges but I think we can get you probation on that. Maybe you might get your license suspended for a little while,” Yelram said.

“We’ll deal with that when it comes up. Right now, I’m going to get ready for a wedding.”

Rashaun rang the doorbell of Tyrone’s parents’ house. He waited outside for a few seconds until the door was opened.

Yvonne stood in the doorway. Her hair was uncombed, and she had on a light blue jumper that did nothing for her beautiful body.

"Hello, Rashaun," Yvonne said, leaving the door open and walking back into the house. "If you're looking for Tyrone, he already left for his church retreat. I'm sure he apologized to you about not being in the wedding."

Rashaun walked into the house. "I'm not looking for Tyrone. I'm happy that Tyrone found God. It's definitely been a good influence in his life. He's come a long way."

"Yes, he has. Do you want something to drink?" Yvonne asked as she walked into the back room.

Rashaun pulled a chair out and sat in the kitchen. "No, but I would like to talk to you."

"Sorry. You caught me in the process of packing. I guess congratulations are in order. You won't mind if I don't attend your wedding but my parents will be there, they adore you," she said.

"Can I come back there?" Rashaun asked.

"No. This place is really messy, but I can hear you fine." Her voice sounded a little muffled.

"Thanks for attending my trial. Knowing that I have support really helps," Rashaun said.

"It was nothing. We can never repay you for what you've done for Tyrone," she said.

"I'm sorry it didn't work out for us," Rashaun said, rising from the table.

Rashaun heard some movement in the back room.

"Not everything that seems good is meant to be. Are you sure you don't want something to drink because you know you can help yourself," she said.

"No thanks. I'm going to leave now. Good luck in Washington," Rashaun said, rising from the chair.

"The same to you and your family. Just turn the knob on the door before you close it." The hoarseness in Yvonne's voice betrayed her feelings.

"Bye," Rashaun said, pulling the door shut. As he walked down the driveway he could feel Yvonne looking at him.

"Paula, don't be late for the wedding," Andria said the small cell phone plastered on her cheek.

"Andria, don't worry. I'll be on time," Paula answered.

"Where are you now?" Andria asked.

"Chris and I are taking Tonia for her checkup. Andria, I found this beautiful dress for her. I swear my daughter will be Miss. USA one day. She is absolutely beautiful," Paula said.

"I know she is. You have a beautiful daughter," Andria said.

"Yeah. A lot of people have been telling me how beautiful she is. I think I'll enter her in a baby modeling contest," Paula said. "I spoke to Chris about it, and he thinks it's a great idea. Thanks for opening my eyes."

"I'll really open your eyes if you have the limousine driver waiting for you. I know how you are."

"Don't worry about me, Andria. I'll be there. Anyway we're at the doctor's office, so I'll talk to you later," Paula said.

Andria hung up the phone.

"I hope you have a lot of minutes," Lethal said to Andria as they drove down Flatlands Avenue.

"Yes. I upgraded to a thousand minutes this month," Andria said, looking at the phone.

"I just switched to Sprint myself," Lethal said, "but their phones are not as good as AT&T."

"I don't care about the phones. Rashaun has to get the one with the latest features. Right now his can take pictures and do a whole lot of stuff. And all he does is take pictures of Wisdom and show them to me speaking of the devil," Andria said, putting the phone to her ear.

"Tell him we'll be there in ten minutes," Lethal said as he turned onto Linden Boulevard.

"Hello, Sir. I was just talking about you."

Chapter 18

"Kim, don't tell me that nothing is wrong. You had him wrapped up in a ball. All you needed to do was kick him as far away as you could," Roger said, standing in the middle of the bedroom watching Kim pack.

"Leave it alone, Roger," Kim said, throwing clothes from the closet into a suitcase.

"Who did you meet at the pier? Is Rashaun blackmailing you?" Roger asked, taking a white skirt from Kim's hands.

"Why would Rashaun wait until he is almost convicted to blackmail me? Even you said that he might have shot Paul in self-defense." Kim snatched the skirt back from him and dumped it in the suitcase.

"Kim, you're giving up everything, even your judgeship. It'll take years in another state before you're offered a judgeship again. I'm begging you, Kim, please reconsider." Roger sat down on the bed.

"Roger, I don't know if I want to be a lawyer anymore. I definitely know I don't want to do criminal law. My father has connections in Washington. Maybe I'll do some corporate law. I'm sure he could put a word in with one of the top firms in Washington." Kim stuffed the clothes into the suitcase then sat on it to close it.

Roger got off the bed. "I guess this is good-bye."

Kim sat down on the bed. "I'm sorry if I've disappointed you, Roger, but I have to do what I need to do, not what I want to do. We had some good times, and I will always remember you."

"I wish I could come with you but I can't. I have to establish myself here first before I could do anything," Roger said, his voice trailing off.

"Roger, I don't expect you to pick up and leave with me. This is not about you and me. This is about me. Maybe one day I'll sit down and tell you about the sins of my past, but let's just say good-bye for now," Kim said, moving closer to Roger.

"Will you give me a chance to get to Washington?" Roger asked, putting his hands around Kim's waist. "I'll be coming to get you. I don't know how long I can stay here without you, but I know I have to do it."

Kim kissed Roger softly on the lips. "Don't worry about us. I'm not in any condition to start a new relationship. I need to spend some time with me."

"I'm happy to hear that because I know that offers will come flying from all directions," Roger said, slipping his hands into Kim's and bringing her closer to him. "One for the road."

"One is never enough for the road but if that's all you want, you got it," Kim said, taking Roger's tongue in her mouth.

Roger pushed the suitcase off the bed. "Promise me that you won't ever make love to another man like this again. I want to be special."

"You are, Roger. You are very special. Now make love to me because tomorrow I'll be gone," Kim said, taking off her blouse.

"I don't know how you did it but I'm happy with the result," George said standing next to Rashaun, his black tuxedo contrasting sharply with Rashaun's all-white tuxedo with tails.

"I still don't know what happened. I spoke to Kim, and the next thing I know is that Yelram is calling my house. Whatever happened I had nothing to do with it. As I told you, Kim wanted me to leave New York with her."

George looked around the church. "That bitch is crazy."

"Yeah, she is, but she is also very smart," Rashaun said.

"And fine. Do you have her number?" George asked.

"What are you boys mumbling about?" Albertina asked.

"We were just saying that it's a miracle that I'm standing in church today and not in a jail," Rashaun said, looking over at his mother who had walked him down the aisle. He could see the pride and love on her face as they walked. It was as much her day as it was his. Rashaun looked over to the front row where Sheila held on to Wisdom as if the wind would break him. Rashaun's father sat next to her with the rest of the family.

"With a little human help, miracles always happen to good people," Albertina said, looking up at the statue of Christ.

The organ started to play.

"Here comes your bride," George said as all attention in the church was directed at Andria walking down the aisle.

Andria wore her mother's wedding dress, both as an honor to her and as a reminder of her father. The dress was an old-fashion one with billowing frills and layers of cloth trailing four feet behind her. Her mother walked with her, a major break from tradition but an application to the modern world where the father is sometimes missing. It had been a long time since everything have fallen into place for her.

Rashaun had received the phone call from Yelram as they sat

talking about what would happen if he got sent to jail. She was trying to convince Rashaun to allow her to bring Wisdom to visit him in jail. Rashaun was adamant about not letting Wisdom see him as a convict. In Andria's heart, she was still hoping for a miracle. She watched Rashaun with Wisdom and wondered why anyone would want to take him away from his son. After his testimony, Rashaun tripled the amount of time he spent with Wisdom. They were already competing on who could spend the most time with him, but Rashaun became relentless.

Andria controlled her wedding jitters as she made every step as pronounced as possible, trying not to run down the aisle and trip. She was happy. As she walked down the aisle, she looked at the people in the church. Many of them she recognized but a lot she had never seen before. They were Rashaun's friends and friends of his family. Andria was surprised but happy to see Steve Francis, her dead friend Judy's husband. She had sent the invite to him but didn't get any reply. He stood out with the sprinkling of white people in the audience. He was wearing a white suit she remembered him wearing at his and Judy's wedding. As Andria approached the front of the church, she was happy to see Mr. Jones in the front row. She had to beg Rashaun to let his father attend the ceremony. As she looked at the man she was about to marry, she thanked God she didn't accomplish what she attempted a few years ago. Life had taken her from hanging over a toilet bowl with dozens of white powdery pills in her stomach to walking down the aisle to marry the man she loved more than life itself.

Rashaun smiled as Andria came up and stood next to him. It really didn't matter what he said to her because he was one hundred percent that she was feeling what was in his heart. Marriage was a mere formality for what he knew he wanted. She had given him a reason to keep living and to keep loving. She had made him put aside the clouds for the sunshine, and as she offered that smile that heated up his blood, he was thankful to be in this place to thank God for her. God had given him life. His mother had guided him through it, but Andria was giving him the reason to get up every morning. First she made him breathe, then she gave him a son to live for. Before, it was all about him, but now it was about his family. He was going to protect them and give them his heart.

George had asked him if he was prepared for the commitment. He wasn't only ready for it, he was ready for a whole new life, from that day forth. He was lying to himself. It wasn't from that day forth because he had made a bond with Andria a long time ago. He had done things he wasn't proud about but hoped God would forgive him. He didn't hear the pastor's words but as he looked into Andria's eyes he heard the I do. Yes, he said to the most beautiful woman in the world. He said I do to his woman who was now his wife.

Rashaun thought he heard an explosion but he wasn't sure because he was still in wedding bliss, but when he saw his mother drop in front of the priest blood pumping from her head, he cried to the only father he acknowledged. "Oh God."

He reached down to cradle his mother in his arms as the explosion went off over and over. He curled his mother's lifeless body in his arms. While tears flowed freely from his eyes he whispered, "Please, Mom, don't leave me now."

His mother's face was glowing from Rashaun's vows. She seemed to be totally happy. She seemed to be at peace, as if she had just finished making one of her masterful dinners and was sitting at the table knowing she had made it great. Rashaun became oblivious to the rest of his surroundings.

When Andria heard the shot she quickly looked around. "Not again," she said as she saw Rashaun drop to the ground with his mother. She looked in the direction where she heard the screaming and saw the scattering of people. It was then she saw the white man in the white suit. It was Steve, Judy's husband. He was screaming obscenities in the worst way. Andria didn't know what she was doing but she knew she had to stop him from shooting. She started to walk to him as if in a daze. She was drawn to the deliverer of death. Steve fired at her as she continued to walk toward him.

"Stop, Steve. Stop the shooting," Andria said.

Andria did not see when Robin reached up to stop her only to fall awkwardly back on the ground. She stopped walking when she saw a priest jump onto Steve. He wrestled Steve down to the ground and started to pound on him mercilessly. It was only then that reality kicked in for her. She looked back and saw Rashaun at the altar, his mother in his arms, tears falling like rain from his eyes as he looked to Andria for understanding. Rashaun's father held on to him, crying loudly as the rest of the church started to recover. Next to Mr. Jones was Sheila, still holding on tightly to Wisdom, tears flowing from her eyes. Andria ran back to the altar and buried herself next to Rashaun who held on tightly to his mother.

Chapter 19

Rashaun's entire outfit was black but it contrasted greatly with his heart, which that day was white. A white mist had covered his heart, and the tears that flowed freely were not even a point two percentage of the hurting in his heart. He stood next to his mother's grave with his father as Andria held Wisdom. His brother and sister and their families all had wet eyes. The priest spoke but Rashaun was not listening.

Rashaun thought back to the great times he had with his mother. She clothed him, fed him and fought for him when she had to. There was no one like his mother, and there definitely wouldn't ever be anyone like her again. He knew she had carved out a piece of his heart and forever it would remain. He knew that when his troubles seemed insurmountable he would reach for that piece of his heart. Rashaun took Wisdom from Andria and went up to his mother's grave. He threw a cup of water onto her coffin as a symbol of what she had been to him, the finder of water in a desert. He went back to join Andria and the rest of the family. He took Wisdom and placed him in the arms of his weeping father. He took Andria by the hand, and together they walked away from his mother. He didn't look back because he knew that he would be back the next day and a lot of days to come.

Andria stopped about twenty feet away from Albertina's grave.

Rashaun looked at her.

She extricated her hand from Rashaun's. As she walked away past the symbols of loss, he knew where she was going.

Andria stopped in front a medium-size gravestone. Next to it was a fresh grave with flowers on it. On the gravestone was the name Judy Francis.

Andria took a flower from her hair and threw it in front of the stone.

"I'm sorry, Judy. The living should never forget the dead. I got caught up in my life, and I forgot about you. Please forgive me. I wish you were here. There are so many things I have to tell you. I'm married now, and yes, I'm a mother, if you can believe that." A slight smile pierced Andria's face. "I don't know what will happen in my life from now on, but I pray for peace and quiet. I hope wherever you're that you are doing what you love doing. On second thought, scratch that, you love doing dangerous things. Thank you for being a friend, and I'll be back. I'll never forget again."

Rashaun watched as his wife made her way among the dead. Their life had been totally chaotic. He reached out when she was close, and she gripped his hand firmly. They exited the cemetery and went to a waiting limousine. Later on that evening he would go with Andria to visit her friend Robin in the hospital. Robin was the only other person who got shot. It was a non-life-threatening shoulder wound that required an operation to remove the bullet. On Monday, he and his new partner, Yelram would visit Pastor Devon Thompson in church. Rashaun did not know what he would say to the man who destroyed his trust who may have saved his life on his wedding day by pounding Steve to death.

The Pastor's church was trying to take away his priesthood for what he had done to Steve.

As the limousine pulled off, Rashaun thought about the ironies of death. They were going to the church hall to eat and drink. A smile penetrated his lips. That was good because he needed to celebrate his mother. True love always needs a celebration.

Kim walked out of the doctor's office on Washington Avenue in Washington, D.C. It had been five months since her departure from New York City, and she had come to the doctor for a routine checkup. The doctor told her that everything was all right and the baby was doing fine. Washington had been good for her. Through her father's connections and her reputation as one of the best lawyers, she got a job in one of the best corporate firms in the city, one whose clients included past presidents of the United States. She was quickly becoming known as a top-notch lawyer, one who used whatever it took to get the job done. What she was most pleased about was the life in her womb. In her womb was a celebration of an unforgettable love.

She crossed the street and went to a Nissan 350 Z.

"Hello, Mrs. Nelson. How is little Roger doing today?" Roger asked

"Better than yesterday, Roger. Much better than yesterday. I think we should take a drive," she said.

"To New York City?" He asked.

"No, Roger, although New York City its always a nice place to visit," Kim said, adjusting the seatbelt over her stomach. "It is not time to go there yet. Right now there is a lot of moaning in

New York City. Give it a time to heal then we'll go back."

"Only for a visit?" Roger asked, pulling the car onto the street.

"Maybe." Kim said, a smile coming across her face. "Maybe to start over again."

COMING SOON

MICHAEL PRESLEY'S

TEARS ON A SUNDAY AFTERNOON

Chapter 1

I was pushed through the revolving exit door of the office building by two ladies rushing to leave the building. As I walked through the corridor leading to the elevators I was constantly bumped by hoards of people heading to the revolving doors. I looked at my gold Movado watch and realized it was ten after five. I navigated to the line of elevators that carried the workers up and down everyday. I stepped aside as more than a dozen business people in suits pushed themselves off one of the elevators. They hurried passed more than as if in a to get to the streets outside. I guess the streets of New York were not as dangerous as advertised. I had been in the building earlier to set up a project with a group of engineers from our office. It was an extensive project that would require long, tedious hours. It was similar to one we had done in Staten Island a few weeks ago. It was during that visit that I met one of the secretaries, Donna Smith. She had been with the company for five years. One of my coworkers, Brian, a tall dark fellow from Brooklyn introduced me. The first hour we were in the building Brian had spent at least forty-five minutes trying to talk to Donna. I paid very little attention to the both of them because unlike me, Brian was single and the world was his oyster.

Brian and I had eaten lunch together since I came onboard Reason Consulting, the largest black engineering firm in New York. Engineers at Reason were not hired based on their résumé but from recommendations by one of their board members. My father-in-law had me working there a few months after the wedding. During our lunch at Au Bon Pai Brian told me that Donna was dripping for me. I looked at him as if he was crazy. I hadn't said a word to the girl and she was "dripping for me."

Brian was a cool guy; he didn't have a jealous bone in his body. He told me that he tried talking to her but she was only interested in me. So after speaking to Brian I went over to her. When I got to her desk she stood and shook my hand. I must tell you I was very impressed. She was about five feet nine inches tall, dark complexion with a body that almost any man would crawl after. I said almost any man, not me. I have had those women who men have killed themselves over.

During our conversation she told me to hold on because she had to file an important document. When she turned around I'll just say that she was a black man's butter. She told me that she couldn't really talk to me and asked if I could come back and see her after work. Now you know why I am going into a building that most people are trying to leave. As I took the elevator up to the sixtieth floor I was wondering where to take her for dinner. I eat out frequently so my head was spinning with choices—maybe I would let her decide. I eat almost anything so it wouldn't make a difference to me.

It was approximately five-fifteen when I knocked on the office door. She came in and led me to a couch in front of her desk and told me to wait. A few minutes passed and a man I hadn't seen before came out and spoke to her briefly as he walked out of the office. He had a large Kenneth Cole briefcase in his right hand and upon further inspection I noticed a gold handcuff kept the briefcase in place.

"I'm so wound up," she said as she slumped down in her chair.

"That's work¯five days a week, then two days to think about it then five days back at work," I said, looking at her from a distance.

"You're very beautiful," she said, sitting on the edge of the chair.

I have heard that comment from the time I was old enough to remember it. It had gotten me into and out of trouble. I think sometimes I could get away with murder because of my looks, the result of a crime perpetuated on my mother when she was incarcerated at the Delvin Correctional Facility upstate New York. Three white correction officers raped her. After I was born my mother took her life.

"I know," I said, smiling. "Thanks for the compliment."

"You're mixed aren't you?" she asked. "With that curly hair and those blue eyes you've got to be."

"Yeah, my father is white and my mother is a southern girl."

"So who did you inherit that over six-feet slender frame from, your mother or father?"

"I don't know." I was being honest because I was never told who my father was. I guess nobody wanted to set up DNA tests for three white men.

She stood and walked to the front of the desk. "Come over here. Let me see how much taller you are than me."

I guess she was into games. Normally, I wouldn't play but this one was worth it. I stood in front of her, her hard nipples pushing against my shirt. She smelled like fresh-picked apricots.

She looked up at me, her luscious red lips glistening against the dark pigmentation of her face.

"I…"

It was all she got out of her mouth as my lips joined hers. She should have slapped me then. Maybe I should have slapped myself for making such assumptions but neither of us did. Instead her mouth feasted on mine as my hand went to the front of her blouse. The snaps came apart like dry- rotted steel wool the kind my grandmother gave me to do the dishes. I pulled her blouse off her shoulders and it fell onto her desk. She pulled me towards her, her breasts rubbing against my white Guess T-shirt. Her hand traveled down my chest toward my dick and she started to rub it through my pants.

"I knew you were packing, looks and a big dick what more can a girl ask for?" she said as I helped her pull my shirt over my head. She started to make her way down my chest, leaving a trail of red lip marks. She unbuckled my pants and slid my pants down. She gently brushed the outsides of my legs with her fingertips as she reached up to pull off my Calvin Klein boxers. I stepped to the side as she gathered my clothes and put them on the couch. I stood naked on the sixtieth floor in an office building in the heart of Manhattan.

"You have what I want in my husband," she said as I started to remove her clothes. I started playing with her breasts and slowly made my way down to her skirt. I lifted it up and worked my way between her legs. My right hand moved over the front of her panties. They were moist. I moved them to the side and slipped my finger inside of her, she was dripping wet. I played with her for a few seconds more before I moved my hand to her butt. She was wearing a thong, and old song played in my head but it quickly faded like the artist who performed it. We continued to kiss until I flipped her around and in so doing her hands scattered all the things she had on her desk. I took her hand away from my dick and slid on one of the condoms that I had bought from Duane Reade earlier. I grabbed her by the hair, her weave feeling like that same steel wool but it shredded much more. I pushed her head down in front the desk. Her two hands held onto the desk for support. I entered her with the force and the vengeance of a man lost to himself and the world. She screamed and rocked the desk as she spread her legs even wider for more support. As she did that a picture fell off the desk and shattered. She was in the picture with a man and two young boys. I looked at it and then at her butt. I slammed into her a few more times until I sent a million of my kids to their death against the walls of rubber. She fell to the floor as I gave my last push.

"I needed that. You have a cell phone?" she asked, putting her clothes on.

"It's 917-777-7777."

"All those sevens?"

"It's better than sixes."

I followed her cue and started to get dress. She quickly put my phone number in her Palm organizer. She didn't offer hers and I didn't ask for it. I finished dressing before her and headed to the door.

"Wait for me she said. I have to clean up this mess and make one phone call." She started straightening the desk. "I think this is yours." She wrapped the used condom in tissues and gave it to me. I put it in my pocket.

"I nearly forgot that," I said.

"If you were an NBA basketball player I might have kept it," she said smiling. She picked up the phone and dialed a number quickly. She spoke briefly in a language I didn't understand.

"Only an engineer," I said and sat down on the couch. It was 6:30.

"Damn! This is the third time this week this has happened." She threw the bits of broken glass from the picture frame into the small garbage pail and placed it back under her desk. "These ninety-nine cent stores are getting rich off me replacing frames."

I waited for her to finish and we took the elevator down to the first floor.

"Good night Mrs. August," the security guard a potbellied man with a heavy West Indian accent, said as we exited the building. When we got outside there was a tall attractive blond white lady waiting for us.

"Thank you," Donna said and waved good-bye to me as she went to join the white lady who lady looked me up and down before she and Donna slipped into a black limousine waiting at the curb.

I walked two blocks south then one east, which took me to the entrance of the Carton Bar. I went inside and as usual there was a combination of suits and casuals. I sat at the bar and the bartender came over.

"Hennessy on the rock," I said, and he turned back before reaching me.

I swiveled the chair around so that I could look at the people like me who found themselves needing a drink at seven in the evening. My left was a white man about fifty-five years old in a postal uniform sipping on a drink that was as clear as water. I didn't think it was water because that would mean he had to drink a lot of those little glasses before he satisfied his thirst. As if on cue, he tapped his glass and the bartender gave him a refill on the way to bringing my drink. A little bit farther down from him were two white boys who may had just reached the legal drinking age in New York City. They had a pitcher of beer and about six shots glasses in front of them. They seemed to be having a good time. I looked over at the tables away from the bar and noticed a couple who seemed to be lost in New York and young black women¯ my guess neither was a day over twenty-five. They both had identical hairstyles long weaves running down their back. They kept looking at me and giggling. One held what I thought was a mozzarella cheese stick, which she twirled around like a baton. I turned back and took a long sip of my drink.

I had recently turned thirty-four and I had been married for four years now. I had a four-year-old son and I was one of the few blacks living in the exclusive Mills Basin section of Brooklyn. I loved my son with every drop of blood that circulated through my system and kept me alive every day.

"Excuse me?" I felt the slight tap on my shoulder. I put my drink down and once more swiveled in my chair. It was one of the girls I had noticed earlier. She was the bigger of the two. I would guess she was five-eight and weighed about 145 pounds.

"Yes." My face showed no emotion.

"My friend wants to fuck you." I looked over at her friend who was holding the cheese stick. She had this big smile on her face.

"And you?" I asked.

"I wouldn't mind," she said, playing with my curly hair.

"How much?" I asked.

She stopped playing with my hair and stood back.

"How much?" she repeated as if her repetition would dissipate the question.

"There's got to be something in it for me," I said.

"How about both of us together," she said, signaling her friend who was starting to get up.

"Been there, done that too many times, so unless your shit got gold fillings, this conversation is over."

"I'll be right back," she said and headed over to her friend.

I took a sip of my drink and rested a hundred-dollar bill under the glass.

"We're willing to do $400 but you have to buy a bottle of Courvoisier as a birthday gift to my friend." She said a stupid smile on her face, "Like the song…"

"I hate the song but I will buy the bottle. Let's go," I said, leaving the bartender with a hundred dollar bill for a $6.50 drink.

I drove into my driveway at Mills Lane at 10:00 P.M. parking my S500 next to the red convertible X type Jaguar in the driveway. As I stepped onto the pavement, a large black pit bull came trotting toward me. I stooped and rubbed the dog on the top of his head. He rubbed against my pants leg, walked with me to the large French doors and stood back as I opened the door.

"Thanks for picking up Emerald from the school. You didn't have to leave as soon as we came home." My wife stood in the middle of the living room. Her right eye was black and swollen.

"Is Emerald asleep?" I asked.

"Like you care. He's has been asleep since eight-thirty." She said.

"I'm taking him to the zoo tomorrow," I said as I took off my shoes.

"Laura, come here," a husky female voice beckoned from the kitchen.

I followed my wife.

"I thought I told you I don't want all that mayonnaise on my sandwich" the woman sitting at the kitchen table in a red night-gown said as my wife picked up the sandwich. She was the house-keeper and my wife lover. "You know I don't like hitting you but you don't listen."

"Sorry Annette, I'll do it over," my wife said.

I went to the refrigerator and took out a Heineken. As I passed by Annette stood. She was a little bit shorter than Donna and God had created ugly.

She looked at me, challenging me with her eyes.

I opened the bottle and leaned against the counter, staring Annette down.

"What! You want to do something about this," she said, pointing to Laura. "Go ahead and see if you won't be arrested for spousal abuse."

"Just as long as you keep your hands where they won't be cut off. If I ever come home and find my child with so much as a scratch on his arm, I will take that artificial dick and shove it down your throat."

"Stop it, both of you!" Laura screamed. "Donald. Dad said he wants to see you tomorrow."

I walked out of the kitchen with the Heineken. I went up the stairs passed the master bedroom into a room littered with an assortment of toys. I knelt next to the bed where my child lay fast asleep. I held the Heineken in my right hand as I used my left hand to move his curly hair away from his eyes. I kissed him in the middle of his forehead. A small tear escaped from my eye onto his bed.

"I love you," I said and stood. I left the room and headed down to the last room at the end of the hall. I put the bottle next to the cases of empty ones in the walk-in-closet. I sat by the window looking out at the darkness of the night. I knew what I had to do. Maybe tomorrow I could stand up to my father-in-law and tell him what I was unable to do for four years.